Early years at Postcard Corner

Real people, Imagined lives, Real places

Early years at Postcard Corner

Real people, Imagined lives, Real places

A Collection of Short Stories

Alan Burnett

TRICORN
BOOKS

Early years at Postcard Corner
Real people, Imagined lives, Real places
Alan Burnett

Design © 131 Design Ltd
www.131design.org
Text © Alan Burnett

ISBN 978-0-9571074-5-8

A CIP catalogue record for this book is available from the British Library.

Published 2012 by Tricorn Books,
a trading name of 131 Design Ltd.
131 High Street, Old Portsmouth,
PO1 2HW

www.tricornbooks.co.uk

Printed & bound in UK by Berforts Group Ltd

Contents

Acknowledgements

*M*y thanks are due to the many people who have encouraged, inspired, advised and supported me in writing this book – especially to my wonderful family, and of course friends in the locality, the UK and across the globe.

I would like to thank my late parents and brother, and very active sister; some great teachers; as well as local (Portsmouth) authors notably the late Jim Riordan, and Betty Burton, Graham Hurley, Julia Bryant, and Rob and Chris Richardson. Many individuals have contributed in different ways to these stories. They include the late Mike Phillips, Donovan Gardner, and Karl Sparrow; as well as Lucian Leon, Ken Webster, Bo Bröndsted, Pamela Holmes, Chris Owen, Martin Murphy, Adrian and Jane Knott.

For the publication of the book I am indebted to Dan and Gail of Tricorn Books whose professional advice and technical skills have been invaluable.

And last, but not least, Miss Elsie Greene.

The author takes full responsibility for any inaccuracies in the text – these will be remedied in the second edition!

Alan's friendly alphabet

A merican friends – Tom and Roses, of Bloomington, Indiana (where the corn belt meets the Bible belt), Washington DC (where there are 30 pages of lawyers' firms in the telephone directory), and Portland, Oregon (said to be the most liberal city in the United States).

B eing friendly is better than being rude or indifferent, especially to those you have to work with in life.

C lose friends – have I got any? I like to think so. But you will have to ask them.

D inner and birthday parties with old friends are liable to leave a lot of empty bottles.

E xam time … that's when you needed school and uni friends; to pick their brains before and celebrate after (Hi there, Ron and Chris).

F amily friends – many live on Portsea Island or nearby – but also in London, Kenilworth, Cheltenham, Nottingham, the Wirral, Suffolk, the Pennines and Cumbria.

G ood friends should never be taken for granted, we definitely need them in old age! Trouble is going to their funerals. But I never cross their names out of the address book.

H elen's kids at Isambard Brunel in North End are learning fast, and know all about Pompey's wins and the Great Ethiopian Run.

I t is true that … while you promise to keep in touch with friends made on holiday – you rarely do so … not so with David and Bess (those who face danger together – stay together!).

Jenny is my loving, lifelong friend/partner/wife, and Keir, Otis, Elsie and Etta our adorable grandchildren at the time of writing, there are more on the way....

Kate keeps in touch with her Priory and Goldsmiths' friends, and started the baby boom in our family.

Lifelong friend is James Duncan – he used to crawl through the hedge from next door in Ghyll Road to play football, and cowboys and Indians (Native Americans).

My brother David is greatly missed but thankfully wonderful sister Didy and the friendly relatives are all around.

Neighbours – are they friendly? Yes, thank goodness. Especially Annie and Andrew.

Overseas friends – to be found in Borneo, Romania, Canada, Spain, Norway, Germany, France, USA and Ethiopia ... now we can keep in touch by e-mail.

Pompey vs Southampton – is that what's known as a friendly match or friendly fire?

Quite a few long-lost friends finally get together after many years, but sadly many don't. Where are they now? Contact me if you are reading this slim volume. (alanburnett@ live.co.uk)

Right Honourable David Blunkett MP for Sheffield Brightside and his guide dog are our friends, although only one of them has ever seen me in person.

Scottish friends include John Mactaggart of Campbelltown, Lord and Lady Abernethy, Jimmy McNair and the Frasers who lived by the castle and now by the Leith.

Tom is good at making friends – like his mum. He writes succinctly like his dad.

University friends from the 60s have grey hair, but – have you noticed ? – the same mannerisms as they did years ago.

Veggie/ vegan friends are fine and healthy, especially the Pope family.

Welsh friends? Not when England play Wales at rugby and lose.

Xmas is a great time for family and friends – but New Year was there first and is my favourite.

Young friends are a treat, and older friends re-assuring.

Zanzibar's Barwanis came to Portsmouth with the exiled Sultan, and still come to visit us after 40 years.

Early years at Postcard Corner

Coming home for Christmas

I strained my eyes to see if I could recognise any familiar
faces among the cheering crowd waiting on the Round
Tower. No-one I knew there. My parents would probably
be waiting in the naval base where HMS Maryton was due
to berth. Then I spotted my brother Ewan and sister Carol,
but no Lesley. Standing on the Spice Island Point, in front of
the Coal Exchange pub, they were holding up a large sign on
which they had printed *Welcome Home Graham.*

It was a joyous scene as sailors embraced their wives and
sweethearts. Bewildered kids were picked up and tossed into
the air. I embraced mum and dad. They looked much the
same. Little sister had blossomed. She jumped up and down,
trying to tweak my explorer's beard.

'You look like Captain Scott,' she teased. 'Where are your
huskies?'

After lunch in the wardroom we packed my box files of
notes and samples of Antarctic flora that I had collected on
my expedition, into the boot of our family car, and drove the
short journey over to Southsea. It was one of those wintry
days when dusk falls in mid-afternoon. The gloom was only
lightened by the colourful lights on Christmas trees in front
windows of homes we passed.

We had so much to catch up on and the evening passed
remarkably quickly. I didn't like to ask if they had seen
anything of my old girlfriend, Lesley. It was past midnight
when I went upstairs and sat on the bed. My room was
unchanged – school and college books on the shelves; posters
of Manfred Mann and Joan Baez on the wall; record
collection.

At first, when I awoke the next morning, I wasn't sure where I was. I put on my old college tracksuit and slipped out of the house. I wanted to see the old familiar places in which I had spent my happy childhood years. Fleming's clock in Castle Road showed 8:20am. A Portsea Island Co-op milk float rattled by, and paperboys huddled around the newsagent's shop. Harry Ricketts, who had mended many a puncture on my bikes, was pottering around his cycle shop, even at that early hour. Alan, the local postmaster, greeted me cheerily; Alan handled all the airmail letters I had been sent; he for one knew where I'd been and for how long. I ran past, towards Southsea Common.

It was a clear, sunny, sparkling morning and I felt great as the excitement of my homecoming flowed through me. Once on the promenade, I turned left past the Rock Gardens pavilion and, on reaching the pier, turned back home for breakfast.

There were bacon and eggs on the table. All except dad were up and eating; he had gone for a checkup at the Royal Hospital. I felt sorry that I had not been there to take him, but Ewan had volunteered. Plans were being made for the next few days leading up to Christmas – the advent calendar showed five days to go.

That evening we all got dressed up to go to the Guildhall for the Salvation Army carol concert, introduced by Richard Baker. I could sense my parents were pleased to have me with them again. The enjoyed showing me off to their friends. Dad was fairly quiet but I understood his report from the hospital had been positive. He wore a Harris Tweed jacket and grey flannels, his British Legion badge and well-polished shoes attesting to his service background. We had pre-concert drinks at the Sussex Hotel; mum was her usual vivacious self. She consumed a huge schooner of sherry and was full of the festive spirit as we crossed the road to Guildhall Square.

After the show, being so unused to crowds and indeed

conversation, I chose to walk home alone. Glancing into the front rooms of neat terraced houses, I saw blazing fires and rooms decorated with cards and streamers – all very inviting. The city seemed so densely populated and cluttered after the clear, clean landscape of the Antarctic that I had lived in the previous months. But the fairy lights brightened up the scene and helped dispel the gloom.

Before I knew it, my route home had taken me into the heart of Southsea. I realised I was very near Rochester Road where Lesley lived. I went past her house. The curtains were drawn and there was no sign of life. I paused, unsure of whether or not to knock at the door. In the past, of course, I wouldn't have hesitated for a moment. I'd lost count of the number of times I'd called to take her out. We had first met at a sixth-form dance and had got to know each other well before I had left.

We had been part of the gang that frequented coffee bars such as the Del Monico and The Manhattan. On Thursday nights we used to go to Kimbells to hear our favourite groups – The Shamrocks from the Isle of Wight, Manfred Mann from Gosport, and Portsmouth's own Simon Dupree and the Big Sound. On one occasion we had heard Simon and Garfunkel at the Railway Club.

But now I was on my own. Was Lesley at home or still away at college? For all I knew she might be with someone else. Give it a day or two, I convinced myself – maybe I'll see her at a party or in the pub. As I walked along Albert Road, the strong smell of Indian curry wafted out. By now the frenetic activity of my first day back home was catching up with me.

The following day the whole family visited Granma Taylor in her trim council bungalow in the village of Hambledon. It was just as I remembered it – the church, village shop, playground, Jubilee Hall – nothing had changed it seemed in the many months I had been away. My granny bustled around in her floral pinny, getting tea ready.

'Graham,' she said 'I bet you didn't have freshly baked scones in the South Pole!'

'No gran', I replied, tongue in cheek. 'The Eskimos kept us supplied with fresh seal meat!'.

'Get away with you', she laughed. 'You will be telling me next that you bumped into Captain Scott!'

Later on, some of us walked up the valley to the famous old cricket ground on Halfpenny Down where Hambledon had played the rest of England. We collected holly as we went. The Bat and Ball pub was as welcoming as ever and we once again toasted my homecoming with strong HSB ale.

Friday the 22 December was a shopping day. I had saved up a tidy sum from my wages over the last eighteen months and was determined to get some really nice presents for the family. Maybe I'd get something for Lesley too. I started in Southsea shopping centre. At Hargreaves I bought a pogo stick for Carol, and a new hockey stick for Ewan. Along Osborne Road I picked up a huge bunch of mistletoe from Alec Rose's greengrocer's shop for the princely sum of one and sixpence. I spent ages in Handley's department store choosing various items for my parents and relatives. The rest of my morning was spent mooching around some of the antique shops in Marmion and Albert Roads. I bought a slim silver brooch with one beautiful pearl at its centre. It reminded me of a frozen drop of water outside the window of my hut in the icy south. It was for Lesley – if and when I saw her.

Late afternoon in Commercial Road the pace of Christmas shopping was altogether more hectic. People had a harassed look about them in their effort to get the shopping done in time. I treated myself to a new record player from Courtney and Walker's and bought satsumas, chestnuts and brussel sprouts in Charlotte Street market. The old familiar shouts of the stallholders assailed me. 'Best bananas – get your bananas here ...' 'Come on ladies, a shilling for ten oranges to clear them up!' After the stark simplicity of living for two years in Antarctica, I relished the bustle of my home city. On the way home I bought a local paper. Turning first to the back page for the sport, I noticed with pleasure that Pompey were near the top of the second division, just below Birmingham City. They had lost 2-0 to QPR the previous Saturday, with Rodney Marsh scoring both goals. Saturday's next game was against Plymouth Argyle. Ray Hiron was fit again and George Smith, the manager, urged fans to forsake their Christmas shopping and turn up at Fratton Park to cheer their team to the top of the division. I fully intended to be there.

What else was going on in the city? The *Portsmouth Evening News* headlined a big fire at John Palmer's brush factory – damage was estimated at a quarter of a million pounds. The theft of 400 turkeys from Cooper & Sons at Lake Road was reported; the stolen van used in the incident had been found abandoned at Portchester Castle. Other news items included an appeal by the parents of James Hanratty to the Home Secretary, Jim Callaghan. The discovery of a body in the sea near the Sallyport was also reported. It had turned out to be that of a Mr James Hillier, a company director with a Mayfair address.

On the municipal front, Lord Mayor Connors was visiting local hospitals. Civic leaders were discussing the future of the Theatre Royal, and Buchanan's Solent City Plan. Also featuring prominently were stories about the possible demolition of houses in Stamshaw, and the imminent arrival in Melbourne of Alec Rose. The grocer and sailor from Southsea was in the middle of his single-handed round-the-world voyage on Lively Lady.

That evening, all of us (the Taylor family) went to the cinema. They left the choice of what to see to me. Julie Andrews and Paul Newman were appearing in a musical and a Western respectively, but it was really a choice between The Beatles in *Help!* at the Classic or Julie Christie at the Palace. I chose the latter. There had been plenty of music during my months away, but certainly no romance, and I had a soft spot for the beautiful actress who had first made her name in *Far From the Madding Crowd*.

I called Lesley's number when I got back but got no reply. Saturday morning was spent chatting over a leisurely breakfast. There was a steady trickle of mum's friends calling to say "hello". But still no sign of Lesley. I had a photo of her, taken on a trip to the Isle of Wight two or three years ago. At that time she had her dark hair cut short and wore a fashionable mini skirt. I longed to see her wonderful smile again. Maybe I'd see her later.

In the meantime, midday, I set off for Fratton Park, having arranged to meet some of my old schoolmates at the Talbot for a drink. This was a custom that we established long before our eighteenth birthdays.

'Graham, how on earth did you survive for two years without beer, girls and football?' My mate Ron asked, half seriously.

'Well,' I replied. 'The first two were a bit of a problem, but from what I hear, missing Pompey's games was no great loss!'

'Get away!' Ron exclaimed. 'You've missed some great times.'

'Oh yes, you mean the FA Cup match when we lost to Aldershot?! By the way, have you seen Lesley?' I said, trying to sound indifferent.

'Sure, she's been around, but not so far this holiday as far as I know,' Ron replied. 'She might be working on the post in Bristol after finishing her college term.'

Well, if that was true, I thought, then at least she had not been deliberately avoiding me.

After several pints and a good chat, we joined the stream of Pompey fans on Goldsmith Avenue. The club's fortunes had seemed varied in recent years. Now they were at least pushing for promotion. The Pompey chimes rang out as the minutes ticked by to kick-off. The green and white scarves of the Argyle fans at the Milton End contrasted with the royal blue of the home supporters.

Regrettably, the game did not live up to expectations. After a bright start with the Pompey attack nearly scoring several times, the game settled down into a dour midfield struggle. Argyle came for a point and got it. They used the offside trap to good effect, and even the raucous wall of sound from the Fratton faithful couldn't help break the deadlock.

'Play up Pompey ... Pompey play up!'

'And it's Portsmouth City – Portsmouth City it is. It's by far the greatest city the world has ever seen!'

'Get stuck in, Hirom, you great giraffe!' urged a frustrated Pompey fan to my left. When Roy Pointer went down in the box during the second half, the referee ignored claims for a penalty.

'You blind git! What's your wife giving you for Christmas – a pair of specs?' Ron bawled.

I enjoyed the occasion more than the football. On the way back, we sought the consolation of a postmortem and took pleasure in learning that Southampton had lost too. After a couple of beers, we began to discuss the prospect of victory in the next match against Crystal Palace on Boxing Day. Nonetheless, I felt a bit down in the dumps as I trudged home. If only Lesley would suddenly appear round the corner.

The next day – Sunday, Christmas Eve – I went on our traditional family outing to the Forest of Bere to buy a Forestry Commission tree. On the way back, Carol excitedly counted the number of houses with Christmas trees. Our route took us through Southwick, Cosham, North End, Kingston and Fratton. The congested city of my birth still hadn't really come to terms with the motor car, although there was talk of a motorway being built in the near future.

That evening I again tried to contact Lesley on the phone. This time I did get through. Her mum said she had gone out with friends and that she would leave a message to say I had called. Later we watched the telly. Benny Hill gave us all a laugh, followed by *The Man from UNCLE* and carols sung by the choir of King's College, Cambridge. The evening's viewing was interrupted only by a group of kids who rang the door bell insistently. The only carol they knew was *While Shepherds Watched Their Flocks by Night*, and then only the first verse! Much to their evident disappointment, they were rewarded not with cash but with a biscuit each.

Later, parcels were hurriedly wrapped, and 'baby' sister Carol, who had recently celebrated her twelfth birthday, announced she was putting out her stocking.

'You don't still believe in Santa Claus?' Ewan and I teased her.

'Yes I do,' she replied cheekily. 'And she's sitting right here in this room!'

Next morning I woke early as usual. Next door, Carol was humming away as she read her new books. I thought of previous Christmases when, aged six, I had been given a carpentry set and, to my parents' horror, had set about attacking some of our furniture. Then the brand-new Raleigh bike I had acquired when I was thirteen. I'd spent most of the day racing around on it and had taken it down to the seafront to watch the lifeguards taking their Christmas morning dip.

Last Christmas, in Antarctica, we British scientists had got together with our South American counterparts and a great time was had by all. We had drunk excellent Chilean wine and scoffed traditional Christmas pudding. We had sung *Auld Lang Syne* in Spanish, and partied well into the night. And it had most certainly been a very white Christmas.

Back home in grey old England there was no sign of any snow, but I certainly relished the rituals of a seasonal holiday at home. We opened our presents; to my intense disappointment no present – not even a card – from Lesley. However, I still enjoyed a great Christmas dinner with all the trimmings.

We all helped to wash up and then relaxed, half listening to the Queen's Speech. When she said in conclusion, "I am sustained and encouraged by the happiness and sense of unity which comes from seeing all the family together," we toasted ourselves in mutual appreciation.

Everyone, apart from me, wanted it to snow but it was a mild damp afternoon. We were all sitting around the fire with books, games, chocolates, glasses of red wine and whisky, when the doorbell rang sharply. For a moment no-one answered it. Finally, Carol went to see who it was. She came back and pointed to me, announcing pertly,

'Graham, it's for you...'

Reluctantly leaving the cosy room, I walked up the cold hallway. The outer door was open, and through the plate glass I could see a figure. It looked familiar. I tried to get a better look. Whoever it was had dark hair; she was wearing a white polo-necked sweater under an anorak. Feeling relief, delight and nervousness all in one, I opened the door. Lesley flung open her arms invitingly. We held each other and kissed. Her cheeks were moist with rain or tears. I felt her soft warmth through her damp coat.

'Shut the door, you're letting the cold in,' shouted an impatient voice from the living room.

My sister stuck her head around the door asking, 'Who is it then?' Then, at the top of her voice, she shouted mischievously ... 'Mum, it's Graham and Lesley, and they're kissing under the mistletoe!'

THE HARD.

H.M.S. SULTAN'S ANCHOR

SOUTH PARADE PIER, SOUTHSEA.

CLARENCE ESPLANADE SOUTHSEA

Satisfied
with Life

The Bandstand, Southsea.

vee Scene, Steamer
New

Early years at Postcard Corner

Early years at Postcard Corner

*A*s I waited anxiously at the entrance of the city museum and art gallery, I heard a familiar and unwelcome voice, that of Director Toady Purkiss, my boss.

'Ah, young Philip, I'm glad you are here. I trust everything is in order for the big occasion?'

'Good evening, Mr Purkiss,' I replied, trying to sound calm and competent. 'Yes, I think everything is ready. The catering staff are just putting out the refreshments, and the exhibition is all set up ready for the grand opening by our celebrity guest.'

'Good, we don't want anything to go wrong tonight,' he barked as he brushed past me, his heavily perfumed wife on his arm.

'And, by the way, keep a look out for the Lord Mayor and his party; they are due to arrive any minute.'

It was only just half past five – half an hour to go before the moment that I had been working towards so hard for weeks. I was excited and nervous at the same time, but above all looking forward to the arrival of our special guest. His agent had promised that he would join us at six to officially open the exhibition.

A few minutes later I stationed myself at the doorway of the special exhibitions gallery. It was packed. This in itself was an unusual occurrence in this dockyard town. Many of the expectant crowd were overdressed and perspiring. They sipped warm *Liebfraumilch* and crunched flaky canapés. They kept one eye out for the arrival of the celebrity, and the other on fellow guests – especially those they particularly wished to be seen with, or to avoid.

The Lord Mayor and his posse duly arrived at 5.37pm and

Amanda and I ushered them to where the other dignitaries were gathered. I left Amanda, my fellow junior curator, to listen, as best she could, to the overbearing councillors who surrounded the city's first citizen. The obsequious Purkiss was pontificating about the exhibition which he had done little to prepare and knew precious little about. The official party would have been larger had it not been for an untimely outbreak of food poisoning following a mayoral banquet some days earlier. Contaminated oysters from Langstone Harbour had been blamed for so much civic discomfort.

Amanda glanced in my direction. She pointed enquiringly at her watch. There were just ten minutes to go but no sign of our illustrious guest of honour. Still, there was no real reason to panic since I had been assured by his agent that he would arrive at the appointed hour.

Normally, municipal exhibitions attracted but a sprinkling of the city's great and good. But tonight was different. It was a unique celebration of the 50th birthday of one of Britain's best known stars of radio, stage and screen. Once it had become known that the great man – born in Southsea half a century before – was to put in an appearance, invitations had been like gold dust. Never had Toady Purkiss been so popular. Usually, his slimy manner won him few friends, but in the last few days he had basked in the limelight of municipal and media attention. He had even recorded interviews with BBC South and Radio Victory.

What he told them, I dreaded to think, for he had not lifted a finger to get the show off the ground. Indeed, it had been my idea from the start. I had hatched the idea with Amanda during a coffee break. At the time, few people in the city had the faintest idea that the star had been born locally and spent his childhood here on the South Coast.

How did I know? Well, it so happened that it was my uncle, Dr Robert Lyttle, who practised at the time from 20 St Helen's Parade, who had presided over his birth. Baby Peter had entered the world at three minutes to midnight on the 8 September, thus increasing the population of Portsmouth to a grand total of 247,343 souls.

Uncle Bob had recounted the story of the birth on numerous occasions – especially once his 'patient' had become so famous – how the infant's mother, Peg, had gone into labour on the stage of the King's Theatre; how, on that blustery autumn night half a century ago, they had raced back to their lodgings in the nick of time.

Initially, Amanda and I had not been convinced that we should try to make a big thing of it. After all, we already had our share of local heroes: Charles Dickens had his birthplace museum at 387 Mile End Road, Landport. His mistress, Ellen Terry, had been laid to rest in the Highland cemetery. There was a plaque on the site of Sir Arthur Conan Doyle's house in Elm Grove, and a monument to Isambard Brunel, the great Victorian engineer, was to be found (if you looked hard enough) in Portsea. The departure point of the heroic Lord Nelson destined for Trafalgar, victory and death was marked by his diminutive statue facing the sea.

Yes, Portsmouth's notable sons – 'why no daughters?' Amanda had demanded to know – were physically, albeit intermittently, remembered.

But not the great P.S. – at least not until today. But where the Dickens was he? The clock showed 5.55pm and it was almost certainly slow. He was due at any moment.

I could feel the excitement and the noise level mounting by the minute. For my part, I was just beginning to feel a wee bit anxious. I fully expected him to arrive on time. After all, he must know the A3 from London well enough, and shouldn't get lost in his native city. I took a look out front into the parking area but there was no sign of him.

As we had painstakingly planned and assembled the exhibition, we had discussed the link between the artistically famous and the places associated with them – Shakespeare and Stratford, Thomas Hardy and Wessex, Kafka and Prague, James Joyce and Dublin, JB Priestley and Bradford – the list was endless, enough to fill an atlas of literature at least.

Was it merely an accident of history or geography, or were celebrities born according to some universal laws of genetics or demography? What was it about Liverpool that spawned The Beatles and Walworth Charlie Chaplin?

Compiling the displays had concentrated our minds on the possible influences of locality on literature. We convinced ourselves that being born into a theatrical family in Southsea in the twenties had made a difference. And we had set out to show exactly how.

Of course, many had left the city of their birth – Dickens within a year. Others had left Solent shores to seek fame and fortune – or to fight and never return. The early settlers to Virginia had all been wiped out in their lost colony on Roanoke Island.

But at least one famous Portsmuthian was due to make a triumphant return in a few moments – and the clock was showing six on the dot.

I saw Amanda pushing her way towards me. She wore a fixed smile, clearly bearing a message from the top brass.

'Patrick, shouldn't he be here by now?' she enquired anxiously.

'Don't panic madam,' I replied, trying to sound nonchalant. 'You go and do a recce outside and I will have a word with those who must be obeyed!'

As she disappeared, I made a beeline for the group comprising the Lord Mayor, Toady, and the Chairman of the Museums and Entertainment Committee. All three had the highest of expectations for the event. To put it bluntly, Purkiss had only agreed to it to boost the ailing reputation of his department and arrest falling attendances at the museum. The city fathers had voted eight thousand pounds to cover its costs, but this was only after they had finally realised that they would be put on the map by the visit of such a celebrity. But where on earth was he?

The assembled crowd, who had earlier busied themselves examining the displays, began glancing at the entrance. Or even worse, at me. This was my first real exhibition. If it was a flop (perish the thought), and *he* didn't show up, I would surely carry the can. My career in museum management had only just begun; I had no desire to face humiliation at the hands of my superiors, nor indeed lose Amanda's respect and affection.

As I eased my way towards the posse of big wigs I felt sweat trickling down my back under my new suit. Other moments of acute embarrassment earlier in my life came flooding back to me – missing a CSE maths exam, scraping my dad's Allegro as a learner driver, losing my passport in Croatia. All these seemed to pale into insignificance compared to this potential disaster.

'Good evening Your Worship,' I mumbled. 'I'm glad to say that he left London in good time and is due any minute. Rest assured, I will inform you and the director the instant he arrives.'

My tone was deferential and, I hoped, soothing enough to allay any doubts they might be harbouring.

'All right Lyttle, but let's hope we are not kept waiting much longer,' the chairman replied curtly, helping himself to another glass of *Côte du Rhone*.

I retreated to the doorway and the familiarity of Amanda's presence. Outwardly, she appeared calm, but as I got close she whispered, 'Where the hell is he? He left at midday and seems to have completely disappeared.'

'We can stall for a while longer,' I answered, trying not to sound flustered.

'Try to get hold of his wife at his home number,' I pleaded. It was at moments like these that you wished such things as car telephones had been invented!

17

'Which one?' Amanda retorted mischievously. 'OK, I'll check his whereabouts, you entertain the troops.'

I must have looked quite glum because she gave my arm an affectionate squeeze before disappearing into our cubby hole of an office.

I don't know what you do when you are nervous, but I pace up and down. On this occasion however, there simply wasn't room for that. Instead, I surveyed the scene, doing my best to exude a semblance of calm professionalism.

At the entrance of the gallery we had placed life-sized, cardboard cutout figures of characters from his films. There was the unmistakable accident-prone French detective, Inspector Jacques Clouseau, with his trilby and white trenchcoat. Nearby stood Mr Fred Kite, the strike-prone, Soviet-loving shop steward. Arranged around them were other Elstree Studios' figures, characters who had become familiar to cinema audiences in Britain and around the world. Harry the teddyboy in *The Ladykillers*. The randy Welsh librarian. The incompetent East End dentist, clasping a mangy cat with which he blotted a single entry in his otherwise empty appointment book. Also, prominently located, was the chillingly eccentric Dr Strangelove, with his right arm extended in an involuntary Nazi salute.

Behind these characters, all played by the one star, were display cabinets full of memorabilia. The London studios had been generous. The costumes, disguises, scripts and publicity materials for films and stage productions all made for a colourful show. *But*, only as a backcloth to the star who was due to appear in the flesh.

The far corner of the gallery was given over to The Goons. We had lovingly recreated a scene from the Grafton Arms in the West End, where they had done most of their drinking and what passed for rehearsals. In the background was Major Grafton MC, landlord and one-time scriptwriter/producer of the show. The centrepiece was the three Goons clustered around a BBC microphone. On the right was Peter playing Colonel Denis Bloodnok, Babu Banerjee, the Right Honourable Hercules Gryptepype-Thynne, and a host of other parts. Harry the chubby, ebullient Welshman stood to his left, acting out his famous Neddie Seagoon character. And in the centre of the gang was the unmistakable, manic, zany, one-and-only Spike, playing Minnie, Moriarty and Eccles – sometimes all at once! They had dog-eared scripts in their hands, and were clearly enjoying each other's company and their own performances.

We had decked out a 1950s pub as the setting. In those days their shows, which usually recorded at the Camden Theatre, were avidly listened to by up to four million people, at home and abroad. In the pub, their audience comprised a few cronies drinking Watney's Bitter and smoking Players. Sitting on the bar was the landlord's pet monkey. Legend had it that he had once peed into a plate of brown Windsor soup. This story had never been proved, since this particular speciality of the house had a bland and dispiriting taste at the best of times.

In the exhibition a recording of *The Goon Show* from 1952 was being played from an old Bakelite radio set. Quite a crowd had gathered round to hear the still familiar voices. They were in stitches.

The same could not be said for others in the room, who were beginning to show signs of boredom and impatience. To my horror, a few guests could be seen sidling to the door and disappearing. Others were refilling their glasses yet again and tucking into the food which was supposed to be consumed after the official opening.

Once again Amanda appeared at my shoulder. 'Still no sign of him ... you'll have to do something to distract them until he gets here ... if he gets here!' she hissed in my ear.

Yet again, with a sinking heart, I approached the Mayoral party. They were, by now tucking into sausage rolls, and egg and cress sandwiches. Some were even starting on the cream cakes and pecan pie which I had ordered specially for the official guests.

'Mr Purkiss, it won't be long now. May I suggest that, in the meantime, I say a few words about the exhibition. Then, we can have the opening as planned. We have heard that he is not far away and should be with us very soon,' I lied.

'Yes, but be quick about it,' was the none-too-encouraging reply. 'The Lord Mayor has another engagement to go to this evening, and our guests are getting tired of waiting!' Despite not being prepared for a set piece speech, I felt curiously lighthearted as I stepped up onto the dais. This had been readied for our famous guest. Not for me, one of the most junior employees on the city council's payroll.

'My Lord Mayor, Ladies and Gentlemen,' (there was no going back now). 'You will be relieved to know that the arrival of our special guest is imminent. May I crave your indulgence for a few moments to tell you a little about the exhibition,' I continued. 'You may have heard the saying the child is father of the man, well our exhibition, which you have been kind enough to show such a close interest in,' (was I sounding like Toady?) 'tells that story.'

'We believe,' I went on boldly, 'that his family and formative life here in our city, moulded his personality, his career and even, dare I say it, his private life.'

At this point I saw the Lady Mayoress give a wan smile. What could she be thinking? I paused, partly to see if the audience was listening. To my surprise, they were mostly attentive. Now I had to think of what to say next.

'The man you will be meeting in person in a few moments was formed, I believe, by a trio of influences. These were his immediate family, the characters he met in his corner of the town during his early years and, lastly, his experiences on tour with his parents in provincial theatres, music halls and temporary lodgings.' I continued on lest their attention flagged. 'This is the theme underpinning the exhibition. We have tried to portray the background of our guest celebrity and the years that he spent with his family a few hundred yards from where we are standing tonight. There to the left of the Lord Mayor you will see the living room of their first floor flat recreated in the style of the thirties!'

The scene depicted was of a birthday party. Peter's seventh. The calendar to the right of the fireplace showed September 1932. Peter was of course at the centre of the group. He was surrounded by a pile of presents – a train set, toy drums and ukulele, sweets and oranges.

His father Bill was sat at the piano, fag in mouth, a beer at his elbow. He was a short, stocky, dark-haired man. Sitting beside the fire was the rounded, grey-headed figure of Ma Rainey, the formidable head of the extended family, and queen of English show-business. Her eight sons and two daughters had followed her into the world of theatre, including Peter's mother.

Peg had married Bill in 1923. She had spotted him playing in the Lyons Coffee House in Palmerston Road. It must have been his spirited rendering of, *I'm Forever Blowing Bubbles* that convinced them that he would make a useful addition to their theatre troupe – and a suitable husband.

Mother and Auntie Ve were fussing over the young, chubby Peter. You could almost hear Peg saying, "Pete, luv, you're the only one that matters ... Peter, what do you want next ...? Ve, bring him another glass of lemonade." If the impression was given by the tableau that Peter was being cosseted and indulged, then that's exactly as it was.

Above the piano was a sepia photograph of a Victorian prize fighter. It was the famous Daniel Mendoza, who had, for a brief time, been the boxing champion of the world. Of Sephardic Jewish descent, he had risen to the top of the boxing world from humble East End origins. Although fame and fortune had been short-lived, he was revered as a family forebear who had made good. In contrast to this muscular, moustached boxer, his great grandson Peter was a curly haired, chubby and overdressed little lad. He was basking in the undivided attention of his family, and loving every moment of it.

I was gratified to see that a fair number of the crowd were now gathering around the family scene to examine its characters with obvious interest. Encouraged, I continued my exposition.

'You see Ladies and Gentlemen, Peter was the apple of his mother's eye. He came from a close and ambitious family. They pushed him to play and perform from an early age. What Peter wanted Peter got – at least when they were there to give it to him.'

The audience were still with me, I plunged on ...

'But, Ladies and Gentlemen, his early life was also one of insecurity and loneliness. His parents were on the road half the time. They either took him with them or left him behind with Ma Rainey. He went on tour with them to Bolton, to Leeds, Glasgow and Torquay. Some of his first impressions were of the bright lights and backstage bustle, but also the shabby dressing rooms and clogged toilets. He was cuddled by adoring chorus girls and cradled by the rapacious landladies in theatrical digs. Is it surprising that he ended up on the stage? The theatre was in his blood,' I pronounced.

On the wall, we had hung a series of billboards illuminating some of the shows in which his parents had appeared. One of these was at the Hippodrome in Keighley.

'You may not know,' I continued (knowing full well that they didn't) 'that on one occasion Peter nearly died. He contracted a severe bout of bronchial pneumonia amidst the freezing dampness of a Yorkshire winter. It was only through the herculean efforts of an African medical student, who tended him all that night, that he survived at all.'

'So, you can see that Peter was a product of his family and

their lifestyle. But he also learnt a lot from the place he spent much of his early life, above the stationer's shop at what was then called Postcard Corner.'

Again, I took a careful look at my audience. To my great surprise they were paying heed to my mini lecture. The fact that it was now quarter past six — well past the time for the official opening — seemed to have been temporarily forgotten. At the back I could see Amanda signalling for me to carry on. I did.

'Do you remember people and places from your childhood? I'm sure you do.'

I found it difficult to imagine Toady Purkiss having a childhood. He must have been a sallow, goody goody, who must have spent most of his time telling his mother all about the misdemeanours of his boisterous classmates at Craneswater Junior School.

We had created our very own Postcard Corner in the far section of the hall. In it we had placed a series of postcard racks, as if in a stationer's shop. The actual emporium had long since been converted into a café, but we had managed to collect postcards of the day from local junk shops, and our own museum and library collections. They depicted scenes from pre-war Southsea, then a fashionable resort. There were scenes of Ladies' Mile on a Sunday morning — fashionable women strolled out in cloche hats, starched white blouses and long dark skirts. They pushed ornate prams and held their husbands' arm.

There were cards of church parades at the Garrison Church, Canoe Lake, South Parade Pier, Southsea Castle, and the bandstand on Southsea Common. It was here that the young Peter was pushed to the front by his ambitious parents so as to catch the eye of the band leader. More often than not, he was invited up onto the stage. Here too he rode his bike along the promenade, stopping only to demand ice creams and lemonade.

'I'm sure that all of you who know and love Southsea will

be interested in having a close look at our little shop,' I said, pointing at the display of postcards. 'You might also like to read the messages on the reverse side and to whom they were sent. You will note that were dispatched by holiday makers and lonely servicemen to their loved ones and relatives. They may have been purchased from the Lightbourne Family shop at the corner of Castle Road. They were sent all over the country – Nuneaton, Norwich, Nunhead and Nantwich to name but a few!

'You will see that the messages scrawled by the senders were short and predictable – "Weather is glorious", "Having a lovely time ...", "Not forgotten you", "Rotten sunburn and headache ...", and one of my favourites – "Ethel fell in a boggy place at Alum Bay today and I laughed 'til it hurt".' All eyes turned to the postcards.

'Ladies and Gentlemen, we are honoured to have Miss Mary Lightbourne with us this evening. I repeat, it was from her family shop, above which our guest celebrity lived, that many of these postcards were sold. Other neighbours of the time were Mr Ernie Thornbank of the Bush Hotel, and Harry Ricketts who still operates his bicycle shop at Number 18 Castle Road. Then there was Miss Whiting who slapped Peter's podgy legs – she was the only one who did – when he was disobedient at the dancing classes he was forced to attend. We are also pleased to have Mr Knight here. He is the photographer at Number 56 who sold Peter his first, but certainly not his last, camera. Also, here is Mr Leslie Champion from Smith and Vosper's Bakery. He used to slip Peter a cake or bun after school. Finally, though he is long since deceased, I must not forget Mr Andrews the ventriloquist, who lived in the flat above them, and performed on the seafront during the summer season. He is alleged to have spent the rest of the year in the Wheelbarrow public house with his cronies.

'Ladies and Gentlemen, these were the characters amongst whom Peter grew up. When he wasn't being dragged around the country on tour with his parents, or being spoilt in the bosom of his family, he was out and about in his neighbourhood. It is our belief that through listening to the characters in his neighbourhood he learnt many of the mannerisms and figures of speech which we know and love today!'

At this point I stood down from the dais and thanked them for listening.

There was a short silence. Then a few claps. I noticed that it was Amanda at the back who started the applause, but it spread. Even a beaming Lord Mayor was showing his appreciation. Only Purkiss remained with his hands by his sides. He was gazing intently at the clock. It was now showing 6.27pm.

I saw Amanda shrug her shoulders despairingly. He still wasn't here. There was a hush and the audience looked at me expectantly.

'Please enjoy the exhibition – I am now going to fetch the star of our show,' I blurted out. With this, I bolted for the door.

'Amanda, give me your keys,' I shouted, 'I've got to find him pronto.'

I ran to her Mini and raced off into the gloom. On the front window were the familiar decals – the official Museum car park pass and Amanda's own, "Historians take time to do it!". But I had no time for amorous memories; I had to find him quickly or all would be lost. Despite my valiant and well received speech, I had to deliver on my promise of an appearance without further delay.

Where could he be?

Assuming he had reached the city and had not been waylaid in a pub on the A3, then he couldn't be far away. I drove furiously towards the city centre. Maybe he had gone to the New Theatre Royal, or the Sussex Hotel, to have a drink. There was no sign of him at either of these venues.

I hated to think what was happening back at the Museum, and certainly couldn't go back without him. I got back in the car and headed back to Southsea. All I could feel was a rising tide of dread. All this effort over my first real career initiative and it looked as though I was going to be let down by the very person whose presence was vital. At the very least, any chance of promotion, not to mention a salary rise, would be gone for good. The local press would have a field day. Toady, and even Amanda, would not forgive me easily. The thought of going back empty handed was too awful to contemplate. I couldn't run away. I drove down towards the seafront. Perhaps he had gone for a breath of sea air after his drive from London.

As I approached the junction of Western Parade and Kent Road, I slowed down to let an elderly woman and her dog struggle over the pedestrian crossing. I looked left up Castle Road and saw a sight which made my whole sense quicken. There, parked outside the Blue Lady café was a shiny, British racing green Jaguar car. Wait a minute ... amongst his large collection of expensive cars, didn't he own a Jaguar E-Type? I parked behind it and leapt out. What an idiot I had been! Where else would he be slinging his hook but the place where he had grown up – Postcard Corner?

I pushed open the door, and was immersed in the warm fug of a crowded café. The owner was standing behind his Italian coffee machine. He let out a loud belly laugh. The whole place was in uproar. All the chairs were taken and every occupant seemed to be in a state of advanced or intoxicated hilarity. Gales of laughter rose from every corner of the cramped premises.

There *he* was, at the heart of his impromptu audience. The centre of attraction and attention. None other than that man whom I had been working on for months, awaiting for hours and chasing all over the city. The one and only:

PETER SELLERS.

He was doing his Inspector Clouseau act. Striding around

the room, tripping over furniture, and poking his magnifying glass towards their plates of faggots and chips; jam tarts and custard.

I stood at the door, savouring the moment. I had, at last, tracked down my special guest. He pretended not to see me. Instead, he approached a customer and gave a loud raspberry.

'Madame, no more curried eggs for you tonight!'

Then he addressed the proprietor. 'Captain Boil de Spudswell of the Zsa Zsa Gabor's third Regular Husbands, I presume? I am your esteemed servant General Kashmai Chek.'

He must have seen me and knew my mission, for he turned to the crowd and bowed.

'It's been a business to do pleasure with you,' he announced. He picked out a ten pound note from his wallet and slapped it on the counter. Scooping up a handful of saucy postcards from the counter, he strode towards me and shook my hand.

'Right sailor ... I'm yours ... where to?'

'Let's leave your car here, I'll drive ... We have no time to lose,' I volunteered.

We set off down Southsea Terrace, but we had only gone fifty yards before Sellers shouted out, 'A pee, a pee, my pension for a pee.'

I reluctantly turned towards the Clarence Pier conveniences, the only such facilities open during the winter months. He disappeared inside and reappeared a minute later, furiously buttoning up his overcoat.

'I'm adjusting my dress, as ordered by the sign above the urinals,' he chuckled. 'I must remember that line for a future Goon Show.'

As we drove, he took a hip flask from his inside pocket and took a deep swig. I smelt brandy. A different sort of anxiety assailed me. Was he going to go over the top and make a fool of himself and me once we got back to the museum? I tried to briefly fill him in on the scene that awaited us.

'Don't worry my son,' he replied, 'I'm game for anything.' And broke into verse from the Goon Show. 'Ying tong, ying tong, ying tong, diddle I po, diddle I po.'

It was nearly seven o'clock as we entered the gallery. Much to my surprise most people were still there, including the Lord Mayor. The place was full and bottles were empty. A hush fell over the throng as I ushered in the one person for whom they had all been waiting. I couldn't help but feel a quiet glow of satisfaction, even smugness, as I steered him towards the Lord Mayor.

Sellers bowed, shook his hand and kissed the Lady Mayoress's hand with an extravagant Gallic gesture. She responded with a nervous laugh. Cheers and clapping went up from the waiting multitude. He mounted the rostrum, peeling off his coat and handing it to me. I waited. Had I snatched victory from the jaws of defeat by getting him here at last? Or, was he about to mess it all up?

Sellers – or was it Clouseau – waved his trilby for hush. 'Ladeez'n Gentlemen, and fellow fespians,' he began, 'I em so 'appy to be in Portsmuss again. I am zo zorry zat I hev been delayed in ze Cafe Filthmuck and I bleme its ownair Monsieur Maurice Plonk.'

Howls of laughter followed his Gallic quips. I smiled at Amanda, who was downing yet another large glass of wine. She held a second glass in her other hand and pointed it towards me.

'You kneuw zat I find it very congenital to visit my piece of birz. Ze gateway to ze incontinent. By ze way, do you still need a pisspot to visit gay Paris? And iz Prince Charles here on navel duties, can yeou tell me zat ...?'

By now, the place was in uproar. Laughter rang out all round, and the Lord Mayor slapped his thigh in glee. Even Toady began to titter, after first looking around to make sure that everyone was in full appreciation of the performance. And Sellers continued without let up.

'May I read you a few merry japes from my bumper book of fun?' And he proceeded to reel off a stream of jokes.

'What's a Greek urn? Answer, a couple of drachmas an hour ... . Have you heard about the pork pie I bought on Preston station? No? The dog's collar I found in it wasn't so bad but the meat was really tough!'

Then he asked if we had heard the one about the Greek and the Chinaman. 'Well, they met in Soho one night. The Greek chided the Chinaman for not being able to pronounce his R's after he had been wished a "Melly Chlistmas". A year later, at the same corner, the Chinaman went up to the Greek and, stressing the R's, said with a hint of triumph, "Very, very, merry Christmas, you Gleek plick!' ... more laughter and applause.

'Then there was a middle-aged man visiting his doctor with sexual problems.'

"What's wrong?" asked the GP.

"Infrequent," was the reply by the distraught patient.

"Is that one word or two?" enquired the doctor!' They were getting worse but the crowd was in the right mood.

'How many canaries can a Scotsman get under his belt? Answer – it depends on the length of his perch!'

"How old are you, granny?" asked a four year old.

"Well dear," she replied, "I can't remember my age anymore." After a few moments the child asked

"Why don't you look in your knickers – mine say 4 to 5 year olds ...!"

After this stream of gags had issued forth, Sellers assumed his Indian doctor guise.

'This is Banerjee here,' he mimicked.

'You know much of the English language has come from India? Goodness Gracious me! Hey, Mr Lord Mayor, sir, can you tell me any Indian words you English have stolen from us?' The Lord Mayor beamed, only too pleased to be made the centre of attention by the celebrated Peter Sellers.

'Let me see. What about pukka Sahib?'

'Very good!' came the repost.

'You too must surely have been in the Indian army; did you meet my friend the Reverend Spike Milligan? I'll tell you all these words are ours and you have taken them – bungalow, chutney, dinghy, dungarees, guru, jodphurs, pundit, shampoo, verandah, yes, and many more!'

I leant against the wall and soaked up the scene. You couldn't help but admire the craft of a great comedian at work. In spite of – or perhaps because of – the brandy, Sellers was on top form. He had the audience in his hand. He didn't give them time to draw breath. Some were dangerously puce with mirth, others wiping tears of merriment from their faces. The long delay had been forgotten. He was the life and soul of the party – *my* party.

The audience was facing the star performer. Behind them, my displays and cutout figures acted as a mere backcloth. But never mind that. At least those who had only come to see Sellers had, by his delayed appearance, learnt more about his early life. I felt more than a quiet glow of relief and satisfaction. I raised my glass in Amanda's direction. She put down her drink and raised her arms above her head in a triumphant salute. I knew my career and our friendship had been sealed in those last few minutes.

Meanwhile, Peter Sellers suddenly bowed to his audience. He reverted to Goon talk and exclaimed in Captain Seagoon's immortal words:

'The hairs on my wrist say it's quarter to needle nardle noo ... it's time to goo.'

I jumped forward to assist his suddenly announced departure.

'A pen, a pen, you fool Moriarty, a kingdom for a pen,' he shouted.

I pulled my municipal biro from my pocket and handed it to him. Out of his coat pocket he drew a sheaf of postcards

– the ones he had bought earlier at the café. He proceeded to autograph them in quick succession. It didn't take more than a minute. He then handed them to the crowd, starting with the Lord Mayor and his party. Needless to say, this act of generosity went down extremely well.

I had arranged that his car be brought around from Postcard Corner. I handed him the keys. He kissed Amanda, shook me warmly by the hand, and disappeared into the night to continue his life of booze, blondes and brilliant banter. But he never did forget Postcard Corner.

Early years at Postcard Corner

May Day ... May Day

*T*housands of people crossed the Thames that morning – by bus, tube, rail and on foot.

Reg Gardner walked slowly over Blackfriars Bridge. He'd had an early start from the south coast and was already feeling tired. He paused to look over the parapet at the grey, cold tidal water rushing downstream. Reg was in poor spirits. The previous evening he had had a row with the manager of his old people's home. Not for the first time he had insisted on turning the lights off at night (to save electricity) and had been threatened with expulsion. Reg had no family or real friends and felt alone in the midst of the commuting throng that engulfed him. But would anyone notice or care if he slipped over the parapet and a grey coat floated downstream with the rest of the flotsam?

'Are you OK, mate?' A passer by called out, but did not stop. He struggled to regain his breath and summon up the energy to go on. He glanced at the burgeoning skyline of the City of London further downstream. All his life he had fought against what it stood for. But to what end? To see the fall of communism, and American capitalism ruling the world?

At exactly the same time a couple of hundred yards upstream a dark-skinned Indian girl in a green sari strode over Hungerford Bridge in the same direction. She was also on her way to North London. Nila had arrived in the country only the day before to start her advanced cancer nursing course at the Royal Free Hospital. She had flown to Gatwick from her home in Kerala, and stayed overnight with a cousin who worked at the airport.

On the train to Waterloo that morning she had been

astonished how all her fellow passengers had totally ignored her. Nor did they greet or speak to each other. They read their *Metros* and some even fell asleep – so early in the morning! Some of the women did up their faces with make-up, indifferent to those around. Nila gazed out of the dirty window at the weeds along the track and graffiti on the walls nearby.

What an unfriendly welcome after the gaiety and tears of her departure from her large family in her village. She remembered her ill father's last words to her – 'Nila, my treasure, go to the mother country and see for yourself all that it has to offer, and make sure that you pay our respects to 'you know who' in London.' She knew he was not referring to the Queen of England.

Now on her first day in the capital, she was about to do his bidding. But England was all so grey and different. Her first impressions were far from favourable. She felt homesick and far from her warm, noisy compound in Kovalem. As she walked on, Nila paused and gazed in awe at Big Ben and the Houses of Parliament. She had only seen them before on calendars and TV.

But her wonderment was rudely interrupted as a passer-by bumped into her and she nearly crashed to the pavement. The flowers she had bought on the station fell to the ground. Tears came to her eyes as she picked them up and carried on.

Having worked as a bus conductor and trade union convenor on London Transport for nearly forty years, Reg knew his way round. The sights and sounds of London were all too familiar. He found a bus to take him to the museum on Clerkenwell Green but to his great disappointment it was closed for refurbishment. And his mood was blackened further by finding that Moriati's, his favourite café, had been replaced by a trendy wine bar. Bill was tempted to go back, but what a prospect – to the bossy staff and sedated clients of his 'home of comfort'? He struggled on towards Kings Cross to catch the No 214 to his Highgate destination.

Nila was bewildered by the grey bustle around her. Everyone rushing to work, and not so much as a glance in her direction, and that included Asian women who she hoped would have at least acknowledged her presence with a smile or cheery word. She was determined to find her way to the cemetery, and summoning up all her courage, she plunged down into the Underground.

Nila rattled north towards Archway. She opened her bag and took out the photos of her family. They were so proud that she had won a place to study in London. She was their ambassador and hope for the future. She knew that she would be expected to get her qualifications and marry a nice doctor – Indian or white, it did not matter. But her first duty was to visit the grave of a man who was revered above all others by her family and especially her father, a life-long activist in the Communist Party (Marxist/Leninist), and campaigner against privatisation in her home state of Kerala.

It was just after eleven o'clock when the park keeper opened the heavy Victorian gates of Highgate Cemetery. The first visitors of the day were a group of chattering Chinese students and a young Italian couple. He sold them some photos and a map and pointed them in the right direction. He then disappeared into his hut to make a brew. He waited patiently for the usual trickle of political pilgrims to arrive. He saw a small man in a pork pie hat and crumpled mackintosh stagger off the bus and towards the entrance. He looked grey and ill, and paused every few steps to catch his breath. He must have been here before, as he passed the kiosk without a word. A few minutes later a young Indian girl approached the gates and paused to take a photograph of the entrance. She looked exotically out of place on this damp, drizzly day. She smiled and asked the way. Just another to add to the thousands who came from all over the world to pay their respects to the great man.

Reg was sitting on a bench when he saw Nila approach. He

had opened his thermos of sweet tea and felt better – and not only because of the drink. The girl reminded him of his army service in India. The temptations that he and his fellow soldiers had been offered in Rawalpindi where, as a gunnery officer he had been stationed for all those years. Nothing much had happened. Corporal Gardner had waited till he got home, and at the age of 26, had found his first woman. The hussy had robbed him of every penny of the £115 he had saved up. He had no wife or daughter. Now he found himself gazing intently at the exotic princess who was standing a few feet away.

Nila was amazed as she stood and took in the scene. She wished that her father could be present to share it with her. In front of her was the man who had changed the world and inspired socialist advances in education and health in South India. Nila felt tears running down her cheeks, and to recover she busily clicked away with her Russian camera. But she had to have a photo of herself in front of the memorial to send home.

'Uncle, would you be so kind as to take a photograph?' Nila asked a small elderly man who was sitting nearby. The 91 -year-old got to his feet slowly and shuffled forward.

'My dear, it would be a pleasure.' Reg stretched his hand towards her and held the camera unsteadily as she stood proudly between him and the statue. The camera clicked several times and he handed it back to Nila.

'Would you like a cup of tea, love?' he asked gently. Nila nodded and smiled. It was the first kind word that had been spoken to her that day.

They sat on the bench together. Suddenly with a nice young woman to talk to, all Reg's trials and tribulations seemed to evaporate. For her part Nila was only too pleased to find one friendly face in a country of indifferent strangers. They sat together – the pair of them. Alone … except for the towering granite figure of Karl Marx.

The Quarterly Bulletin

of the

Marx Memoria

Library

No. 91

JULY/SEPTEMBER, 1979

J. Dywien

Andrew Rothstein

Frank Walker

J. R. Shanley

0025-410X

Early years at Postcard Corner

Scotch Pines

*I*t all looked exactly the same. The square, solid, Scottish farmhouse with a neat lawn in front, silhouetted against the familiar cluster of pines. The only change he noticed in the two years since he had left was that the driveway had been tarmacked. The "Myreside" farm sign was still nailed to the gatepost. It was written in cheap plastic letters bought by him many years ago at Woolworths in Hawick. He had fixed it with a newly acquired Christmas carpentry set.

His father's Ayrshire herd was in the milking parlour and sheep were huddled by the stone wall on the brackened hill. Further in the distance the Eildons were shrouded in a fine drizzle.

His father had met him off the Royal Scot at Carlisle a couple of hours earlier. The train had been packed by families returning north for Hogmanay. His dad hadn't altered much either. Just greyer. He had put on his best tweed jacket and regimental tie for the occasion, but still wore his everyday cap and well-worn brogues. They had driven up the A74 through familiar border country, its small, grey, mill and market towns bright with Christmas colour.

He saw his home with a feeling of ambivalence rather than elation. Hens scattered in all directions and the collies leapt up as the land rover pulled into the yard. He felt close to tears as his mother appeared on the back doorstep. She had been making scones and was hurriedly taking off her pinny. He struggled out to hug her.

Tea was a bit awkward. They didn't know exactly what to say to him nor he where to begin.

Two years ago when he had left for California on the

Young Farmers Club exchange visit he had written regularly. The flight, seeing New York from 30,000 feet up, the huge cars and enormous distances – had all been described in detail. He'd mentioned the black customs officer who had welcomed him cheerily with an – "OK, Malcolm, have a nice stay."

His letters had informed them all about the wonders of 'agribusinesses' in the California's Imperial Valley. He had written at length about private swimming pools, drive-in movie theatres and commercial clutter along the highways.

Since then communication across the Atlantic had become intermittent. From him, photographs of visits to Yellowstone and the Grand Canyon and postcards of the Golden Gate Bridge and Mexico City. He had sent some T-shirts for his nephews the previous Christmas. He had received from them, copies of the local *Teviotdale Gazette* regularly, and letters full of family and farming news.

But during the last eighteen months they had heard little from or of him. He had never really explained why he had decided to stay in the States, obtained a work permit and found himself – it was in the Vietnam years – being drafted into the Marines. They knew little of his time at Fort Bragg, a sprawling military complex located amongst the brown flakey-barked pines of the North Carolina Piedmont. Nor of his time at Fayetteville, with its former slave market, segregated streets and schools. Here he had learnt what 60s life was really like in the segregated American South.

Of course as next of kin they had been notified by the US military authorities of his injury but they had never been told exactly how it happened.

He had been playing in a game of American softball. The game had started at a friendly pace but had hotted up. He had been running for a pass from his friend Hank Williams when someone tackled him. He had twisted and fallen to the red soil of the exercise field. He had felt only a terrible searing pain in his back, and remembered being surrounded by a cluster of concerned players.

His spine was damaged and he was semi-paralysed. He had been kept in the Veterans hospital for five months until he could walk with the aid of crutches. Then he had been sent home. But all this was too painful to tell.

Later in the evening, sitting in front of the fire, they all began to relax a bit. He was gently chided for asking for some ice in his whisky. He recounted some incidents from his journey home – selling his car for one dollar before embarking from pier 42 in New York. About the American hippies on the Italian liner who smoked pot in their cabin. They were convinced that rice was good for the brain. The Southampton taxi driver who had taken him to Euston station for a fiver.

Only when his father had gone out to shut up the hens did his mother ask him shyly how he was. Did he feel much pain? Should they contact the specialist they knew in Edinburgh after Christmas?

"I'm fine Mum," he'd said. "Really ... We'll see about further treatment in good time." He didn't have the heart to tell her the truth which was that there was no hope of any improvement and that he would be paralysed for the rest of his life.

He woke up about seven the next morning to the sound of a tractor being started up. He lay with his eyes closed for a few moments. No bugle and barrack room swearing, nor the bustle of night nurses in the Veterans hospital going off duty. Only farmyard sounds and a blackbird singing in the holly bush outside his window.

When he opened his eyes he was struck by the smallness and sameness of his room. A Lakeland picture on the wall opposite. School rugby photographs. The bookcase filled with old film and sports annuals from the '50s. In the corner his cases and bags were piled up, as yet unopened. Crutches by the chair.

"Breakfast's ready, Malcolm," his mother called.

He had already smelt the bacon and toast. At least she hadn't brought it up on a tray. In the past he would have flung on his clothes and be sitting at the table in a couple of seconds. Now he took an age to wash, dress and struggle awkwardly down the narrow staircase. Over breakfast his father suggested that they go to a local rugby match that afternoon. Kelso were playing Melrose, the club for which he had played after leaving school.

Many of his old acquaintances would be there. His older brother Jamie, who had 'married well' and now farmed 400 acres near Lilliesleaf, would be serving behind the bar. Sally Cairns, who he used to take home on the back of his motorbike after dances, would be making teas for the players. She would be wearing her high-fitting cashmere jumper and jeans. He had read in the local rag that she was engaged to a teacher from Motherwell.

What would they make of him? A wounded hero returned home? A worldly traveller first to be envied, now to be pitied?

"No thanks Dad, I think I'll take it easy today," he said.

At about two he saw his father off from the back porch. As always it was stuffed with coats, keys, twine and torches. A shotgun for shooting rabbits was propped up in the corner. There was a half-full box of cartridges on the shelf.

A little later he went out into the farmyard. The December weather was bleak and grey. Familiar smells of hay, manure and sheep dip greeted him. The stable was now full of yellow bagged ICI fertilizer. The pipes by the horse trough were bound with sacking and a block of soap was still wedged in by the tap. He passed the hay loft where the Irish farm workers used to stay in the summer. From an upper window he and his friends had once emptied a pale of water over a crusty old aunt. The duckhouse and pigsty were full of rusty machinery. He came to the open-sided barn where, during the war, his granny had allowed tramps to stay the night. She had even given them a cooked breakfast (you didn't need coupons in the country). No wonder they kept on coming back with a new hard-luck story.

He sat down on a hay bale. He knew that, however much he loved the place in which he had been born and brought up, he would not have come home if he had had any choice. Why did it have to happen to him? What could he do now?

He couldn't take over the farm from his father as planned. He doubted that West Cumberland Farmers would employ a non-driver as a salesman. Run a sports shop in Hawick or Gala? It was too late – a Scottish ex-international rugby player had already cornered the market. He knew a desk job in an insurance office wasn't for him. However well he got on with his parents, he couldn't see himself staying on the farm able only to feed the hens and help with the accounts. He would be cut off and dependent.

The cold, damp evening was closing in, and so was his world. He made his way back to the porch and then returned to the barn. He remembered the occasion when he and his sister had hidden high in the hay and watched – breathless but emotionless – a pig being killed below.

He loaded the shotgun, gripped the cold gun metal tightly and pulled the trigger. His mother looked up sharply from the kitchen stove. The rooks in the Scotch Pine trees exploded in noisy confusion.

Early years at Postcard Corner

Lord Nelson and the Dinner at the Admiralty

An Informative Treatise on Lord and Lady Nelson and Lord and Lady Hamilton by Admiral William Willmot Henderson CB KH. This strictly veracious account being largely written on HMS Victory, the Royal Dockyard, Portsmouth, in 1843 and completed on board the mail steamer Tyne, off Madeira, June 1854

*D*ear Readers.

You will all be familiar with Lord Nelson's famous victory at Trafalgar. You will know that, when news of this epic sea battle reached England in 1805, church bells were rung and bonfires lit throughout the land. The whole nation mourned and thousands of us attended his funeral and burial at St Paul's Cathedral. You need no reminder of Lord Nelson's redoubtable naval career and valiant exploits as the greatest naval commander that England has ever had the fortune to possess. Can it really be four decades since the Hero of the Nile was killed in action?

But I am of the firm opinion that the memory of his glorious victories lives on in the pages of our history books, Her Majesty's Royal Navy training manuals and in the hearts of all true Englishmen. Why, there are even hundreds of taverns and hostelries up and down the country that have been named after Lord Nelson. I'll wager that in two hundred years from now our loyal antecedents will be celebrating his famous victory!

But, esteemed readers, I warrant that barely a single one of you knows what went on at a certain dinner at the Admiralty. (This event took place after Nelson and his entourage had returned from the Mediterranean in 1800.) I do, for the simple reason that I was one of the few who were present that evening in the dining room of the First Sea Lord.

Of course it is common knowledge that Lord Nelson, despite being the devout son of a clergyman, had what I must term an 'intimate' relationship with Lady Emma Hamilton. Perchance you do not know, and indeed find it strange to believe, that there existed a deep mutual friendship between Sir William Hamilton and Lord Nelson. It is a matter of fact that, for all but two months of the three years Lord Nelson and Lady Hamilton were 'bosom friends' in Mediterranean ports, they were also in the company of the ageing Sir William.

There was, as the French say a 'ménage a trois.' And I am able to confirm that all three, as well as Fanny, Lady Nelson, were seated round the Admiral's dinner table that very evening. For my own part I was delighted to receive an invitation to this seemingly auspicious supper party. I feel it my duty to report to you what transpired that evening, not in the interests of idle or malicious curiosity, rather in the spirit of genuine understanding of my fellow naval officer, and his duties, deeds and delights.

For I have with me in my cabin a first edition of the 'Life of Nelson' by Robert Southey. In many ways it is an admirable testament to the life of our hero. It faithfully recounts his exploits from midshipman to Admiral of the Fleet. It depicts the famous victories he masterminded at the battles of St Vincent, the Nile, Copenhagen, and Trafalgar. Yet I must profess serious objections to

Southey's account.

I do not question for an instant the accuracy of his dates, nor the fitting interpretation the author gives to the qualities of Admiral Lord Nelson's seamanship, patriotism and leadership. But my belief is that the pages of his book offer but a partial, and altogether too dry version, of Nelson's life. There is precious little told of how he spent his days at sea and nights ashore. His Lordship's afflictions and passions are all too summarily dismissed. He is condemned by Southey as 'guilty of criminal immorality' for having a 'vicious liaison with Lady Hamilton with whom he was infatuated.' Nelson, we are told, 'behaved scandalously and inexcusably in casting off his dutiful wife'.

Honourable readers, I leave you to decide upon questions of morality. But let us not wilfully or rashly judge the actions of others without first gaining some understanding of their situations. It was Lady Hamilton herself who termed the close bonds between herself and the two noble Lords as a 'tria juncta in uno'. Now this unusual domestic, not to say platonic and amorous arrangement, may not accord with our Christian principles. Some may have been genuinely scandalised and certainly Mrs Henderson, my beloved spouse, did not approve. But does that mean that the actions of those concerned were to be roundly condemned by all and sundry?

Discerning readers — Since I have taken the liberty of being critical of the eminent historian Southey you will be asking yourself about my own credentials for offering an alternative account. My supposition to you is that being a serving naval officer – I joined the Navy in 1793 – the very year that Lord Nelson first met Lord and Lady Hamilton, I have no little knowledge of those naval times. I fought at Trafalgar as a junior officer on the 'Belle

Isle.' I witnessed some of the 1,587 men lose their lives on that glorious but fateful day. On my ship some thirty-four brave souls perished. I, thank the Lord, survived and have been fortunate to have lived on in pursuance of domestic happiness and professional advancement.

But of course that gives me no monopoly of wisdom. For there are, as I write, many thousands of officers and men in Her Majesty's senior service. They will all have their own tale to tell and interpretation of events. I have it on good authority there are presently no less than 40 admirals, 50 rear admirals, 103 vice admirals, 717 captains, 843 commanders, 2,694 lieutenants, 36,337 men (including Royal Marines), and 6,678 boys in the Royal Navy.

But unlike me they were not present at the dinner party that night. Nor have they read many of the hundreds of Lord Nelson's letters – at least those that have survived. For the long months when I was laid off on half pay (five years, two months, two weeks and one day in total to be precise) I have worked diligently on diaries and documents. I have scrutinised newspaper reports and cartoons depicting Lord Nelson's alleged frailties and foibles.

But not being content to rely on dusty Admiralty reports, I have spent a fair part of my prize money on travelling long distances to search out and speak to well placed informants. I conversed at length with Mr Tom Allen, Lord Nelson's personal servant. This blunt man was, much to his regret, not on board Victory at the Battle of Trafalgar. He believed to his dying day that had he been beside his master he could have looked after him and prevented his tragic death. Sad to recount, Tom later returned to his native Norfolk and fell on hard times. From him I learnt that his lordship rarely drank more than a glass or two of wine; that he often took catnaps in his cabin; that his green eye patch was attached to his hat, that he took camphor and opium to relieve outbreaks of pain and melancholy. All this and much more was gladly imparted to me by this loyal servant.

I greatly regret not having being able to trace Signor Gaetano Spedilo, who was valet to both Sir William and Lord Nelson. I understand that he has long since returned to his native Genoa. But I did find Fatima. She was Lady Hamilton's Nubian personal maidservant who also bore witness to many of the events of which I write. It was she who accompanied the trio on their overland journey back from Naples to England. Being an African she hated the cold and damp of our English climate. She did her best to be at home here, even to the extent of agreeing to be baptised as Fatima Emma Charlotte Nelson Hamilton!

Fatima duly confided in me that her conversion to Christianity felt uplifting at the time but did not stop her being later dismissed when, through poverty, Lady Hamilton could no longer keep her in her employ. Not did it save her from being placed in the infamous Bear Lane workhouse in Deptford, where she barely survived on a pitifully small allowance. It is tragic to recount I found her in the St Luke's madhouse before her death. She was able to tell me snatches of her life with Lady Hamilton. But alas, her distress was such that she was unable to impart more. Out of sympathy I did not press her too onerously.

One final piece in the jigsaw – apart from first hand experience at the Admiralty dinner that is – was supplied by my sister-in-law Mary. It was she who, as a young girl, was playing in the garden of Berkeley Cottage in Deal in the County of Kent. On that occasion she was met by Lord Nelson and Lady

Hamilton who were strolling arm in arm down the path in front of the cottage. She tells me that they looked over the garden wall to admire the roses. They had spoken fondly to each other and kindly to Mary who recalls quickly gathering flowers to make a nosegay for the loving couple.

But I am getting ahead of my account of the dinner in question. All my investigations took place after Nelson's death in 1805. The social event that I am about to describe occurred before Trafalgar on a winter evening at the turn of the century.

A year earlier in the Neapolitan court in Palermo, Lord Nelson and Lady Hamilton had not only lived under the same roof but, in all likelihood, shared the same bedchamber. Lord Nelson and his entourage, which included the Hamiltons, had then returned to London in triumph and were now being officially welcomed to a private dinner by the First Sea Lord.

As our carriage traversed Hyde Park towards Admiralty House on that memorable occasion, I remember speculating on the evening ahead. It had been widely reported that the Nelsons and the Hamiltons had set up their own houses in separate localities in the capital. They were often in each other's company, though significantly their triumphant tour of the West Country had, for whatever reason, excluded Lady Nelson. I could not put out of my mind the scurrilous reports that had been circulating. But surely this was an official engagement where such personal matters would be politely ignored. As it was to turn out I could not have been more mistaken.

Dinners at the Admiralty were known to be sumptuous occasions. With Lord Nelson as the guest of honour this one promised to be no exception. My expectations were high, and Mrs Henderson was in an unusually jovial mood. As we arrived in *the Strand I observed the Nelsons' carriage pull up and its occupants alight. Lord Nelson looked dejected. He did not greet us with any warmth. It seemed with reluctance that he offered his arm to his spouse. Lady Nelson sniffed the cold winter evening air and gathered her shawl around her.*

The banqueting hall was set out as befitted such a splendid naval occasion. Though I believe it would be in no way so grand or happy an event as Nelson's fortieth birthday party, which had been held a few years earlier at the Palazzo Sessa in Naples. On that occasion eight hundred guests were invited to supper and they had danced till dawn. Lord Nelson had been the centre of attention and Lady Hamilton had been the belle of the ball.

But tonight's dinner was altogether a more sedate and decorous occasion. Some of Nelson's trophies had been placed around the room. A warming fire crackled in the huge fireplace and the walls were resplendent with oil paintings of famous ships and naval battles. The dozen places at the dinner table were set out with magnificent silverware. Excellent food and wine awaited the guests.

Naturally the Nelsons and Hamiltons were seated on either side of the presiding First Sea Lord. I had the honour to sit close by, as it happened between Lady Nelson and the sharp-eyed and handsome Lady Spencer. The latter was to prove herself a skilful hostess before the night was out.

Sherry was served to the company and the meal began with watercress soup. Initial conversation was polite and stilted. Fanny, Lady Nelson, was discussing her ailments with her hostess. Lord Hamilton appeared to be entreating the First Sea Lord to authorise the transport by the Navy of some of his precious belongings which had had to be left in Naples. Emma was being her usual vivacious self. In contrast Lord Nelson's demeanour was downcast. My quiet observation of these four eminent personages – who were bound together by such a bittersweet set of experiences and emotions – was gently interrupted by Lady Spencer.

'Captain Henderson, your wife tells me that you are seeking an Admiralty post in Portsmouth. Would not a young officer like your good self prefer to be at sea?'

'Ma'am,' I replied – ever so diplomatically, 'Naturally I would prefer to be on active service but it is my firm belief that the proper and diligent provisioning of ships is indeed a worthwhile task.' And I added mischievously – 'Perchance Mrs Henderson has the inclination to have me at close quarters!'

Lady Spencer laughed dryly, and we resumed our meal. My gaze again fell on Lord Hamilton, if for no other reason that he was the tallest guest at the table. For than thirty-four years he had served as the British ambassador to the Neapolitan court. I have it on good authority that he had used his connections to become a worldly and respected diplomat. But also, when in Italy, he used his first wife's dowry to amass an unrivalled collection of classical vases, figures and glassware. He had acquired paintings by Rubens and Rembrandt. He was also a keen natural historian, and, I am reliably informed, he climbed Mount Vesuvius on no less than twenty-two occasions.

But on this particular evening Lord Hamilton – this avuncular, aristocratic and accomplished gentleman – displayed a sad and resigned countenance.

That had not always been the case. Certainly not when he had first met Emma Harte – the future Lady Hamilton – back in 1792. This meeting had taken place at the Paddington home of his nephew, Charles Grenville, who had taken the attractive young Emma into his household. Sir William, like many others before and after, had been mightily impressed with Emma's beauty and vivacity. But he had returned to Naples to resume his none-too-arduous duties.

Subsequently Grenville's ambitions got the better of his affections for his mistress. The discarded Emma had been sent to Naples with her mother and took up residence in the Villa Sessa. This arrangement, I am led to believe, allowed Sir William the pleasure of her company in return for Grenville being declared as his sole heir. I have it on good authority that at first Sir William was a reluctant partner to this arrangement, but he soon came to appreciate her talents. Indeed her attractions were such that he took her to London and they were married. He was 61 and she 26. The cynical cartoonists of the day were to portray the match as an unequal one, and not only in age, but also in social position.

Across the dinner table I could hear snatches of a conversation Lord Hamilton was having with his friend Lord Nelson. He was complaining in a somewhat resigned tone of the treasures he had had to forsake in Italy and beseeching the man that he deemed to be 'virtuous, loyal and brave' to assist in the task of recovering them. For his part Lord Nelson seemed distant and preoccupied. He had enjoyed his time in Naples but this was London, and circumstances had changed. His answers were short and non-committal. Of course I was not to know that Lord Hamilton was to live but a few years more. He was to die in the arms of Lady Hamilton and holding Nelson's hand. Being a freethinker his passing was 'without the help of the Church.'

But on the evening in question he cut a sad and tired figure. He was definitely under the weather.

His sole wishes seemed to be that his treasures were recovered from abroad, and he be allowed to stay at home in peace and quiet.

As the soup plates were cleared, Whitstable oysters were served. I could not help noting the enthusiasm and evident enjoyment that Emma Hamilton gorged herself on this seafood delicacy. She must have eaten half a dozen by the time I slipped one into my mouth. Each of her mouthfuls was accompanied by half a glass of sparkling white wine.

It was difficult to believe that this larger than life socialite sitting next to the First Sea Lord – and opposite her lover Lord Nelson – had been born in Nesse, Cheshire in 1765 in such humble circumstances. She started life as Amy Lyon. Her father was a hard-working colliery blacksmith, but had died when she was but two years of age.

She received scant schooling and eventually was packed off to London and into service. Being by all accounts a pretty lass, she soon attracted the attentions of several well-to-do young men in town. She was taken up by Lord Harry Featherstonhaugh, who took her to his Up Park estate in Sussex. Alas, she found herself pregnant and returned north to bear her child which was soon to be adopted. Later back in London she kept house with the young Grenville. Emily – as she then liked to be called – was taught to write, read and sing and play the piano. She had grown remarkably beautiful. She was tall, with dark blue eyes, long auburn hair, a pretty face and full figure. The portraits of her by Romney – she sat for him on no less than a dozen occasions – certainly do justice to her fine features and give us more than a glimpse of her exuberant personality.

At the dinner table Emma was, as usual, the life and soul of the party – as she had been in Naples, and since their return to England. She was stouter now but still a fine-looking woman. I could clearly detect her Lancashire accent. She said 'booth' for both, 'as' for has and 'ous' for us as she described their journey overland back to London to the First Sea Lord. She was saying how much she missed the warm Mediterranean evenings and the sea bathing, the rich Italian food and local sweet wine. She had impressed those at the Neapolitan court with her fluent French and Italian.

But there was a great deal more about her years in Naples that she wasn't imparting to her fellow dinner guests that evening. She omitted to mention the beguiling theatrical performances she gave when her lithe and voluptuous body was barely concealed by the muslin dresses she wore without the encumbrances of drawers, petticoats or stays. Nor did she recount, although it was common knowledge at the time, of the famous occasion when she had literally thrown herself into Lord Nelson's arms upon his arrival in Naples after the Battle of the Nile. How, day and night, she had attentively tended his wounded and aching body and soothed his fevered forehead. How she praised him and danced for him so that he recovered his health and spirits.

Of course the First Sea Lord knew, as we all did, that when Naples was threatened by an imminent French invasion it was Nelson's fleet that had carried the staid ambassador, his sociable wife and their court to the safety of Sicily where they had set up house in the Palazzo Palagonia. What was less well known was that it was there that Emma's charm, flattery, and womanly attractions had caused Lord Nelson to draw ever closer to her. I have it on good authority that it was Sir William who went early to bed and Lord Nelson and Emma who drank, danced and embraced till dawn.

I have to confess that I do not find it strange that this turn of events should transpire. After all Emma had been 'passed between' sundry rich and high and mighty men since she was in her teens. And her present ailing husband had all but encouraged or at least condoned her close friendship with the victorious Admiral Nelson from the start. As one of my contemporaries has written – 'He knew his tenure on her affections would sooner or later be terminated by death or a younger and more suitable partner.'

All this I considered as I watched Lady Hamilton's demeanour at the dinner table. Her feelings for Nelson were but thinly disguised. Although she regaled the whole company with her vivacious and earthy stories, it was towards Lord Nelson that her affections were clearly drawn.

I have subsequently discovered that she wrote him hundreds of letters when they were apart. Many were burnt, but in one that I was shown Emma had written to a friend –

'I adore the happiness of being beloved, esteemed and admired by the good and virtuous Nelson.'

But who would have guessed on that evening, which was to end in such high drama, that Emma's life would be so full of tragedy thereafter. Her increasing girth only partly disguised her impending motherhood. She cared for the child she bore Nelson, albeit of necessity at one stage removed. For the little Horatia was looked after by a Mrs Gibson, in a subterfuge that was designed to conceal the real circumstances of the child's parenthood.

Throughout all her later tribulations and social rejection, (she died penniless in Calais in 1815) I am led to believe that she was fiercely loyal to every one of her intimate companions, both men and women. Perhaps the only exceptions were to some of Nelson's family who treated her with disdain after Trafalgar and the woman who was sitting opposite her that evening. The woman she disparagingly referred to as 'Tom Tit', namely Frances, or Fanny – Lady Nelson.

While the company at the dinner table were served with braised lamb and roast potatoes, and listened to Emma's amusing tales of the Italian peasantry and earthy jokes at Bonaparte's expense, they barely spared a glance at the timid and self-effacing wife of Lord Nelson. But she did not escape my not unsympathetic gaze, nor the cosy attention of Mrs Henderson.

Frances Nelson, née Nisbet, was petite, neat and elegant in her own way. Although I have seen her on only a couple of occasions including on this occasion, she struck me as genteel and dutiful. Hers was a faded prettiness, like a flower that has barely bloomed. Her reticent manner was accompanied by a habit of nervously fluttering her hands.

She clearly suffered from a chesty ailment, probably as a result of living in cold rectories in Norfolk where she often looked after Lord Nelson's father when her husband was away on naval duties. It was plain to see that their marriage had been 'ordered', yet not without affection. It was the loyal Fanny's lot to watch in the background as her husband's fame spread with every battle that he won.

She was a devoted naval wife – Mrs Henderson will be upset by the use of this term, but I can think of no better to describe the lady who sat opposite me at the dinner table. By all accounts she had remained steadfastly devoted to her husband whether he was at sea facing physical danger or engulfed in the temptations of the flesh in Mediterranean ports. She must have seen the cruel cartoons depicting her husband's 'outrageous infatuations' with the 'uncouth' Lady Hamilton who now sat at the table in such close proximity. But she conversed with us with a commendable dignity and calmness. After years of waiting she must have been deeply injured by her husband's cold reception when he had returned to London. I discovered some years after the occasion of which I am writing that he had told her – 'Do not come to London on any account, but keep quiet where you are.' From Portsmouth he had written – 'Nor would I have you come here for I never come ashore.' (I have to tell you that this sentiment must have been a deceit, for officers were often ashore even if ordinary seamen were detained on board for fear of them deserting). Yet this is the same man who had written to his wife earlier in affectionate, nay, very reassuring terms – 'There is nothing in you that I would have otherwise.'

Over the years he must have welcomed her fortnightly letters and the small jars of cherries and apricots in brandy she sent to him whilst far from his home in Burnham Thorpe. How different was to be the impact of such small tokens of marital loyalty and affection on this very evening. Lady Nelson was all but ignored by her husband, and had to content herself with small talk to her neighbours about the London social scene. As I have said she was largely engaged by my spouse.

Dear readers, the said admirable Mrs Henderson would wish me to re-state the qualities of steadfast fortitude and loyalty which were displayed on this occasion and many others by Frances, Lady Nelson. She may have lacked the sparkle of at least one other woman at that dinner but it would be grossly unfair to dismiss her lightly. She must have suffered sharply from the personal injury and insult of rejection but up to the later incident, which I shall shortly recount, she showed no sign of reproach or distress.

The meat plates were cleared and puddings lay before us. There were trifles, fruits and ice creams. Once again I surveyed the scene at the dinner table.

Lord Nelson cut a morose figure, as he had done from the start of the evening. The wine had loosened Emma's tongue as she now continued a loud monologue on the fashions of the day. Lady Nelson, as I have noted, was a diminutive and nervous figure amongst the assembled company. Lady Spencer was using all her social skills to keep the dinner party progressing satisfactorily, and her task was not helped by Lord Nelson's demeanour.

Need I remind you, esteemed readers, of the character and achievements of this noble Lord? I dare say not. I am certain you will know all about him. You may have seen the monument on Portsdown Hill erected and paid for by those such as myself who fought at Trafalgar. This very year the statue and column in his memory have been completed in Trafalgar Square in London. Indeed you may be reading this epistle in a street or inn that bears his name.

Surely all the world knows that Lord Nelson was born on the 29th September 1759, at Burnham Thorpe in the County of Norfolk, the fifth son and sixth child of Edmund Nelson, a Norfolk rector. That his mother died when he was but nine years old. Like many of our standing he was destined for service in the Navy from an early age. He was involved as a midshipman in skirmishes in the West Indies. He married at the age of twenty-two. A fellow naval officer once recounted to me that this did not stop him falling for a woman in Montreal. He had to be forcibly persuaded by his fellow officers not to desert his ship and career for her. Was this an omen of events to come, I wonder? A veritable flaw in Nelson's character exposed – so at least says my esteemed wife. It is her view that his early childhood had made him susceptible, or indeed gullible - to use her own words - to the charm of ladies. For my part I deem him no different from any other man who had spent long years at sea in the service of his Majesty.

That all who sailed with him from his early years to the glorious days when he was Admiral of the Fleet held him in high esteem is not contested. I have to remind you that this was the age of seditious revolution in France. These were revolutionary times. But Lord Nelson was interested in deeds rather than words in support for the common man. He saw at first hand the rural poverty in East Anglia, where day labourers struggled to keep their families alive on a tiny wage.

A few years later when seamen of the fleet at Spithead petitioned the Admiralty over poor pay and hard conditions he was at one with their demands. The records show that he concurred that the mutineers should proceed 'with caution, peace, clear minds and determined hearts.' Behind the scenes he urged the Admiralty to accede to their petitions for improved wages, more vegetables to keep scurvy at bay, better treatment for the sick and injured and 'an opportunity to taste the sweetness of liberty ashore' when they returned from sea. As we now know Lord Howe did eventually accept most of their entreaties. It is little wonder that his lordship was respected so much by all ranks in the Royal Navy.

Even as we ate our sugary pudding on the evening in question the guest of honour and his host were engaged in detailed discussion on the provisioning of the fleet. But I observed that Lord Nelson's attention was not wholly on this serious business. He kept glancing at the woman who sat but a few feet away - none other than the lively and alluring Lady Hamilton.

He had first met Emma on the 11th September 1793, when he returned in triumph from the victorious Battle of the Nile. His health was poor. He suffered from malaria - first contracted in the West Indies. His elbow had been shattered at the Battle of St Vincent, and he bore months of pain following the amputation of his right arm. The loss of an eye and a head wound gave him severe headaches. But it wasn't only the scars of war with which Lord Nelson was inflicted. As Fatima was later to confide in me, he needed the loving tenderness of womanly company. It was not long before the attentive flattery of Emma, the undisputed Queen of the Neapolitan court, won his heart. In sensuous Naples, in welcoming Palermo, on the overland return trip back to England, and now in cold, foggy London and this very night at the dinner table in the Strand there was no mistaking his quiet passion for her.

Dear readers, pray do not treat my account of this love affair with doubting scepticism. May I quote a passage from one of the letters that were written by Lord Nelson to his lover.

'My dear own wife - for such as you are in my eyes and in the face of heaven, I love you and never did love anyone else. Would to God I had dined with you alone - what a dessert we would have had. You may readily imagine what must be the sensations at the idea of sleeping with you; it sets me on fire, even the thought, much more the reality. I cannot eat or sleep for thinking of you my dearest love. Last night I did nothing but dream of you. I kissed you fervently and we enjoyed the height of passion.'

Yet here was the author of this love letter dining in the close company of both his amour (and her aged husband) and his loyal wife. His was not an easy position to be in, that night at the Admiralty dinner. When later in our carriage on the way home Mrs Henderson and I discoursed upon the evening's happenings, my spouse indicated that she for one had little or no sympathy for the plight of his noble Lordship.

'Lord Nelson,' she remarked tartly, 'should have thought about the consequences of his actions before he entered Lady Hamilton's bedchamber.' We did not pursue the matter further. For my part, I am content to observe, without censure, the delicacies of the situation which was to transpire that evening.

So now dear readers, I have informed you the essence of the four people involved and the circumstances which led up to the fateful incident which I am about to recount.

The dinner was all but completed. To some of the party this was evidently a great relief. Notably Lord Hamilton who was clearly tired, unwell and to ready to depart home, and our hostess who was, I suspect, pleased that the evening had gone ahead without 'mishap.'

It must have been around half past ten. The port and Madeira were being passed round in the normal naval custom. I noticed, without any particular interest, that Fanny was shelling some walnuts that had been placed upon the table to be taken with the wine. She was dressed in simple and demure white and purple satin and had drawn her shawl around her shoulders as if feeling the cold. The men were in readiness to withdraw to the smoking room. Lady Hamilton held court in her uninhibited manner. She had drunk freely throughout the meal and kept up a loud and lively conversation with all the men in earshot. And then it happened.

Lady Nelson placed the walnuts in a wine glass and handed them in a somewhat submissive yet kindly way to her husband. I was not the only one to notice this simple act of marital attentiveness. Nor was I alone in being astonished and dismayed by the reaction of Lord Nelson.

With his only arm he roughly pushed the glass away from him. It smashed against a china pudding bowl and shattered. The walnuts spilled out onto the dinner table in our midst.

There was a stunned silence amongst the assembled company. The conversation and laughter suddenly ceased. It might not have done if this had been a careless accident, but it was clear to all present that evening that this was a rude act of disdain to his wife on the part of the First Sea Lord's guest of honour.

My recollection of what happened next is less clear. I remember Fanny standing up and bursting into tears. Lady Spencer, our accomplished hostess, hastily beckoned the ladies to withdraw to her boudoir. They fled the dining room. There followed a lengthy and very awkward silence, only broken by the scrape of chairs as first Lord Spencer, closely followed by his male guests, stood and made ready to retire to the smoking room. We did so leaving the remains of the dinner party – including the broken glass and spilled walnuts on the now soiled damask tablecloth.

Dear friends ... I trust I may, by now, address you thus. Do I surmise correctly that you are wondering why I have chosen to recount this unfortunate incident? Indeed some might say that I am making heavy weather of it. You may even be critical of my singling out this one incident for mention and indeed special attention. Why, given the great esteem that I naturally hold for Lord Nelson, have I made specific note of this mean or, at best, thoughtless act towards his wife?

I cite three points in my defence of inclusion of this apparently obscure incident at the Admiralty dinner. First, I have to admit that it was partly included at the suggestion – nay insistence – of my wife Sarah. When my spouse learnt that I was writing my own personal account of the life and times of Lord Nelson, she looked at me quizzically.

'My dear Will,' she exclaimed in her calm but determined way, (after all she is the oldest daughter of an army general) – 'if you do not include reference to the dinner party and the incident with the walnuts in your report then do not expect me to accompany you to any more admiralty dinners.' Mrs Henderson, you see, took a dim view of Nelson's very public and rude response to his wife's action on that night. In fact thereafter she never had a good word to say for him. One of her favourite sayings a propos Lord Nelson is 'England expects every man to do his duty' and there she always pauses, 'to his wife'!

But to be truthful I myself would also wish to recount the incident for the very reason that I am telling you about the social and private life of the noble Lord. I alluded earlier to the desirability of providing a full and well-rounded account of Nelson's life. For sure you need no reminder of his naval exploits and heroic deeds. Nor the reminder of the loyalty he inspired in the men who fought under his command. Nor, indeed, the universal and heartfelt sorrow that greeted the news of his untimely and tragic death in October of 1805.

Finally it has to be said that in my humble opinion this incident constituted a turning point in the lives of Lord Nelson and those of the dinner party guests who were so closely interwoven with him. Things, as they say, would never again be the same. The immediate aftermath saw the Nelsons and the Hamiltons return to their respective lodgings at Dover Street and Grosvenor Square. But not before Fanny had confided in her hostess and Mrs Henderson of her husband's coldness towards her. Evidently the only consolation for this unhappy and injured wife was her social position. On this point they strenuously reassured her that she would retain her standing in society.

As for Sir William he is reported to have said that he 'didn't give a fig for the world'. His health was poor and his patience over the extravagant expenditure incurred by his wife all but exhausted. It is well known that before his death he joined Lord Nelson and Lady Hamilton when they set up home in Merton. Right to the end this aesthetic and noble man maintained his steadfast admiration for Lord Nelson – his 'virtuous and brave friend'.

Emma had been drawn to Nelson from the first but they rarely enjoyed happy times together even when settled in Surrey. She had their Horatia but lost another stillborn bairn. Her position was frowned upon and deemed unacceptable to many in fashionable London, including at the Royal Court. As Lord Nelson's consort she had in a sense displaced Lady Nelson. Her generous style of living, her dinners, dancing and card playing continued unabated. Her stoutness in part disguised her impending motherhood. But her life was to take a turn for the worse upon the demise of Lord Nelson. She remained loyal to all those she knew, but few of them reciprocated her goodwill. Nelson's decree that she should inherit some of his worldly goods was crudely ignored. Perhaps it is less well known that she was later to die in lonely and impecunious circumstances across the Channel in Calais.

Of the social travails that confronted Lord Nelson and Lady Hamilton in their life together, I will say no more. I commend to you, my patient readers, the philosophy of Captain Hardy in this matter. His stated belief was that all this was of little consequence so long as it did not interfere with the duty of a naval officer to his King and country. I hasten to add that Mrs Henderson in no way concurs with this sentiment.

And in this respect, we know that Lord Nelson was second to none in his adherence to duty. For on the 14th September 1805 he prepared to say his farewell to his loved ones – namely Emma and Horatia before departing their house in Merton. He was to catch the overnight coach to Portsmouth to board HMS Victory. He was ready to engage the enemy for the last time.

Their last few hours together were joyless. Emma was desolate. For once she could neither eat nor drink. Indeed all she did was to cry throughout their last meal together. Her tears fell on the table. She was inconsolable.

Lord Nelson prayed at his daughter's bedside and prepared to depart. He shook hands with his brother in law, embraced his beloved Emma and set off an hour before midnight.

The post chaise rattled through the Surrey countryside. They passed through Esher and Guildford. At Liphook whilst they changed horses Nelson wrote out a prayer that he had been composing on the journey. As dawn was breaking the coach approached Portsdown Hill and from it could be seen the fleet off the Isle of Wight.

Once in Portsmouth they made for the George Inn on the High Street. It was there that I myself was waiting with Thomas Lancaster, whose son was due to join Nelson on board his flagship. That morning I have to tell you that his lordship had a determined look about him, as if his mind was already on the *battle ahead and his plan of attack. Yet the first thing I saw him do when inside the inn was to pen a short letter – I can only assume to Lady Hamilton.*

By this time word had got round that the noble and much-loved Lord Nelson had arrived. A huge crowd gathered outside the hostelry. There were shouts from the populace. Hardy suggested we left by the back entrance, but it was in vain, for he was crowded and cheered all the way to the ramparts where the jolly boat was awaiting. He waved his hat to the people whose wholehearted respect and affection he had long earned. His mind was set for action but his heart was with the woman and child he loved back in Merton.

Dear readers, you know that Lord Nelson met his end at Trafalgar; that his brilliance as a naval commander was the deciding factor in this and his earlier victories; that the nation then and now mourned his tragic death.

As for myself I have pursued my modest naval career. In 1841, as I have informed you, I was appointed to HMS Victory. What better place to write these notes than in the very cabin in which Lord Nelson planned for victory, gave his masterful orders, wrote to his wife, and dreamt of his beloved Emma?

Now I am on my way home from South America where I was engaged in the arduous task of ending the despicable system of slavery. I have had some limited success, although with precious little help from Her Majesty's Government. I am laid low with yellow fever and fear I may die before reaching port.

My account I dedicate to my estimable late wife, and my family back home in Kent. In her life she never ceased to scold Lord Nelson for his misdemeanour that night at the Admiralty dinner. Her exact words, I well recall –

'England expects every man to do his duty ... to his wife.'

For my part, I have long since forgiven him for his ungentlemanly behaviour on this occasion, and pay him my utmost respect as a man of great humanity, and a brilliant naval commander.

Early years at Postcard Corner

The wise old owl in Fratton

*I*am 82, and maybe a bit of a wise old owl – or so some of the locals would have you believe.

Whilst I must admit my hearing is not as good as it once was, you would be surprised what I have seen through my net curtains over the years.

Tawney owls can swivel their necks and have a 110-degrees field of vision, although arthritis has take its toll on my neck movements. But not much that goes on in Sheffield Road escapes my perceptive gaze.

So, like it is said of Yorkshire folk – 'we see all, hear all and say nowt'. In my case that's because there aren't many of my old friends and neighbours around any more for me to have a chat with. But maybe it's not such a bad thing that I don't have such a gossip as Mrs Stanley next door as I used to.

> *'A wise old owl sat in an oak*
> *The more she saw the less she spoke*
> *The less she spoke the more she heard*
> *Why can't we all be like that bird?'*

But what about age, and wisdom, and owls? Are we given the due respect that we were accorded in the past?

Certainly we have all been around for a long time. Fossil remains of owls some sixty million years old have been discovered in Ten Mile Creek in Wyoming. Barn owls are at least 12 million years old.

Owls (and elders) have been celebrated and venerated through the mists of time. In ancient Greece owls were held in the highest regard ever since they warned of the approach of the enemy at the Battle of Marathon in 490 BC. Ancient Greek coins were called owls and it was believed that if a pregnant woman saw an owl they would give birth to a daughter. No hi-tech scans in those days then.

In Yorkshire, in days gone by, owl broth was said to be a reliable cure for whooping cough, and in India owl flesh is reputedly an aphrodisiac.

And we have our cruel side, for we do kill small creatures and birds and one of Chicago's most infamous gangsters was called 'Owly Madden.' President Obama may have been based in the windy city but so were a lot of hoodlums. I hasten to say that I myself am just a gentle 'old dear', or at least that's what they called me recently at the clinic.

And owls today must be still seen as symbols of integrity and physical prowess – otherwise why would modern hi-tech firms use us as their corporate logos and Sheffield Wednesday FC proudly display us on their shirts.

But what about this particular wise old owl, who lives in the heart of Fratton, on Portsea Island, on the south coast of England, in this most under-rated of British cities – Portsmouth?

You will find me at No. 19 Sheffield Street, where I have lived for 57 years. If you head over the railway bridge and turn right at the Co-op funeral parlour (established 1935) you will come to Jolly Taxpayer pub. I am just round the corner so *please* come in for a chat, as I get mighty lonely and would love to have a visitor or three.

Mostly you will find me perched near my front window watching the world go by. We mostly live our lives at home, some of us aged folk are indeed prisoners of our front room. I don't get down to the Southsea front much these days, nor visit Albert's grave in Kingston cemetery. But that doesn't mean that I am out of touch with what's going on in the wider world.

You see, for migrating birds and even sedentary owls

international frontiers have always been irrelevant, and I know my neighbours are affected by the bad news from Wall Street, go to Disney World with their kids, and work for IBM, and may be flooded when global warming arrives in the Solent.

It is true that neighbours are not usually friends these days, and most people rush about in their foreign cars to Tesco's, or to a 'better' school outside their local catchment area. But the pattern of life in the new millennium is still very local – at least for some of us.

I say all this as a gentle reminder to you that, whilst sparrows, pigeons and starlings may keep their heads down in Sheffield Street, this still clear-sighted and contemplative tawny owl at No. 19 has a keen memory and a tale worth telling.

So what, you will be wondering, do I think of Sheffield Street?

Well it can't be described as rural for sure. It is no Badgers Brow, Blackberry Lane or Dogwood Dell that are all to be found in suburban Waterlooville. Its not even like the 'Welsh' estate in Drayton, the 'Isle of Wight' estate in Wymering, or the 'Lake District' blocks of flats in Paulsgrove.

Although there is still an HMS Sheffield in the senior service, I'm glad in a way we are not tagged with a naval connection. No, you can keep Nelson Avenue, Hardy Road and Weevil Lane for sea birds and seafarers.

Of course you might think I would be envious of those living in roads where the famous were born, stayed or even were murdered. Charles Dickens started his life 200 years ago at 299 Commercial Road, Landport; Peter Sellers entered the theatrical world of his parents in 1925 on the corner of Castle Road; the famous writer of Sherlock Holmes mysteries – who played in goal for Pompey – lived in a house in Elm Grove, which was destroyed by Mr Hitler in 1941.

No, there are no blue plaques in Sheffield Street, although

there is a case for one at No. 43 where a Mr Tibling lived a century ago. He was the Salvation Army officer who collected pennies for the poor outside Fratton Park on Saturdays and gave it to needy families and the elderly. He was one of the few locals who campaigned for the first state pension in 1908. So lets hear it for Mr Tibling.

Never mind that no-one famous or infamous breathed their first or fell off of their perch in my street. Ordinary folk down the generations have lived, learnt, loved in our two-up/two-down brick terraced houses. Just as some birds use their same nests year after year.

Nonetheless I do have a sneaking inclination to live in a road with an intriguing name like Flying Bull Lane and I can't help wondering if those who live in Manners Road are always polite to each other even on a cold wet Monday morning. Nor would I fancy Nobbs Lane in Old Portsmouth amongst neighbours who might be plumy voiced and standoffish. As for Mafeking Road – why hasn't the local Labour party suggested that it be changed to Mandela Road? I bet some of the residents would have kicked up a stink if it had even been mooted.

But there is nothing wrong at all with living in a street called after a northern industrial city famous for its fine cutlery. And we are in good company, for nearby are Manchester and Liverpool streets – and they are top of the premiership. Sheffield may have lost much of its steelmaking but, judging by the Full Monty, they do have a good sense of humour up there in t'north.

I, for one, am more than content to live in Fratton. For one thing I can hear when the goals are scored on match days. I know the stadium is a bit of a ramshackle place, but over a hundred years, countless goals, tackles and saves have been seen there by the Pompey faithful. Who wants a soulless, out-of-town sporting edifice like Brighton?

Certainly not me nor the blue scarfs who live around me in

the shadow of the stadium and drink at the Shepherd's Crook.

In fact I will follow the example of the Brent geese. These greasy, shit-everywhere creatures were the main reason cited why many a development in the city was refused planning permission. Their grassy feeding blocked a new hall of residence being built at Milton. What a cheek! They only fly in from their breeding grounds in Siberia for a few winter months. As temporary residents they shouldn't even have a say in local public affairs. Admittedly there are over twenty thousand of them so they are bound to carry more clout than a few resident foxes or squirrels and certainly a single, aged owl.

But lest you think that the interests and welfare of us owls are not properly represented, I would remind you that we do have the World Owl Trust based at Muncaster Castle in Cumbria, as well as the RSPB gunning – I mean standing up – for us winged creatures. And the recently merged Help the Aged and Age Concern into Age UK are there for us wrinklies.

But I digress. I know you want to hear more about Fratton. Within the neighbourhood are some notable Victorian edifices. The Carnegie library for example, and the community centre in Trafalgar Place. This former school welcomes all comers through its doors. There is a sign to prove it.

'*This centre welcomes everyone, regardless of age, ethnic origin, gender, disability, and sexual origin.*'

Do gays and Bangladeshis use the centre? I suspect that they have their own places, but I may be wrong.

For those who do cross the threshold of this battered building there are no shortage of activities. For a start 7-11 year olds an join up with the Starlight Majorettes on Monday and Thursday evenings. For the more muscular there is karate, and, for those who might fall into temptation, Alcoholics Anonymous and Weightwatchers meet weekly. The Portsmouth Bonsai Society meets here on the second Friday in the month and the comrades of the Socialist Workers Party on Wednesday evenings from 7.45 to 9.45. I wonder if an hour in the pub afterwards is long enough for them to plan the overthrow of world capitalism and the creation of a society where every man contributes according to his ability and receives according to his needs. Good luck to them I say. I know I've got precious little to show for a lifetime's hard work.

But I do love watching all the comings and goings. Even if they are all too pre-occupied with their lives and hobbies to pass the time of day with me.

What other landmarks dominate the Fratton scene? What was Snow's BMW Morris/Austin garage is now Motorcycle World. A car repair garage is to be found in the premises formerly occupied by the once famous Henry Mott's Dainty Cream Cheese biscuit premises. Fontana's ice cream parlour has disappeared and so has Vollers' corset factory.

Happily the Electric Arms survives and is open all day and most of the night. You don't hear 'Time gentlemen please' anymore, but the ex-dockyard workers who share a pint in its snug surroundings don't mind that as long as they can have a chat about the good old days. It used to be a Brickwood's pub, but today they sell Labatts iced beer and Magners cider.

Last, but by no means least, I have to mention the corner shop. It was run by Brian and Gladys Butterfield for years, but they have retired and its now Mr Haque's emporium.

One feature of the shop that hasn't changed is the *Evening News* board outside with its intriguing and usually doom-laden headlines. Local accidents, fires and crimes are featured regularly. Is this pure *schadenfreude*, or does bad news really sell newspapers? Who am I to say. All I know is what I see in the 'come and buy one' headlines. And over the years there have been some choice stories filling the pages of the local rag – 'City burglar stabs goldfish', 'Boy aged ten collides with super tanker', 'Hants pair jailed for stealing Mars bars', and another of my favourites – 'Revolting students in library sit-in'. Even big wigs can appear in its pages, and on the front page if they commit a misdemeanour.

But most of everyday life in my patch of the city goes on unreported. Some anecdotal evidence is provided by the postcard ads which can be seen in the corner shop window. My keen eyesight can pick out some of the current homely commercial messages – 'reward for lost tabby cat which answers to the name of Oliver or Ollie', 'pond water snails for 25 pence each', 'clairvoyance sessions with Neil – home visits optional', '6 berth holiday caravan in Dunoon, Scotland at £80 per week' (no mention of the rain or midges!).

So never underestimate the corner shop (it used also to be a post office) as a centre of news and gossip – by the way what's the difference? If you want to know what's going on at first hand/claw then get on down there. Watching the coming and going of the customers is enough for me. They come for milk, fags, crisps, and sugar when they run out. They also buy lottery tickets – hundreds of pounds worth every week, and not one jackpot winner yet. I am sure I would have heard the hoots of joy if there had been. That's not to say I am against the National Lottery. I know for a fact that it is eagerly anticipated twice weekly and has helped to build the Spinnaker tower at Gunwharf Quays.

But never mind the giddy heights of that landmark, what is this Fratton territory I see from my perch? Brick houses and postage stamp gardens for sure. Most of the outside lavies have gone, as have the Welsh slate roofs in favour of Marley tiles. Most houses now have TV aerials, satellite dishes or cable boxes. The street is full of cars and vans. There are few brand new vehicles, but more than a sprinkling of Fords and Rovers, as well as a few Mazdas and Daewoos (I wonder if Korean owls make a Daewoo cry?)

Flimsy black bags have replaced metal dustbins for the Tuesday collection. More is the pity, as foraging foxes tear them open and strew the remnants on the pavement. I swear that the mangy old vixen knows which day the rubbish is collected in Sheffield Street. She must do the rounds of central Portsmouth according to the weekly rota.

Then there are the 'for sale' and 'to let' and 'no junk mail' signs, flower baskets, and birthday balloons which appear regularly in the streetscape. But I particularly like the treasured '*objets d'art*' that are displayed inside front windows. I can see Spanish dancers, African antelopes, China vases, Scottish bagpipers and other assorted figurines. I am delighted to report that the occupants of No. 7 Sheffield Street have placed two china tawny owls in their window. Maybe they were placed there as a kind gesture to cheer me up, when I'm feeling lonely and a wee bit depressed with life.

So these are the familiar sights from my window. But there are also smells and sounds to report on. Exhaust fumes all the year and the drains don't half pong in summer. And there are the curry smells from Bangladeshi and student houses in the road. I have heard it said that there are now more people employed in the country in the curry business than in coal mining, steel making and shipbuilding combined. That being the case, why should even Sheffield Street be any different?

I don't know how old I am in owl years, but thankfully my hearing is still very good – like David Blunkett, the unsighted MP for Sheffield Brightside. I hear the opinionated Humphrys, and the windbag Nauchtie on Radio 4, I hear classic FM, Five Live and Radio BBC South. I hear laughing and crying. I hear foul drunken shouting on Saturday nights and 'Songs of Praise' on Sunday mornings. I hear the signature tunes of *The Archers* and *Eastenders*. I hear car alarms and emergency sirens. I hear the chimes when Pompey score on match days, although not when the opposition are gifted a goal. And not to forget the hooters of ships at sea in foggy weather, and in the dockyard at the stroke of midnight on New Year's Eve.

I am reliably informed that there was a grand total of 157 people living in Sheffield Street at the last census. At least one less now as Mr Goodspeed died last week, and was buried this

Tuesday. You can imagine the twitching net curtains as the Dashwood and Denyer hearse drew up outside his house.

And I know many of them by name – even if they don't know me. I hear the odd – 'all right, Bill?' And hear mums calling after their kids. There are us old folk that I have known for years. Nellie Foster at No. 20, and Florrie Bessant at 49, and the Earwicker sisters at No. 14. There are also quite a few children including Tracy and Lee at No. 9. I remember that little saucebox well, as he once threw a coke can at me when I told him off for swearing. I got my own back by puncturing his soccer ball.

Then there are the young couple just opposite me. They are newly married and I call them the Dearloves. They painted their house when they moved in and seem to spend a lot of time enjoying each other's company, sometimes forgetting to draw their curtains! And while on the question of sex, I have it on good authority that humans and owls do differ in their behaviour. Under the bedclothes or in mid air – whatever takes your fancy. For me opportunity would be a fine thing. As for owls – their courtship consists of sitting on a branch together. We sway about, ruffle our plumage, offer food, and flap our wings to show we are willing. The more ardent make grunting noises. Afterwards they preen ourselves, and roosting side by side, press their flanks together. Not bad, eh?

By the way, have you seen the way middle aged men hold in their paunches when they see a pretty girl? I am not sure how often couples have sex in Sheffield Street, but its just as well they do have offspring otherwise the birth rate would plummet. Extinction has faced some species, like the Whekau laughing owl in New Zealand, and the Dodo which drew its last breath in Mauritus in 1681. By the way, do you know that the saying, 'getting off at Fratton,' refers to a form of birth control approved of by the Pope!

The O'Flahertys at No 13 certainly have done their bit to balance the age structure of the locality. They go to Mass regularly, support Celtic and have five bairns. Then there are the Alis at No. 35 – Ali Armina, Ali Khyrum, Ali Nishar, and Ali Razna. I notice that Bangladeshi women always walk down the road behind their menfolk, and that their kids speak Pompey English when they are with their mates.

A few local names appeal to me. Sheena Sheath at 18, Christine Coldbreath at 15 and Diana Dance at either 34 or 36. There are some Pinks, and Dickensian Magwitches also in residence. You will think I am making it up. Never! I can also report that there are birdy names close by. Yes, Pam Moorhen down at the end of the road, the Sparrows next door to me. Any persons less like their ornithological namesakes I cannot imagine, for they are raw boned, slow moving and deep voiced. So there you are, it shows that even in the 21st century, on the 200th anniversary of Charles Darwin's birth, people are in tune with their natural origins. Of course none of them actually fly – unless you include flying to Florida or the Costa Brava, flying off the handle or flying down the road to catch the bus.

So now you know a fair bit of the residents of Sheffield street. But nothing as yet about their rhythms of life – their hourly, daily, weekly, monthly and annual routines.

In the old days 'milko' used to deliver his bottles before 6am. I enjoyed hearing the clink of bottles, his whistling and the re-assuring whirr of his electric cart. Not long after, lights would go on and the breadwinners would get ready to leave – this being a blue-collared neighbourhood you understand. Then there was postie doing his rounds; he stopped at most houses, delivering bills in brown envelopes, free offers, holiday postcards, and, at Christmas, a mass of cards and packages.

Next out are the kiddies. The older ones jostling and shouting, and the nippers holding their mum's or granny's hand. (Incidentally it is a fact that the male tawny owl will feed its brood for three weeks and the babes are flying after a month.) No holding them back then, and no need for paternity leave that the trendy Labour government started a few years ago.

We pensioners usually do our shopping after 9.30am. The simple reason being that our free bus passes don't start till then. We are sometimes known as '*twirlies*' if we arrive at the bus stop early! I have a Black Watch tartan shopping trolley, which helps me to keep my balance and allows me to stow away my purse and errands safely.

Then there is a lull in street activity until the schools come out between 3 and 4. I can report that there are two latchkey children in my road, although no harm has befallen them as far as I know – and I usually do. Certainly there are no paediatricians – that's what some folk call paedophiles – living around here. By six the cars are back and family teas and telly-watching begins. I sometimes make a meal, but it is hard to make an effort just for myself. More often than not, I have soup and toast, some fruit and a cup of tea while I watch Sally Taylor present the local news on BBC *South Today*. Later in the evening some of the young and middle aged go down the pub to down some beer. We old folk don't venture out after dark – it's cosier and safer at home. There is not that much late night drunken noise round here, although a student party got out of control last June. A young lad was playing his saxophone out of his bedroom window, which didn't go down well with the neighbours who had to get up for work the next morning. I was awake anyway so it didn't make much difference to one 'late-to-bed and late-to-rise owl' at least.

Then there are the weekly routines. Black bag rubbish is collected on Tuesdays – that's when the foxes come round. Some family washing is still done on Mondays, but not many Littlewoods' pools collected on Thursdays any more – it's all the National Lottery now. The weekend is for shopping, car cleaning, DIY'ing, gardening, visiting and church/mosque going. And the pattern repeats itself for 52 weeks a year, except for high days and holidays. I like the Christmas lights but not the trick-or-treat door knocking. I like the long sunny June/September days but not the long cold nights of November and February.

But I must remind you of the fact that, in Sheffield Street, the locals are not filthy rich. Some buy their clothes at charity shops, and food at Iceland. Maybe you do too and nothing wrong with that. A few get away to Turkey, but others can't afford a holiday and their free-school-meal kids spend the summer on the Southsea seafront, getting told off for jumping into the Solent from the ramparts. Men repair their own cars or get the help of a mate. Some of the old folk claim pension credit and get a few more pounds a week to pay their electricity and gas bills. What would the good people on this street do if they won a fortune on the lottery or unexpectedly inherited a large legacy? I'm not sure, but no doubt some would move up off the island to Cosham or over the hill to Cowplain. But most of us are proud of where we live. On the only time I have visited Port Solent, I overheard an irate father telling off his kids for fooling about on the swanky marina broadwalk.

'Behave yourselves you two,' he shouted. 'Where do you think you are – the back streets of Fratton?' What an ignorant and unfounded thing to say. I bet he had never set foot in the place, and nor would we like him to do so.

Most don't move away, but instead stay and make the best of it. And there is help at hand for those of us in need. I'm not talking about myself you know, but those like Mrs Pope at No. 23. She gets visits from the Salvation Army befriending service, meals on wheels and is picked up to go to Age Concern's spanking new Bradbury Centre at least once a week.

Don't get the impression that all is sweetness and light around and about. Not so, for there are arguments over late night door banging, car parking, dog fouling, and over-hanging foliage in back gardens. There are issues that cause aggravation such as dumping stained mattresses in forecourts, and vans parked in front of front-room windows. Everyone grumbles and some complain to neighbourhood bobbies or hopeful municipal candidates at May election time. Very occasionally we all pull together – like at the 50th anniversary of D Day, when we had a street party. For a few hours the street was transformed with flags and bunting, trestle tables laden with food, and there was singing and dancing. Next day it was back to normal.

I once heard that the guru of neighbourhood life – Jeremy Seabrook – say on the radio:

'People don't live in the street at all, they simply exist. The living is done inside; inside their houses which may be shabby but are warm, but also inside their heads where the fantasies and images of the media and telly permeate the poorest and well-to-do alike – with their invitations to escape, to dream and to forget.'

I think he may be talking about us in Sheffield Street, and the place where you live.

What I do know is that spouses, children, the younger generation and local councillors are all blamed when things go wrong. But to my mind the real culprits are miles way – out of town landlords, greedy city bankers, and one-day celebrities. But don't take it from me. My NHS, old-fashioned spectacles make me see the world in my own peculiar way. Come and see for yourself. After all, I am but a wise old owl, sitting at my window, flying in my mind over the smokeless chimney pots of Portsmouth, chatting to an ever-declining circle of friends.

You may be thinking to yourself – why doesn't this old clever claws do something herself? What's the use of all this detailed observation? Why sit on the sidelines like a season ticket holder at Fratton Park? Go and take an evening class in local history or genealogy. Turn off the telly and get down to sing in St Mary's church. Go and volunteer in the owl sanctuary shop in Highland Road. Save lives and limbs by organising a petition to slow down traffic in the narrow streets of Fratton. Join Portsmouth Pensioners' Association or a neighbourhood watch scheme to keep an eye on the youngsters, or spend a few hours a week reading to children in schools.

You are right of course. And so is Marcus Aurelius, a wise old Roman when he reminded us old ones – 'Do not waste what remains of your life in speculating about your neighbours, unless it is with a view to some mutual advantage!' As soon as I have filled this Woolworths notebook with my scribblings, I will get up off my window seat and become involved in local community activities. As soon as you have finished reading about my experiences of Sheffield Street, I know you will do the same…

Early years at Postcard Corner

Waking up on the way to Minton's Playhouse

I Waking up to the tanks

*R*obert, they are attacking us, come quickly!' It was his mother at the other end of the telephone. Its insistent ringing had dragged him out of his deep, warm, pre-dawn sleep. Glancing at his watch – it was only 5.25am – Robert had stumbled to the phone in the hallway of his flat, and was now listening attentively to his mother's anxious words.

'The Germans have invaded Belgium and Holland ... their tanks are crossing the frontier and *Luftwaffe* planes are bombing us. What must we do?'

'All right Maman, stay where you are and I'll come over right away,' he said, trying to collect his thoughts and at the same time trying to sound reassuring to his elderly and very agitated mother.

Robert flung on his clothes. Looking out of the bedroom window he could see red streaks of drawn – or was it the glow of fires which were lighting up the tiled rooftops of central Brussels? Turning on the radio he listened to the solemn voice of a Belgian government spokesman confirming his mother's frantic message. The Seventh Panzer division under General Rommel had crossed the Belgian border south of Liége. Brussels and Tournai were being bombed. German airborne troops were being dropped behind the Maginot Line to capture key bridges and rail links. Prime Minister Pierlot called for calm from the populace and resistance from the Belgian Army and their allies.

Robert looked around his flat. It was a mess. Lecture notes spread untidily on top of his desk, the sink full of unwashed dishes and a Sydney Bechet record on the turntable of his wind-up gramophone player – the last of many records he had played the night before. There was no time to clear up. He slammed the door and rushed down the communal stairs into the street.

The elderly concierge of his block of flats – dressed in her customary dirty smock – was standing at the entrance of the doorway watching the unusual bustle in the street outside.

'Monsieur Goffin, it's like 1914 all over again, what will become of us when the Germans arrive,' she whined.

'Don't worry Madame Laurier, I'd stay indoors if I were you. Keep out of the way until we see what is happening. I'll be back in a minute.'

Robert ran the few blocks to his family home. They had always lived in the centre of town. It had suited his father when he was alive and worked in the Belgian foreign ministry. It had also been convenient for Robert when he had been a student at university nearby.

So the long awaited invasion had at last occurred. It was May 10th. For months they had been expecting it. Over recent years they, and many others in Europe, had watched the rise of Hitler and the Nazis and the build up of the German military machine. Then in the east, Poland and Czechoslovakia had been invaded on the spurious pretext of 'liberating' their German speaking populations. This had been followed by France and Britain declaring war.

More recently German invasion plans had been discovered amongst the belongings of high-ranking German General Helmut Reinberger when his light aircraft had made a forced landing at Mercelin sur Meuse. King Leopold and some of the Belgian cabinet had hoped that their neutral stance would protect them but Robert and most Belgians had never shared this optimistic and naive view. It was now clear that Hitler's army was heading west through the Low countries and onto France and possibly England.

Robert's grey-haired mother and his younger brother Louis greeted him at the top of their stairway. He smelt coffee. Madame Goffin had not departed from the habits of a lifetime despite the seriousness of the occasion. They sat down together at the kitchen table, listening to the radio and thinking aloud what to do next. It wasn't as though they had not already made some plans. Money had been transferred to a London bank months ago. His late father had taken the precaution of sending some of their most precious family possessions out of the country some years earlier. His brother was already in the army and he had already forewarned his mother that she might have to flee at a moment's notice. They had all suspected that for the second time in the century, Belgium would fall under foreign occupation. After all what could a small nation of only eight million people do against their mighty neighbour? At the back of their minds they all took for granted that occupation by the Nazis would bring hardship, and probably worse, for anyone resisting.

'Maman,' he said 'we will leave for England today. I'll take you to London where you will be safe. We will lock up the flat and leave the keys with Uncle Emile. Louis will keep an eye on the place when he is able. Collect some belongings together, and I will meet you at the central station in a couple of hours to catch the Ostend train. We should be able to get a ferry later in the day.'

There was no time to argue or discuss it any further. Robert took a glance round the family home. For a moment his mind turned to childhood memories of Christmases and birthday parties, long hours of doing school homework, gatherings with his friends. Also special occasions when in recent years he had invited visiting jazz musicians back for a drink after their performances – Cab Calloway at the Gaiety Club who, after a few brandies, had played and sung *St James' Infirmary* and

Minnie the Moocher, and the memorable time when the great man himself had stayed the night with them – Louis 'Satchmo' Armstrong when he had suddenly arrived from Amsterdam.

He kissed his mother and set off at the double for his own place to put a few of his belongings together. By now it was fully light. A clear, fine May morning. The streets were full of housewives out buying bread and exchanging anxious gossip. Ambulances and fire engines were converging on the scenes of bomb damage near the railway goods yards. Robert quickly filled two suitcases. In one he put his clothes and other personal belongings and the other he reserved for some of his most precious jazz books and records. He carefully stowed away several copies of his own published books and articles including '*Jazz aux Frontiers*'. It was a heartbreaking and impossible task to choose a few records from his priceless collection of over 3000, lovingly acquired from music shops in European capitals and publishers abroad. In the end a few of his favourites were placed carefully in the suitcase and padded round with papers; he took with him a few of his Bix Beiderbecke, Louis Mitchell, W C Handy, Bessie Smith and of course Louis Armstrong records.

His two cases were heavy and bulging. But that didn't worry him. It was his beloved records and library which he was deserting that troubled him most. Would he ever see them again, Would billetted soldiers of the German occupying army destroy everything? It was with a heavy heart that he made his final preparations including a few quick telephone calls – one to his professor at the university, another to his friend Michelle who lived in the village of Leefdaal outside the city, and finally to his Uncle Emile. To all three Robert explained his plans and the need to take his mother to safety. They were neither shocked nor surprised. Only Michelle seemed unconvinced by his reassurances that he would keep in touch and be back soon. Robert was half scared by the speed of events and the suddenness of decisions, but there was no time to be lost lest the opportunity to get his mother safely across the Channel would be put in jeopardy.

Within an hour Robert was at the Gare du Nord. It was packed. Grim determination rather than panic showed on the faces of the throng. His mother had far too much luggage but refused to part with it. As the crowded train pulled out Robert felt relief and sadness in equal measure. Pleased that he was getting his mother away, but sorrow that his kid brother was being left behind to face the dangers of resisting the invading German army, and likely Nazi occupation. And he still hadn't realised the full extent of his loss in forsaking his beloved record collection. He knew that it was irreplaceable and unique and he vowed that never again would he buy another record.

At Ostend they joined the stream of refugees onto the packed ferry and by mid afternoon were out of sight of the low-lying Flemish coast. In the passenger lounge they met a Jewish family called Goldstein whom they knew. They shared their anxieties and sandwiches together. A kind offer was made for Robert's mother to stay with cousins of the Goldsteins in North London. Robert said that he would find a room in a guest house or hostel.

II Waking up to a Woodbine

Someone was coughing. But it wasn't noise which first intruded into Robert's senses, it was the sickly sweet, yet strong aroma of Virginia tobacco. He turned over and buried his face in the pillow but the stench of cigarette smoke was engulfing him. He lay for a moment before raising himself on one elbow and looking around. In the next bed to him, at a distance of less than a foot away, a vested, unshaven man of indeterminate age was sitting up in bed reading the *Evening Standard*. On his rough grey blanket close to him lay a half-empty packet of Wills Woodbines and a half-full ashtray.

'How do, mate – want a fag?' his neighbour asked in a friendly, casual way. He spoke with a strong accent Robert recognised as Irish.

'Thank you, no,' Robert replied, trying not to appear ungrateful or unfriendly. After all he had spent many a night in smoke-filled Brussels's clubs and bars, and had been known to smoke cigars when he got together with his friends over glasses of Juppiler beer.

His affable neighbour resumed his perusal of the racing pages before asking in ethnic brogue –

'Is it French that you are, Sir?'

Robert felt like accepting a new nationality for the sake of convenience but replied that he was a French-speaking Belgian. This information elicited no further response.

Robert sat up and looked more carefully around the room. There were more than a dozen beds crammed in. Motionless shapes lay under uniform grey blankets interspersed with beds covered by coats added by their owners for extra warmth.

Under and between the iron beds were trunks, suitcases and cardboard boxes. It was clear that he wasn't the only refugee in the Camden hostel to which he had been directed the previous night. They had arrived at Victoria station – it had seemed that half Europe was passing through – at least the nationalities on the receiving end of Hitler's unwelcome advances. They had been given cups of steaming sweet tea by cheerful volunteers and directions by helpful bobbies. He had seen his mother safely off with the Goldsteins before striking out to find a bed for the night.

As he was about to go down for something to eat, his new Irish friend offered Robert his well-creased newspaper. Although his English was not good he had no difficulty in reading the headlines.

'Churchill condemns invasion of Low countries' was splashed across the front page. '600 killed in basement of the Grand Palace in Tournai' he read with horror. There was a map showing the positions of opposing forces with arrows indicating the rapid advance of German troops. Fierce resistance was reported, but little by way of detail.

The rest of the newspaper was filled with stories of English preparations to defend their country against Herr Hitler. Troops were being sent to the south coast and children evaluated to the Midlands and Wales. There was to be a ban on ringing church bells except as a warning of invasion.

Other stories caught his eye on the inside pages. Sir Oswald Mosley, the leader of the British Fascist movement, had been arrested and imprisoned, and a Prince Obolensky had been killed in an air crash. The British Labour Party was holding its annual conference in Bournemouth and had voted by 2.4 million votes to 170,000 to support the national government now under Winston Churchill's leadership. The price of milk was to go up to 4d except for pensioners, expectant mothers and the needy (those whose joint weekly wage came to less than 40 shillings or 27 shillings for a single person). Robert couldn't help but marvel at the calm way in which the British were organising their wartime welfare plans. He also couldn't help wondering what was going on across the Channel where invasion and imminent occupation were a reality.

Robert left the newspaper on the table, and sought out the caretaker who, for half a crown, agreed to store Robert's possessions safely away in his cubbyhole. It was just after nine o'clock when he set out on foot for the Belgian Embassy in Eaton Square.

It was a bleak, chilly day in Camden town as the gaunt Victorian red-brick hostel spilled out its polyglot lodgers into Arlington Street. Robert turned left and found himself in the bustle of a street market. The fruit and vegetables looked inviting enough but he could understand little of the patter of the street vendors. He walked briskly up Gloucester Crescent, passed elegant Georgian houses, some with Austin and Morris cars standing outside their gates. Regents Park was shrouded in smog, but he could make out soldiers marching and gun crews practising in the murky atmosphere. There were also air raid shelters being constructed. Yet amongst these scenes of frantic wartime preparations elegant women continued to exercise their pet dogs. He kept heading south through Marylebone towards Marble Arch. The streets and shops were pretty empty, although the red double-decker buses were full. There was plenty of activity in the elegant squares of Belgravia. Here teams of workmen were busy cutting down the wrought iron railings of the gardens and squares and throwing them into lorries. Some residents were clearly very unhappy at this particular element of the war effort and were remonstrating with the contractors. A couple of bobbies were in attendance. Only the railings of the embassies were escaping this indignity in the affluent heart of the Duke of Devonshire's estate. Once again Robert was left fascinated by the *sangfroid* of the British people who were apparently willing to sacrifice their beautiful iron railings to make tanks, planes and guns.

At the Belgian Embassy, Robert joined a lengthy queue. By the time he had reached the head of it he had heard all about news from his homeland. Fact was difficult to separate from rumour but it was clear that Belgium's defences were crumbling.

After he had registered himself at the reception he asked to see the cultural attaché, who he knew had been on the staff of the University of Brussels at one time. He was ushered into a small office at the back of the building and recognised the man sitting in front of the gas fire – it was Maurice Maeterlinck, one of Belgium's best-known playwrights. They exchanged handshakes and news. Maurice, it transpired, was at the embassy to fill out papers to enable him to apply for a visa to the United States. He promptly advised Robert to follow his example.

'What's the use of staying in London if it is going to be

overrun in the same way as Brussels has been?' he asked in a whisper. Robert replied that he was not in any position to think too far ahead but he took the precaution of taking Maurice's address all the same. Shortly after, he left to see his mother in her temporary accommodation in Hendon. This time he took the tube and was soon travelling north in a carriage full of uniformed servicemen.

He found her in good spirits. She was ensconced in the Goldstein house surrounded by elderly French-speaking Jewish ladies. They were discussing their plight over tea and cakes. A couple of hours later he emerged to find the sun had burned its way through the smog. But the atmosphere on the Northern Line Underground was not so fresh. The platforms were littered with discarded possessions from people who had spent the previous night sheltering from air raids. The trains were full and dirty. They lurched their way south towards the West End – Highgate, Archway, Tufnell Park, Kentish Town, Euston, Goodge Street, Tottenham Court Road to Leicester Square. The only person Robert spoke to on the journey was a thin young man who, he had noticed with surprise, was reading a book by Guy de Maupassant.

'*Ça va Monsieur?*' Robert asked, hoping to find out more about the man sitting next to him. A conversation followed – a unique occurrence amongst his other passengers.

'*Je m'appelle Erik Phillipps, Bonjour.*'

It turned out his French-speaking fellow passenger was a refugee from Vienna where his family had been arrested by the Gestapo, and murdered. There was a short explanation for Erik's use of the Underground. That was simply to keep warm. They emerged together into Charing Cross Road, Mr Phillipps to spend time in the secondhand bookshops and Robert to hunt out some of the places he had previously frequented on nights out listening to jazz before the war. Robert had a cup of coffee in a Lyons Corner House. He listened to the tales of air raids and bomb damage being recounted by those around him. He was served by a pretty waitress in a smart black dress with white starched cuffs and collars. The place reminded him of similar establishments in Brussels. Pleasant art deco buildings with an inviting atmosphere, and friendly service. He wondered what was going on at home – had the Germans entered the capital of his country yet? Where was his brother and how were his left-wing students surviving? Was their property still intact or had his record collection been destroyed or stolen by looters? Not for the first time he felt alone in a foreign country, but remembering the experience of Mr Phillipps he counted himself lucky to be free and with his mother.

Making his way into Soho he stopped outside where the Monseigneur Club had been located. It was boarded up. His mind went back to the heady days when he had come to London to hear and meet Louis Armstrong. He had attended rehearsals in Poland Street, a wonderful concert in the Dominion Theatre. Afterwards a few of them had come back to this club to drink and talk jazz. Since it had almost been 'closing time,' Nat Gonella had ordered 30 pints of beer for the group. They had drunk hard and fast before being thrown out into the London night. It was clear that the Dominion Theatre was also closed for business. Robert spoke to a small, rotund man he assumed was the manager.

'Any shows booked in the future?' he asked hopefully.

'You're joking mate, all we get are variety shows these days, and they don't pay. People are afraid to go out at night because of the air raids and anyway all the American stars won't come across because of the war. You'd be better off going over to America, that's where all the action is.'

These words kept coming back to Robert as he lay awake in his hostel room trying to ignore the coughing, wheezing and farting of those around him.

III Waking up to the Statue of Liberty

'We're here, it's New York', one of the men in Robert's cabin shouted. He had lain half awake on his bunk most of the night. He had worried about his family, his invaded and occupied country, his decision only taken after a lot of heart searching to cross the Atlantic – to the home of jazz. About 4am he had finally fallen asleep and was now awoken by shouts and frantic movement in the confines of his steerage class cabin.

He joined the excited throng on deck. Sure enough there on the port side was the Statue of Liberty – the unmistakable symbol of American freedom and opportunity. He remembered the inscription often associated with it – 'Send us your huddled masses yearning to breathe free'. A message that had warmed the hearts of thousands of immigrants and refugees to the promise of the New World. Though not, Robert reminded himself, the slaves brought from Africa in conditions of the most atrocious cruelty and degradation imaginable. In the past had come Irish fleeing from famine, Italians from poverty in the south, English from religious persecution. Now it was mostly Jewish refugees from Nazi persecution and comparatively wealthy Europeans, like himself, who had escaped.

On the Jersey side lay Union City and on the east side of the Hudson river, the skyscrapers of Manhattan. There was a keen sense of anticipation amongst the passengers and that included himself – Robert Goffin, a slightly stooping, bespectacled, homesick, nervous, jazz enthusiast Belgian, arriving in the land of the free, the land of plenty, the land of the Wall Street crash and the Depression, the land of slavery, the Model T Ford and the birthplace of blues and jazz.

The longshoremen tied up the ship at Pier 94. The formalities took surprisingly little time – at least for himself whose papers were in order. The next thing he knew was that he standing on 52nd Street gazing in awe at his first sight of urban America. The huge automobiles and trucks, raw redbrick buildings and the number of black faces make an immediate impression. From his reading and research he knew that 52nd Street was an entertainment centre of New York and soon spotted theatres and dance halls as he walked eastwards. He spotted 'The Onyx' and the 'Hickory House' where famous jazz musicians played regularly. At this hour all was quiet. Robert booked into a small hotel next to 'The Famous Door Club', which he had also heard of in connection with late-night jam sessions amongst the New York jazz fraternity.

The receptionist at the Hotel Paris was a huge black man who was smoking a large cigar. Apart from the name, the place had no obvious resemblance to France. The black man was reading the baseball reports and showed no obvious interest in Robert apart from securing from him the 10 dollars deposit for a room in his dingy establishment.

'OK bud, leave the key here when you go out, no liquor on the establishment, and no peeing in the basin.'

Robert had a reasonable grasp of English but realised that the accent of the American South was not at all like the BBC English that he had been taught in his lycée back home near Brussels. He unpacked his luggage before carefully double-locking his room door and depositing the key. He set out eagerly towards Broadway. The contrast to London could not have been greater. Whereas London had been grey, damp and war-torn, New York was hot and bustling. As well as, two thousand miles and a world away from Germany.

The sheer size of buildings and vehicles was almost intimidating, and the variety of languages being spoken enthralling. He recognised Italian, Yiddish and Spanish. He drew comfort from the familiar landmarks of downtown Manhattan. He sought out an oasis of tranquillity in a music shop on First Avenue. It was like an Aladdin's cave. All the well known phonograph labels – Paramount, Victor, Decca, as well as specialist jazz companies like Okeh and Black Swan records were on display. Robert gladly spent a few dollars on copies of *Downbeat* and *Metronome* to see who was playing where in Harlem. To his delight he saw that Benny Carter was at the Apollo with Billie Holiday, Cootie Williams at the Renaissance Ballroom, and yes, Louis Armstrong at the Paramount Theatre. The Jewish owner of Mann's Music Store confirmed to him that the New York hotels and ballrooms were swinging now that the Depression had lifted, the days of Prohibition had passed, and thanks to the jobs in military production, people had dollars in their pocketbooks. Benny Goodman, Count Basie, Duke Ellington, Harry James were all packing them in and business was booming. After vowing that he would not buy any more records after what had happened to his priceless collection in Brussels, Robert contended himself with buying a few books and some sheet music. He was particularly pleased to pick up a copy of Alan Lake's 'The American Negro and his Music' which he had seen favourably reviewed.

That night Robert sought out his mentor and idol at the Paramount Theatre. The audience was, like himself, mostly white, and youthful. There were some Negroes downstairs. Louis Armstrong played with all his customary verve, passion and showmanship, and was frequently clapped and cheered throughout the two hours of the masterful performance. It was all very different from the polite, deferential audiences at concerts which he had attended in Europe. There was even some dancing in the aisles.

After the concert he nervously knocked on the maestro's dressing room door. Louis was sitting in the middle of a group of friends with a whiskey glass in his hand. Black faces turned enquiringly towards him as he was shown in. Slowly a smile came over Louis' glistening face.

'My man Robert' ... 'great to see you' ... 'welcome to

America'. 'What are you drinking – Scotch or bourbon?' Turning to his wife Alpha he beckoned Robert over.

'Honey, this is Mr Jazz of Brussels over in Europe. He knows more about our music than anybody else, even in America.'

Robert was clasped by the hand and welcomed like a distant but revered relative. He was plied with questions about the war in Europe and how he had come to be in New York.

'Honey, go get my friend Robert some ice from that mean -mouthed manager.'

Louis waited till she was out of the room before leaning forward and confiding in Robert.

'OK gate, what can I do for you ... Do you need money?' He pulled out a thick wad of dollar notes and slipped more than a few bucks into Robert's jacket pocket.

'Take it quick, before my lady returns,' he said putting his finger to his lips to confirm that this offer was between them only. Robert wanted to protest but he knew that this gesture was genuine enough. He felt overcome. Tears came to his eyes. Here he was just off the boat, in a strange land and was being befriended by arguably the greatest jazz musician in the world. They talked and drank for over an hour before Louis announced it was time to go and play some more elsewhere.

'Come on man, let's go!'

Harlem streets were full of life and people – mostly black people. They were elegantly dressed. Men wore wide-brimmed hats, had padded shoulders, flashy ties and shiny processed hair. Women wore frills and feathers, powder and perfume, silky gowns and striking hats. There were Cadillacs and Oldsmobiles on the roads and all manner of hustlers on the sidewalks. They passed the Abyssinian Baptist church where Paul Robseson and Revella Hughes were top billing. Only with difficulty could Robert stop himself believing that he was dreaming. Ushered into a club called the 'Garden of Joy', and given a seat close to the stage. Willie 'The Lion'

Smith was playing piano and the crowd was whooping in their seats and dancers gyrating sensuously in front of the band. Robert could only look on in fascination and amazement at the scene. By popular acclaim 'Satchmo' or Pops to his friends was called onto the stage. He matched and complemented the lyrical intricacies of the stride piano and played and sang in a whirlwind of syncopated sound.

In the days that followed, America was inexorably sucked into the War, especially after the Japanese attack on Pearl Harbour. Robert immersed himself in the New York jazz scene. He listened to the white big bands in the glitzy hotels downtown and got into the heaving dance halls in Harlem. As an outsider – 'a mouldy fig' – he was sometimes ignored and occasionally abused, especially when he took little heed of the commonplace segregation operated in many of the theatres. But generally his knowledge of jazz and willingness to listen gained him a measure of acceptance. He was introduced to musicians and solicited by prostitutes. They assumed that his presence signalled sexual desire rather than an appetite for music. During the day he wrote up his notes and toured the music shops talking to agents, publishers and fellow enthusiasts.

All the time he had not forgotten home. Sitting in his room with neon flashing and occasional squeal of car brakes from the highway he imagined the rest of his family in London and Belgium. He frequently telephoned his mother. She was well, though apprehensive at the prospect of a German invasion. Many bombs had fallen on London but none near her. His fellow Belgians at home were suffering, with curfews, censorship and concentration camps. A plan by Hoover to provide soup kitchens to the populace in cities of the Low countries had apparently been blocked by Churchill. He pronounced that it would be counter-productive to the war effort. The Belgian government in London was calling for active resistance. He received letters smuggled out from his students – they were boycotting lectures. In July, he and a handful of fellow Belgians celebrated Independence Day. It was a muted affair since most were due to return to take up arms for their country. His new American friends advised him to see more of their country before returning. Louis Armstrong urged him to stay – 'Go down south young man, go to New Orleans where it all started, go talk to the folks down there.'

IV Waking up in Bourbon Street

The sound of breaking glass woke Robert from his long, deep sleep. Empty bottles were being thrown into a garbage truck in the street outside his room. And it wasn't any old street but the one and only Bourbon Street, in the heart of the French Quarter of New Orleans. He had travelled the 1,400 miles from New York to Louisiana by Greyhound because of the railroad strike called by International Brotherhood of Pullman Car Employees.

His route had taken him through the industrial cities of the Northeastern seaboard; through Philadelphia where USS Washington had just been launched and where the great jazz trumpeter Louis Mitchell was born; through Baltimore where Billy Holiday was brought up in poverty and prostitution. There she had first sung *Strange Fruit* – the poignant ballad about the lynching of Negroes by white mobs led by the Klu Klux Klan. Then they had passed through the lush green fields of Virginia and tobacco barns of North Carolina before reaching the pine forests and red red soils of the South.

Robert had known he had entered the Southern states when he saw rebel Dixie flags and Confederate statues in the small towns along the turnpike highway between Atlanta and Birmingham. He also saw more black faces and the telltale signs of segregation. In the bus stations there were even separate toilets and drinking fountains. Throughout the journey whites were all at the front of the bus and Negroes at the back.

The other thing which really impressed Robert was the sheer size of the country – certainly compared to Europe and Belgium – and its unrelenting preparations for war. Cities and towns, north and south – the signs of the home front were everywhere.

Factories were working at full blast, rail sidings full of tanks destined for Europe and the Far East; huge posters extolling the virtues of buying war bonds alongside the highways; victory gardens being cultivated in parks and vacant lots; and Boy Scouts collecting scrap metal, rubber and cloth – all for the war effort. One of his fellow passengers had also pointed out the little blue stars in house windows indicating that a member of the household had joined the armed services. Finally everywhere were men and some women in uniform. The war was not being fought in America but there was no doubt that America was going to war.

The final section of his journey had been from Jackson south through the cotton fields and plantations of Mississippi. At Natchez the bus became crowded with people going to a country fair. A thin, white woman took the seat next to Robert and he was obliged to engage in conversation. She was a school teacher from Baton Rouge and was truly amazed and clearly disconcerted to hear that her foreign travelling companion was going to New Orleans for the sole purpose of listening to jazz.

'Why on earth would you all want to come all the way from Europe to listen to that jungle music!' she exclaimed for half the bus to hear.

'It's voodoo music and causes depravity and immorality.' She went on to expand her thesis to Robert and anyone else who was within earshot.

'It's devil music that reduces self control and encourages lust, drug taking and rebellious behaviour amongst the Negroes and young whites who should know better. How can you come from Europe with Bach, Beethoven and Brahms and stoop so low to listen to that jazz?' she admonished Robert. He declined to get involved in an argument. But politely pointed out in his broken English that jazz and the blues was a genuine, and uniquely American form of music which had European and African origins, and it had all started in New Orleans, and the south.

There had been no meeting of minds and Robert had felt a sense of relief when she alighted and he was left in peace to anticipate with great excitement his arrival in 'the crescent city'. He had the sound of jazz in his head as they crossed the New Orleans city limits. The music of the famous sons of New Orleans – Louis Armstrong, Buddy Bolden, Bunk Johnson, Sidney Bechet, Fats Domino and Jelly Roll Morton to name but a few.

On arrival Robert got a cheap room in the French Quarter. He could see the clear blue sky through the torn curtains. The springs of his iron bed were broken and the floor and bedclothes were none too clean. But so what, he was here at last. He had read so much about the city and its musicians and at last had the chance to see and hear it all for himself.

He was eager to explore, although he knew perfectly well that life didn't get going until after dark. He wanted to see how much was left of Storeyville, the 38 blocks of the city which had existed from 1896 to 1917 as the red light and entertainment district. Did houses of pleasure still exist on Basin Street? Madame Lulu White's infamous Mahogany Hall had long since gone, but Preservation Hall was very much alive and jumping.

In the days that followed, Robert relished walking on the levees and taking the ferry over the river to Algiers. He found the dive where Lizzie Douglas had sung. It had been converted into a funeral parlour. He also walked uptown where Louis Armstrong was born in 1900, the Negro quarter bordered by a church, prison, school and the aptly named Funky Butts Ballroom.

He went everywhere he wanted, apart from the docks which were closed to the public because of the activities of the US Navy. He kept well away fearing that he would be mistaken for a German spy, on account of his strange European accent. The fact that New Orleans had once been French would hardly save him from arrest by the military police.

He explored the music and pawn shops on the lookout for memorabilia, and followed parades and funeral marches to hear the magic sounds of jazz being played in the city where it had all started around the turn of the century. He drank Regal beer in the clubs and frequented the dance halls to see who was playing with whom and where. To his profound disappointment most of the musicians he thought should be playing had gone. Departed to Memphis, St Louis, Kansas City, Chicago and New York. Or else they had joined the forces to play to the troops.

But Robert did not just immerse himself in what was left of the jazz scene in the city; he established contact with the University of Tulane and due to a shortage of staff got himself hired – (he was getting used to the American language) – to give lectures to sociology and law students at the nearby campus. He also paid several calls on the mayor of the city to sound out the possibility of establishing a museum of jazz. At first the idea had met with blank faces and non-commital replies, but after a while the city bosses had come round to such a tourist-drawing project. Gradually his reputation as a knowledgeable enthusiast spread to the local media and he was interviewed by a reporter from the *Picayune Times*, and on several local radio shows. To his surprise and delight he was invited to write an obituary for Fats Waller when he died during the early months of 1943. He used the immortal words – 'it ain't what you do – it's the way that you do it'.

The obituary was placed in the edition headlined 'Scrap champ of the USA,' which told of Warren Beaux, 11 years old of Vermillion parish, Louisiana who had collected 800,000 pounds of scrap for Uncle Sam.

V Waking up in Oxford, Mississippi

After the dinginess and disarray of his room in the French
Quarter of New Orleans, the small university dormitory study
he woke up to was bare and bright. He was on the campus of
the University of Oxford in Northern Mississippi to attend the
37th annual conference of the American Sociological Society.
He had travelled up-state the previous day by train. Along the
same railroad that had taken thousands of black Americans
out of the South and to the big cities where opportunity
beckoned. Through McComb, Haslehurst, Jackson, Winona
and Grenada, and then changing at Batesville to the red brick
buildings set on the edge of the Holly Springs National Forest.
As Robert lay on his bed in the warm summer morning
he flipped through the conference programme. Although
Belgium could claim Adolphe Quetelet, one of the founders
of social science as its own, American sociology was more
advanced. Delegates from all over the States were there from
the Ivy League Colleges in the north east to small Southern
Baptist teacher's colleges.

The range of papers being given was certainly nothing if
not varied. There were academic contributions on intra-
regional migration patterns of Negroes, the season of birth
and its relation to human abilities; the ecological patterning in
Rochester, NY which related indices such as families on public
relief, foreign born, TB cases per thousand households,
juvenile delinquency, child neglect and membership of the
Boy Scout movement, all were correlated and mapped for this
extremely well-studied city. There were also papers reflecting
wartime preoccupations such as early school-leaving near
military bases and family breakdown amongst service
personnel. Finally a paper concerned with the methods of
contraception practised by American couples caught his eye.

In it the author described the use of condoms, douche, diaphragm, safe period, and withdrawal amongst different socio-economic groups in American society. It also noted that some American Indian tribes in northern California used a drink made from crushed mistletoe berries to avoid pregnancy. He was due to give his paper in a session devoted to the music of black America during the latter part of the morning.

After a shower, he dressed leisurely and proceeded down to the massive dining hall. After an excellent breakfast of eggs – done 'sunny side up' with grits, the staple diet of southerners, he took a stroll amongst the beautiful shrubs and trees on the campus. He felt at home in this academic setting, albeit one very different to the crowded buildings of his faculty in Brussels. It was very peaceful after the bustle of New Orleans and people were friendly. It was, in many ways, a bit of an oasis from wartime European violence he was now reading about, and southern segregation which he could see everyday.

At eleven o'clock he took his place in the lecture room. There was a mixed-race audience with a sprinkling of women. The professors wore bow ties and linen jackets, and the women fanned themselves with their papers. The paper being given before his was by a Chicago University professor. It was entitled the 'Differential attitudes of whites in northern and southern colleges towards Negroes'. The two sets of respondents had been asked to agree/disagree with a series of statements, and the results obtained were dramatic. For example 83% of northern students agreed 'that the Negro should have the same opportunity for education as whites'. Amongst southern students 64% agreed 'that the Negro should always occupy an inferior position in the community'. 88% of the southern sample agreed with the statement 'that I have no objection to the Negro provided he keeps his proper place, and 57% agreed that 'all the Negro needs to make him happy is the satisfaction of his material needs'. Finally only 9% of the southerners concurred with the statement 'that if given a chance the Negro would be just as good as the white man'.

Many of the audience – including Robert – were surprised and shocked by these findings, as they were announced by the lecturer. There followed a heated debate, and general agreement that the gulf between north and south was as wide as ever. Some of the audience pointed out that there was plenty of prejudice and discrimination all over the States, not least in the US Army itself.

Robert rose to give his own paper. He was nervous – not because he wasn't sure of his subject matter but because his command of the English language was still far from perfect. His accent singled him out from the New England twang and the Southern drawl of his academic colleagues. His paper was on the role of the American Negro in the development of jazz. He first pointed out that little serious research had been done on this topic with the possible exception of Alain Locke's book 'The Negro and his Music' which had been published in 1936. He developed a thesis – which he had long held and had been further confirmed by his recent experience since coming to the States – that jazz was in a permanent state of flux. Jazz, he argued, was African in its origin with its syncopated rhythm harmonies having been brought by the slaves and fused with European musical traditions in the nineteenth century. While the essence of jazz and blues arose out of Negro experience, it had been, was being, and would in the future be taken up, modified, and transformed by whites to reach a wider audience in America and abroad. Ragtime, blues, hot New Orleans, swing, were all part of a process involving music and songs being spun out from the black community to the larger, wealthier white society. Music was hatched in Storeyville, Beale Street, Chicago's Southside and Harlem, and through the medium of phonographs and radios spread to the entire population.

Robert was careful not to overstate his case. He noted that

W C Handy – a Negro – had done a great deal to popularise blues through his own music publishing company, and mentioned the role of Marcus Garvey's Universal Negro Improvement Society with its branches in cities and towns throughout the country. He also acknowledged that some white musicians such as Bix Beiderbecke had been innovators, while acknowledging the black musicians who had inspired them. He used a quotation from Hoagy Carmichael who, hearing Louis Armstrong play, had exclaimed – 'Why isn't everybody in the world here to hear that!' And ended up with a comment by W C Handy which he had recently read –

'A constant struggle is needed to keep commercial forces from destroying the genuine expression of Black music that comes from the soul of the people'.

Few in the audience showed any inclination to disagree with his hypothesis, partly Robert suspected because they did not know as much as he did about the history of jazz. An elderly Negro professor from the Tuskagee Institute agreed with him profoundly. Whites, he announced gravely, had 'bleached out the sound of black music'. The only other contribution from the audience was from a female Dean from Georgia State College. She pointed out that, in her opinion, jazz had an enormous potential as a unifying force in American life since it was appreciated and played by both sections of their society. He readily agreed. At that point the chairman closed the session, calling the participants to a picnic lunch in the grounds of the college president's mansion.

Over tasty snacks and cool drinks Robert found himself with a University of Chicago professor who was describing the race riots which were taking place in Detroit. At that point a tall, slim woman edged closer to his group at the edge of the lawn. It was she who had been involved in the discussion about the positive role of jazz in American society.

'Good afternoon, Dr Jazz from Brussels,' she greeted him in mock seriousness. 'My name is Ada Gordon. I enjoyed your lecture. By the way do you know that here in Oxford you are right next door to the birthplace of blues?'

She went on to explain that there were a dozen counties around Clarkedale in the cotton-growing bottomlands, on either side of the Mississippi-Arkansas state line where the Blues started its life. Many of the great bluesmen grew up in these settlements – Gus Cannon in Red Banks; Joe McCoy in Raymond, Furry Lewis in Greenwood. That they travelled around the region performing at country shows and informal gatherings amongst black plantation workers and sharecroppers. Some ended up in the state penitentiary at Angola like Leadbelly. Now many have gone north to make a living in Chicago.

Robert was impressed that a well-educated black woman knew and cared so much about her musical roots, when apparently all around there was indifference.

'Thank you kindly for that information,' Robert said. 'I must do more research on the subject and obviously I am in the right place to do it.'

'You sure are, you should get down to the Yazoo delta and hear some real blues.'

Ada sounded encouraging, almost impatient. Then she added: 'Look, the conference is nearly over, why don't I take you there. There is a young blues man playing tonight in Indianola, it's only a few miles from here.'

Robert was getting used to American friendliness and hospitality by now and he accepted the invitation at once. After a few moments he wondered whether it was such a good idea after all. He was in the deep South – would it be wise for him – a white man – to travel alone with a Negro woman and charge into a black community?

'Are you sure that it will be all right for us to do this?' he asked quietly.

'Sure it will be OK,' Ada replied without hesitation. 'If it was a black man with a white woman then that would be a very different story, and anyway I know some of the folks over there. Anyway you are a European and that's better than being a local white!'

It was mid afternoon when they set off in Ada's Chevrolet. She explained that it belonged to her father and that her parents lived near Oxford. She had the use of it for the day. They drove slowly due to the wartime speed limits and the need to save gas. Robert examined the Mobil map of Mississippi and chuckled to himself at some of the names of places – 'Progress', 'Zachary', 'Necessity', 'Trout', 'Jigger', 'Bobo' – he wondered about the origins and history of these places.

The origins of others were clearer – 'Hushpukena', obviously an Indian name, and 'Alligator' where presumably that species were to be found.

Ada switched on the auto's radio, a luxury that Robert had never seen before. A Memphis station was playing country music. Ada retuned the radio until she heard a black station. They were playing songs by Paul Robeson and then a blues number sung by Chester 'Howlin Wolf' Burnett. Robert sat back and closed his eyes. He felt a long way from home, his family and the war. The hot air blowing on his face, the music, the landscape of yellow pines and roadside shacks and being driven by this fine-looking, articulate, and friendly woman. He felt lucky to be where he was, compared to being back home.

They talked about music, civil rights, the changes taking place in America, her job and his plans to write up the history of jazz and establish a museum in New Orleans. They joined the interstate 82 and passed more gas stations, motels and travel inns. There was more traffic on the highway, mostly trucks transporting oil, bales of cotton, and lumber. Robert noticed Ada look in the car mirror occasionally and she suddenly remarked out of the blue.

'If anybody stops us, you do the talking. Say that you are a European army officer, and I am taking you to a military base in Arkansas.' Robert did not comment, but it made him realise that his companion was not quite as at ease as she had first pretended. In the event they arrived without incident in the town of Indianola round about 7 o'clock and went in search of the hall where the concert was to take place.

VI Waking up with Ada

Somewhere nearby a dog was barking and church bells were ringing. He must be somewhere in the country. There was the smell of coffee. He was in a spare bedroom, with a table with white linen cloth and wooden bed and chairs. Outside through the net curtains he could see pine trees and a track leading up to farm buildings. There was a horse and buggy. Robert washed and got dressed. Downstairs breakfast was laid out, and a delicious smell of bacon coming from the kitchen. Ada appeared from the kitchen. She was wearing an apron over her white blouse and blue denim jeans.

'How many eggs do you want, and by the way the john is outside, round the back.'

Over breakfast she explained that her parents had gone to church but that she had been excused to look after their visitor. Her family had lived for generations in this small settlement outside Oxford, and close to the Alabama state line. They had of course been farmers, but her father had worked for many years for the US Army Corps of Engineers on flood control projects in the Vicksburg district. Her mother also worked as a janitor at the university which Ada had attended as a student.

The previous evening when they had returned late from Indianola, Ada's folks had already gone to bed. When later in the morning they returned from the Charismatic Baptist Church they were formally introduced to their visitor with the strange-sounding accent. They were polite and courteously curious as to who their daughter had brought back to stay.

In the afternoon Ada invited her guest to walk in the

surrounding countryside. They went down a mile or so to the Buttahatchee river. They passed through the pines and watched the dragon flies darting over the surface of the slow moving, brownish water of what Ada described as a creek.

'This creek,' she announced, 'flows into the Little Tallahatchee river and then the Mississippi, all the way down to New Orleans and the Gulf of Mexico. This is the centre of my world, and where my forebears who suffered slavery were bought. They are still exploited as sharecroppers. And injustices are still continuing. Do you know,' she said, 'that there was a lynching nearby in Aberdeen only a few years ago? Only in 1939 did Congress pass an anti-lynching law which instructed all public officials to take all diligent efforts to protect Negroes in their charge. Jim Crow laws discriminate against us all the time.'

'I've been lucky to get a good education and job but most others don't get that chance,' she went on. 'Music and in particular, jazz and blues also provide a chance to advance but there again most of the outlets are controlled by white companies, entrepreneurs and the mafia in the big cities. And as for the war, why should Negroes fight for democracy abroad when they can't even vote at home? Do you know that in the recent presidential election only a tiny fraction of Negroes were registered to vote? 52 millions voted, but precious few black Americans.'

Robert must have looked chastened by this mini lecture, because Ada suddenly laughed.

'Say, now I don't blame you for all this, although I don't like to think what Belgians got up to in the Congo.' Then she turned for home.

That evening, after supper, she showed off her record collection of women singers – Ethel Waters, Ozie MacPherson, Ida Cox, Julia Davies, and Josephine Baker. They ate some ice cream and drank some beer. Cousins and friends came in to join the party and to meet the friend that Ada had brought back from College. They danced and whooped to Bix Beiderbecke playing the *Jazz Band Ball*, Coleman Hawkins playing *Body and Soul*, and Fats Domino crooning *Ain't Misbehavin*. Robert was even coaxed into dancing, as Billie Holiday sang *Summertime*. He felt happy and grateful to this family that had taken him into their home – just as Louis Armstrong had done those months ago in New York when he had first arrived as a lonely exile in a strange country.

It was after midnight when he said goodnight, and farewell to Ada's folks who, he was told, would be long since gone to work by the time he left in the morning to return to New Orleans.

For a while Robert couldn't sleep. He lay listening to the crickets, and recalling his bitter-sweet experiences of his Sunday in the Deep south. He tried to imagine what it must be like to be black in a white society, for men to be threatened and even killed if they stepped out of line, for women to be vulnerable to rape and abuse. And the feelings of black servicemen in segregated units being asked to risk their lives for the freedom of others in far-off continents, including his friends and family in Belgium. Of Negro musicians being discovered by white entrepreneurs or researchers like himself and in danger of having their music stolen by white parasites.

Robert fell into a deep sleep and dreamt that he was rescuing Ada from drowning in the Tallahatchee river. Next morning it was 8 o'clock when he was awoken by a knock on the door. Ada stuck her head round the door. She brought in some hot water.

'Sleep well, honey?' she asked. She looked fresh and more good looking than ever. She was wearing a loose smock and her feet were bare.

'*Oui, merci*,' Robert replied, 'and I saved you.' He told her of his dream. She gave a rich deep laugh.

'I wouldn't swim in that creek if you had given me a hundred dollars, the catfish would tickle my toes and then there are the alligators.'

Ada sat on the bed and smiled. 'I've found something that might interest you,' she said lightly, and much to Robert's surprise, held up a sprig of mistletoe.

He stared at it for a few moments wondering what she meant by such a present and then he too burst into laughter. He had forgotten that Ada was amongst the audience when the sexual mores of American Indians had been mentioned in the previous Friday's conference lecture.

'My folks have gone to work,' she said with a smile. Robert felt overwhelmed with desire. He had not held a woman for many months and her presence and subtle invitation combined to touch him deeply. Their eyes met and he took her hands in his and kissed her. He felt her body under her muslin chemise and they embraced. They made love.

For the rest of the summer as the Allies invaded Sicily and the Italian peninsula, and swing bands played to packed audiences all over America, Robert studied and lectured on jazz. He saw Ada whenever possible, but that was on only a few precious occasions. Geography and race all militated against them. It was with affection that it ended. By the end of 1943 Robert was back in New York.

VII Waking up in Minton's Playhouse

Robert lay listening to the roar of the traffic outside his room at the Cecil Hotel on New York's 118th Street. He felt disturbed, and yet curiously elated. He had spent the previous night – indeed until the daybreak – at Minton's Playhouse downstairs. He had experienced an incredible night of jazz – music that he had never heard before either in Europe or his time in the States.

Naturally he had heard about the joint. Where Henry Minton, and now Teddy Hill, welcomed musicians to jam after they had played downtown. How they gave them loans and fed them when they were down on their luck and out of work.

What he had heard he was told was 'Rebop', Bebop or just plain 'bop' jazz which was quite different, more subtle, improvised, tormented than New Orleans and certainly very different from swing. The old tunes and materials had been reshaped. Melodies had been paraphrased and harmonies revised. The music was disturbing, with taunting riffs and a revolutionary angular, flowing, harsh yet lyrical flavour.

He had heard Dizzie Gillespie, Charlie Parker, Thelonious Monk, Charlie Christian, Nick Fenion and Kenny Clark play. Nothing had prepared him for their new and invigorating performance. And it wasn't just how they played but their whole demeanour. Quite the opposite from the smooth, velvety commercialism of the swing bands. These young lions wore crumpled suits, black berets, shades and in some cases goatee beards. They seemed different. Gone was the Uncle Tom showmanship which Negro musicians often slipped into for their white audience. Bop was played by cool cats who were playing for themselves and against each other – not for those who happened to be listening.

Monk had played *Round about Midnight* at four in the morning. It was lodged in Robert's brain.

Why had he not heard this stuff before? The answer was simple, the wartime record ban meant that very few people outside New York had been able to hear this new, cool, improvised, refreshing, technically brilliant, urban, black music. He had talked to Ralph Ellison who was there recording and listening at Minton's and a few other hot-beds of wartime jazz. Ralph's view was that Monk, Parker and the others were reacting against the sugary commercialism of swing and wanted to create jazz which could less easily be exploited, watered down, and taken over. Bop was a manifesto for Negro equality.

Robert took a long time to get himself up and into action. He was finding it difficult to adjust to the type of jazz that had engulfed him a few hours earlier. It was so stimulating and yet disturbing. He loved the improvisation and yet found the discordancy hard to appreciate. As for his theories of the development of jazz, it was all too soon to decide whether or not his jazz history book would have to be rewritten. He wondered what Louis Armstrong and some of the established kings of jazz thought of it. How they would react. According to one or two of the music magazines he had read they were none too impressed.

Robert had but a few days to explore further. He had to get himself organised to fly to Europe. For weeks now he had faced the growing dilemma – stay in the US or go back home to take part in the liberation of his homeland. He had read with horror in the *New York Times* of the atrocities being committed by the Nazis as the tide of war gradually turned against them. In Belgium and elsewhere there were reprisal executions taking place, and concentration camps being discovered. But the brave resistance being put up by an increasing number of partisans was also being reported widely. In the case of Belgium, this was mainly taking the form of sabotage.

He had grown used to the American way of life – its friendliness, its sense of opportunity and informality. He loved travelling. He still loved Ada, but he could not face the prospect of remaining out of the war forever and detached in his comfortable exile on the wrong side of the Atlantic. He felt he had achieved a grasp of the essentials of jazz and experienced its vitality, power and diversity. In a strange way he felt that the music he had heard played in Minton's Playhouse provided a fitting finale to his search. When the war was won he could continue to write up the true story of jazz and persuade Americans that they possessed a unique and valuable art form. He determined to make the most of all the material that he had assiduously collected over the months of his sojourn since he had first sighted the Statue of Liberty.

VIII Waking up in a Telft barn

Robert didn't know if he had been woken up by the chill which had crept into his body or the scratching which was caused by the hay which served as his bedding. He had spent the night in a farmer's barn outside the village of Telft, a few miles from the city of Liège. Around him were English soldiers of the Guards Armoured Division, to which he had been attached as a guide and interpreter as they had swept into Belgium, on 3rd September 1944 a few days ago. He had undergone basic training in the south of England. His division had played a key role in spearheading the advance towards the German heartland.

The scenes which had greeted the liberators were both terrible and wonderful. They had been shocked by the sight of the Breedinck camp outside Brussels and the stories of cruelty and terror to which his fellow citizens had been subjected to these past years of occupation. Thousands had been sent to German labour camps and it was rumoured that, in the last few days, trains full of captured resistance fighters, and Jewish internees were being taken east to provide cover for the German retreat. The RAF was bombing strategic targets and the Allied armies were still being faced by stiff resistance.

Yet the welcome they had received from the local populace was unforgettable. There was dancing in the streets, bonfires, and everywhere the red, yellow and black of the national flag of Belgium. They had been garlanded with flowers and offered wine and beer, though goodness knows where it had come from, for the population had earlier been reduced to eating cats and rats to stave off hunger.

Slowly the company stirred into life. Ablutions were performed swiftly and rations hurriedly eaten. Instructions were issued down the line from Major General Adair via shortwave radios. Their goal of the day was to intercept a train which had been spotted by reconnaissance aircraft carrying Belgian prisoners heading for the German border.

Although he had only been on active service a week or so he was already getting used to the dangers. His early fears had given away to a grim determination to get on with the job of clearing out the German army from his country and then chasing it to Berlin.

Occasionally he thought of his mother who he had briefly met in London; and America and Ada. All this was too precious to lose. He also kept wondering what had happened to his brother, who had been last heard of fighting with the Resistance in the Liège district.

Later that morning reports came through that the train they were trying to find was crawling; literally going a snail's pace, about a mile from where they were. Apparently it was being driven by a Belgian captive who was deliberately going slowly so that the Allies could reach it before it caught up with the rest of the retreating Germans.

Half an hour later they caught up with it and prepared to attack. The German guards were in no mood to fight and ran from the carriages with their hands in the air. The driver gave a series of blasts as if to send a message of hope to the packed occupants of the carriages. They could see faces peeping out from the cracks. Cheering started as the British flags on the armoured vehicles were spotted. They rounded up the German guards and Robert was instructed to liaise with the prisoners once the doors were torn open.

There were scenes of jubilation. The motley crew of prisoners, dressed in the remnants of uniforms and scraps of clothing, were thin and unshaven. They knew that if the driver had not delayed their progress they would be facing an unknown and perilous future in Germany during the last few months of the war. There was jubilation all round. Robert tried to get some sort of order into the chaotic scene. The last carriage was being opened as he conversed in French to the several leaders of the group. He heard a shout.

'*Robert, Robert, c'est mois, Louis.*'

He had saved his mother, lost his jazz records, experienced real life and jazz in America, and now found his kid brother.

Postscript

Robert Goffin was born on 21st May 1898 just outside Brussels. From 1920 his interest in jazz developed. During the twenties and thirties, Goffin became a devotee of jazz. In 1922 he published *Jazz Band* and ten years later *Aux Frontières du Jazz*.

In 1939 he went to New York, where he stayed at the Peter Stuyvesant Hotel. In 1942 he visited the Deep south and New Orleans and later was to be appointed as Professor of the History of Jazz at the New York School for Social Research.

The Armed Forces edition of his book *New Orleans, Capital of Jazz* sold over 300,000 copies. He was made an honorary citizen of New Orleans. In 1945 he returned to Belgium, writing *From Jazz to Swing* in 1946 and *Louis Armstrong – Le Roi du Jazz* in 1947.

In the post-war period he became a distinguished man of letters publishing many books, poems and giving lectures all over the world. He died in 1984 '*apres une vie bien remplie*'. On 12th September 1998, to mark the 100th anniversary of his birth, a Grand Jazz Concert was held in the Commune of Lasne, outside Brussels. The 'Sweet Substitute Quartet' played compositions by Louis Armstrong, Earl Hines, Duke Ellington and Jimmy Dorsey.

Early years at Postcard Corner

The Ellen Langer experiment
– *savour the sixties and see the difference!*

*I*n **1979** Ellen Langer and her colleagues at Harvard
University conducted an extraordinary project into
awareness and behaviour in ageing. She asked a group of men
aged 75 or older, and in good health, to meet for a week's
retreat at a country resort. They were told not to bring any
newspapers, magazines, books or family photos dated later
than **1959**.

The resort had been set up to duplicate life as it was twenty
years earlier. Reading material from two decades ago was
available, and the only music that was played was twenty years
old. In keeping with this 'flashback' exercise, the men were
asked to behave entirely as if the year was 1959. All talk had to
refer to events and people of that year. Every detail of their
'week in the country' was geared to make each subject feel,
look and behave as if they were in their mid fifties.

During the study period Langer's team made measurements
of the men's 'biological' age. They measured physical strength,
posture, perception, cognition, and short term memory, along
with thresholds of hearing, sight and taste.

The Harvard team wanted to change the 'context' in which
these men saw themselves. The premise of the experiment was
that seeing oneself as old (or young) directly influences the
ageing process itself. Thus the men were also required to wear
ID photos taken twenty years before, and learned to identify
one another through these pictures rather than the present
appearance. They were instructed to talk exclusively in the
present tense of 1959 (I wonder who will win the 1964 General
Election?). Their wives and children were referred to as if they

were also twenty years younger, and they had to talk about their careers as if they were still ongoing.

The results of this gerontological 'play-acting' project were remarkable. Compared to a control group that went on the retreat but continued to live in the world of 1979, the 'make-believe' group improved in memory and manual dexterity. They were more active, and self-sufficient. They behaved more like 55-year-olds than 75-year-olds.

Perhaps the most remarkable change had to do with aspects of ageing that would normally be considered to be 'irreversible'. Impartial judges who were asked to study before-and-after pictures of the men detected that their faces looked visibly younger by an average of three years. Measurement of finger length, which tends to shorten with age, indicated that their fingers had lengthened; stiffened joints were more flexible; and posture had started to straighten as it had been in younger years. Muscle strength, as measured by hand grip, improved; as did hearing and vision.

'Intelligence' is considered fixed in adults, yet half of the *experimental group* showed increased intelligence over the five days of their 'return' to 1959. Only a quarter of the *control* group improved their IQ test scores.

Professor Langer's study was a landmark in proving that so-called irreversible signs of ageing could be reversed using psychological intervention. She attributed this 'success' to three factors : (1) the men were asked to behave as if they were younger; (2) they were treated as if they had the intelligence and independence of younger people – unlike the way they were treated 'at home'! (Their opinions were elicited with respect and actually listened to); (3) they were asked to follow complex instructions about their daily routine.

Langer enabled these men to be *'time travellers'*. They journeyed back twenty years psychologically and their bodies followed. They looked and felt better and younger. Isn't it about time this study (to include women also) was replicated?

市会議員
Dr. アラン・バーネット CBE
ヘイブロック区－労働党

経済開発委員長
商業ドックス委員会－委員長

シビック・オフィス・ギルドホール・
スクウエア、ポーツマス PO1 2AL、英国
電話：01705 842492
　　　　　834172

自宅：
8 サセックスロード、サウスシー、
ポーツマス PO5 3EX

Portsmouth
CITY COUNCIL

Early years at Postcard Corner

Pompey Haikus (5-7-5)

On Portsea Island
Thousands of people – side by side
Many good neighbours?

Southsea Common is
Busy, brown, even snowy white
But we like it green

Gleaming French ferries
Overshadow, cheer and wave
Still and West drinkers

All Pompey was there
When Sol went up to lift t'Cup
Sing, jump all day long

Use sunscreen 24
Or toast ourselves burning hot
We choose, earth does not

August on the beach
But not in Paulsgrove, where
They are on the march

Pubs to coffee shops
Deco cinemas to mosques
Nothing stays the same

White sails, sparkling sea
Hot jazz/blues on the bandstand
Sundays are just fine

Early years at Postcard Corner

Pat's palimpsest of Port Carlisle

*P*at lay dozing on the edge of sleep and wakefulness. She stretched her legs out lazily. Her husband's side of the bed was empty. He had not long been gone since the place he had occupied was still warm.

Then she heard Robert clattering around downstairs, followed by the front door slamming and his car being started up. He must have set off early to play another round of golf with his county council cronies.

Pat felt warm and cosy in bed, and thank goodness it was Saturday. No need to hustle off to work. For a while she lay dreaming. It was one of those worrying dreams where everything is going wrong. In this case her school was in the middle of an OFSTED inspection. Her class was unruly. To her horror they were writing with chalks on old-fashioned slates. The inspectors were clearly most unimpressed. Some dreams you want to get back into but Pat was relieved to escape from this one. Downstairs the dog was barking and she needed a pee.

She dragged herself out of bed and threw open the curtains to see what sort of day it was. Grey and blustery, with the clouds scudding in from the Solway and a few spots of rain hitting the window panes. Once downstairs she fed the dog – why hadn't Robert done it already on his way out? Neither the mail nor the paper had been delivered yet so she picked up yesterday's *Telegraph* and carried it back upstairs with a mug of tea. She was irritated that Robert had rushed off like that but at least she could relax on her own for a few minutes. In the old days she would have been stirred into action by the children, but now – apart from the dog – she was on her own. No-one was demanding anything of her for the moment at least.

She sipped her tea and glanced at the crossword. Her husband must have done most of it the night before. As usual he had meticulously crossed out the clues which he had filled in. It was obvious that he had got stuck in the lower right hand corner. He'd got 15 Across: 'Nickname for a south coast city' – Pompey (not surprisingly since he had been in the Navy) and also 'laughter' as the answer for 17 Across: 'It is the best medicine – the Readers Digest says so!' But 21 Across was uncompleted – the clue was 'Can be read from left to right or reverse' (10 letters). As a regular crossword buff and English teacher Pat could spot a palindrome a mile off. She remembered that it was Miss Wharton who had first explained to her that it was a word or phrase that was identical from both ends. Her favourites were 'rotator', and 'nurses run' and she just about remembered an old Latin favourite from her school days – *Roma tibi subito motibus ibit amor.* She was making progress and sipped her tea smugly.

It was clear that 18 Down was the key. It had ten letters 'P-L--P----'. The clue seemed very obscure: it read 'Traces left on a classical magiboard'. Her usual tactic was to guess from the known letters – pal,... pel,... pil,... pol,... palomino, pelmanism, polemical. This was getting nowhere, so she concentrated on the clues to help complete the missing letters. 23 Across was a northern river of four letters and 'Tyne' fitted. Then 24 Across: 'Vicar's wage packet' (7). Pat's presence on the parish council gave her an advantage there – it must be stipend. Back to 18 Down ... P - L - - PS - - T? What on earth could a classical magiboard be? She had 'O' level Latin but that didn't help. She was stuck. The book she had been reading the night before – a Virago biography of Angela Carter entitled 'Flesh and the Mirror' – lay temptingly on the bedside table.

Then in a flash she half remembered a reference to palim something in a local history course she had done a year or two ago. It was a term describing how elements of the past could be observed in that of today. Pat sneaked a look at the Penguin English -ictionary she kept handy for such eventualities. Yes, there it was ... PALIMPSEST – a twice used writing material on which partly erased earlier writing can be seen below more recent writing (origin Greek palim = again, and psestos = rubbed smooth). In archaeology the term often applies to landscapes in which traces of earlier settlement can be seen amongst and below the modern pattern.

Pat filled in the space with the greatest of satisfaction. Robert would never have got that one. He was more interested in keeping his handicap down to single figures on the golf links. She decided to leave it out in a prominent place so that he could observe her clever handiwork.

Meanwhile Pat lay thinking about the palimpsest idea. It had been used by Professor Burley in a local history class to describe how in the Cumbrian countryside successive traces of Celtic, Roman, Anglo Saxon, Norse and Norman occupation – including place-names – were evident. Also how our modern cities reflected the impact of the industrial revolution. He had shown the class wonderfully illuminating slides of ancient Turkish cities such as Troy and Iznik which incorporated layer upon layer of different civilisations.

The more she thought about the notion the more she realised just how widely it could be applied. To an individual building; a village like Port Carlisle where she lived; the county town of Carlisle where she had been brought up, as well as her home county of Cumbria. But there was possibly more to it than that. If it could be applied to places couldn't it also provide insights into people? After all geographical areas were merely the settings in which people lived. Why not a palimpsest of people? The British were a real mixture, so were the Roman army that had occupied northern England. The inhabitants of Port Carlisle were from all sorts of backgrounds, especially those who were classed as the incomers – who had been neither born or brought up in the locality.

And what about herself – Pat Bell – married and middle aged, passed the eleven plus to go to the grammar school, graduate of Manchester University, deputy head of St Ann's primary school, with two children and soon to be a grandparent. She began to think of all the people who had influenced her development, and made their mark on her character, appearance, disposition and beliefs. The early experiences ingrained by parents, grandparents and siblings, certain teachers and classmates, tutors at college, and boyfriends including Peter.

She remembered a saying by Jean Paul Sartre, that went something like – only on the bodies of others can you discover your own. When she and Robert had first got married they had enjoyed staying in bed on weekend mornings – making love, drinking coffee and relaxing together. How times had changed.

Now he was off on the golf course chasing birdies and eagles. Meanwhile here was she, left alone to her thoughts in her bedroom. Pat looked around the room for reassurance. It was a real repository of memories. For nearly twenty years she had slept, loved, dreamt, wept in this, her bedroom. The past was all around her. The fireplace was original and she had scraped layers of paint off it. The rocking chair was a family heirloom – on it she had sat on her grandmother's knee. As usual Robert's clothes were draped all over the chair – just one of his longstanding and irritating habits Pat had to put up with. There were Tassell's photographs of her wedding and also more recent school ones of their two children, source of satisfaction and solace.

The history of her home area was represented by two paintings which also had been handed down to her. One by Sam Bough RSA of the Solway marshes and a second by William Nutter (1818-1872) entitled 'Carlisle from the Canal.' Pat kept these near her to remind her of her roots in this quiet, isolated corner of England.

On the mantelpiece was evidence of the history of the former vicarage that they had bought a few years after getting married and had lived in ever since. The builders had found several ginger beer bottles when putting in central heating and also the remnants of a child's farm set.

Other personal evidence of the past was to be found in the wardrobe. Although most of the clothes she no longer wore had gone to Oxfam a few long skirts from the 60s remained, even if Robert's flared trousers had long since been dispatched. She had three hats for special occasions, one of which she had worn on her wedding day. Her jewellery was also something of a palimpsest of birthday and Christmas presents from those close to her. But possessions, though treasured, were only tokens of her past. Far more important were the years of experiences and memories which were bound up in this the most private and intimate of the rooms in their house.

Memories of passionate and adventurous lovemaking in the early years – lying with Robert, under him, beside him, on top of him. Of fulfilment and frustration. Of seeing her good looks fade and figure fill out. Of Christmas mornings when the children ran in at six o'clock in the morning to show them the toys she – Santa Claus – had carefully placed in their stockings a few hours earlier. Of illnesses and feeling anxiously for lumps. Above all it was a place to reflect on the past, plan for the present and occasionally try to imagine the future.

Pat leapt out of bed – it was well after nine – time to get moving. She looked out of the window to see what sort of day it was turning out to be. The view was always changing according to the seasons and weather. She loved it dearly. In the foreground was their garden and their very own fragment of Hadrian's wall. Beyond lay the line of the old canal and railway – now converted into a coastal cycle path – and then the Solway estuary and the Scottish hills. Pat paused. For the first time began to reconsider this so familiar scene as a palimpsest of local history.

Above all there was Hadrian's Wall, built AD 122-130, a total length of 73 miles (80 Roman miles) from Wallsend in the east to Bowness, a few miles from where Pat was standing. Only a few foundation stones remained in their property, but it was real enough for she had found a Roman coin a few years ago when digging in the kitchen garden. On it the head of Emperor Severus had appeared when she had carefully cleaned it up. The wall – the Northern-most frontier of the Roman Empire had been built and garrisoned by legionnaires and camp followers from all over Europe. Pat had tried to imagine the reaction of soldiers on being given their orders in Provence or Andalucia to march north to the remote, cold edge of the known world. She imagined that they would not have been best pleased. She still remembered some verses by WH Auden –

> *'Over the heather, the wet wind blows*
> *I've lice in my tunic and cold in my nose*
> *The mist creeps over the land of grey stone*
> *My girl is in Tungria, I sleep alone*
> *The rain comes pattering out of the sky*
> *I'm a wall soldier I don't know why.'*

But the wall was barely visible in the garden that Pat had lovingly created over the years. True, the fruit trees and rhubarb patch had preceded her tenure, and the rockery had been constructed earlier in the century. But, especially in the summer months, it was a product of her green fingers, and a blaze of colour with her favourite flowers – marigolds, sunflowers, cosmos and cornflower. Who knows but some of the herbs which grew in the south-facing back garden had originally been brought by the Romans from their Mediterranean base. In which case the garden which Pat looked out on with pride could truly be a horticultural palimpsest.

Beyond the beech hedge which marked the boundary of their land lay the Powmaughan beck and the cutting which marked the route of the former canal and railway line. If ever there was clear example of a palimpsest of transport history, Pat thought to herself, then this was it. She knew all about the development of this communications link. The canal had been opened on 12th March 1823 by Sir James Graham Bart. MP with a lavish breakfast for 200 dignitaries. Some 20,000 of the local populace had lined the canal basin quays in Carlisle and watched the bedecked boats which it was hoped would link the city with Liverpool and the outside world. For thirty years the canal did indeed carry timber, coal and passengers (they could reach Liverpool the same day with a bit of luck), but alas the ambitious scheme to join the Solway to the Tyne in the East came to nought and with the coming of the railways its viability was shortlived. The canal was drained and the Silloth – Carlisle railway was constructed on exactly the same line. It later became part of the LNER company, and part of British Railways before being axed by Beeching in 1964. From where Pat stood at her bedroom window there were few relics to be seen – only the converted railway station, overgrown quay walls and now the cycleway.

Pat had no wish for her quiet corner to attract the interest of the heritage industry, but she was more than happy to take occasional visitors around her section of the Roman wall and at the same time inform them of how Port Carlisle had once been a significant hub in the links between the border city and the rest of the world. A bit like a modern motorway junction it seemed to her.

The story about the Roman wall which Pat never failed to recount to her visitors was the disagreement between Chief Venutius and his wife of the Brigantes tribe. They had resisted the Roman invasion and occupation for many years. But she had changed her allegiance to the Roman side, possibly being attracted to the pleasures of Roman lifestyle or merely taking a pragmatic stance in view of the military might of the Roman fighting machine. Eventually Venutius was put to death and his followers enslaved and sent to work in the Swaledale lead mines. What befell his wife, or for that matter what her name was, Pat had no idea, even though she considered herself a bit of an amateur local historian.

Pat heard the postman whistling in the drive. She was just in time to open the door and save him from having to stuff the letters and assorted bills through the letterbox.

'Morning Mrs Bell,' he remarked with a cheery smile. 'Fraid spring hasn't sprung for you today.'

'Joe, I hope you have brought me good news,' she said, shuffling through the pile. Yes there was an official looking letter from Cumbria County Council.

'Why, what's up?' he said. 'Have you won the pools or summat?'

'No, nothing really.' And to change the subject Pat said, 'By the way Joe, do you know what a palimpsest is, when it's at home?'

'No Mrs, I do not, but it sounds painful whatever it is; it's not a new kind of sheep dip is it by any chance?'

Pat laughed and said cheerio before taking her letters into the kitchen. She had applied for and been interviewed for a new post as co-ordinator for the whole of Cumbria's schools. She definitely wanted a change from the everyday drudge of teaching, and was optimistic, for the job was just up her street. The interview had gone well, and her colleagues had confided in her that she was likely to get the job. She tore open the letter and read with growing disbelief and dismay the following ...

Dear Mrs Bell,

Thank you for your interest for the post of director of the Cumbrian Schools English project. Your application has been carefully considered. I am afraid that the news will be disappointing to you in that your name is not among the shortlist of candidates invited for final interview. I am sorry the outcome is not what you will have hoped, but we had a huge response to our advertisement which produced an extremely strong field of candidates.

May I nevertheless thank you for your interest, and hope that your disappointment on this occasion will not prevent you from applying for a comparable post in the future.

Yours sincerely
Miss V. McGlasson

Pat didn't want to believe what she was reading. She scrunched up the letter and threw it towards the fireplace. Not even on the shortlist! How could that possibly be? She tried to think – what on earth was wrong with her application? It was unthinkable that she should be rejected in this way – after 15 years of dedicated service to the LEA and the teaching profession. Pat gave a shout of frustrated rage and burst into tears. She was glad that she was on her own at this time of weakness and misery. Or perhaps it would have been nice to have a shoulder to lean on.

Her only consolation was her Labrador which nudged its head against her leg. At least a sort of act of condolence, Pat thought, and tried to pull herself together. It wasn't easy. She felt painfully rebuffed, disappointed, hard done by. This was a major setback to her career. Some of the keen disappointments Pat had faced in her life crowded in on her – being left at home when her older brother had been taken to a Guy Fawkes Night party; coming second in the Brampton music festival; not getting a wendy house for Christmas when she was eight. Failing the maths 'O' level on the first occasion. Being ignored by Peter Thompson at a sixth form dance. And worst of all finding out that her husband had been friendly with a female educational psychologist employed in the county education offices – just how friendly she had never asked him and didn't want to know.

Pat felt stifled. She had an urgent need to get out of the

house. She picked up the dog's lead, put on an old garden coat and banged the front door shut. She headed for the Solway marshes. She felt like the loneliness of a long neglected walker.

The air was damp but fresh. Pat blew her nose and gulped it in deeply. She made her way up to the village – such as it was. Port Carlisle or Fishers Cross as it had been known before the canal days, was little more than a huddle of farms and houses. It had no village green worth speaking of though it still had a church, pub and shop/post office. If the truth were known it had become little more than a dormitory suburb for Carlisle a few miles to the east. Pat, together with the rest of the village, had campaigned against the closure of the village school, but in vain. The local children were now bused to Bowness and the Hodgson Bequest which had stipulated in his will of 1792 that all children with the name of Hodgson should be educated free of charge 'without limitation of time or locality' had long since been dissipated.

Mrs Liddell was behind her shop counter but customers were few and far between. A couple of cars were parking near the pub – whereas before there might have been a Morris and Hillman now there was a Peugeot or Honda. It was said that the 'Crown and Thistle' had once been a centre of smuggling, with contraband being brought across the Solway from Scotland, but that must have been before the Union. What was not in dispute was the fact that all the licensed premises in the Carlisle area had been nationalised and in public ownership from 1917 to 1971.

They had been taken over by Lloyd George to stamp out drunkenness amongst the munitions workers. Many had been closed, but the 'Crown and Thistle' had survived selling state beer under the State Management Scheme until the Tory government sold it off to the Youngers Brewery. Fortunately the new owners had not torn the place apart and it was a popular watering hole for locals and visitors alike.

To take her mind off her disappointment Pat had once

again begun to think about palimpsests. Most country pubs, it occurred to her, retained at least a name from the past and something of their former character, even if its authenticity was not always guaranteed. Perhaps some themed pubs were only really pseudo palimpsests after all.

Turning sharply right Pat took a shortcut through the cemetery. On the gravestones and engraved on the war memorial were the names of local families, whose members had been lain to rest or fallen for their country. Generations of Armstrongs, Elliots, Feddons, Nixons, Hetheringtons, Stockdales and others who had laboured on local farms. Many, still in their teens, had enlisted into the Border regiment only to end their lives in the horrific battles of the First World War. These people had moulded the village through the ages, but there were precious few monuments to their contribution. There was no way of telling that the weekend cottage next to Mrs Nixon's house had been a smithy; or that the village recreation field had been dug up during the Second World War to grow vegetables, or that Charles Wesley had preached under the copper beech tree.

Some local worthies had made their mark on the place. Sandy Postlethwaite who owned much of the land had kept its hedges, rotated its fields and refurbished its sandstone farm buildings. The Graham family had paid for church renovations and built a new sports pavilion. More recently, a few active young professional families from the city had organised a campaign to brighten up the village with flower baskets to enable it to win a prize in the best-kept Cumbrian village award.

Pat's mood had not lightened. She considered how little was left to remind us of those who had built up the village and kept it going through the centuries. In particular those who had built the wall, canal and railway on which the settlement had been based. If the village as it stood today was a palimpsest of local history, then whilst most of its buildings showed some traces of the past, there were fewer glimpses of those who had lived there through the generations.

Pat's gloomy thoughts were interrupted by a greeting from the direction of the church.

'Hello, Mrs Bell, are you on your way to church or here studying local history?' asked a friendly voice.

It was the vicar – a young man who had recently come from Newcastle to take care of this and two other adjoining parishes. He had had some difficulty in gaining acceptance by his canny Cumbrian flock. Pat liked his down-to-earth attitude, and paused to have a word with him. Her bad news still made her feel upset, but she didn't feel inclined to tell him about it. Instead she sidetracked onto safer historical ground.

'I was just thinking how little we know of the past local populace of the village,' she said.

'Well,' he countered with a smile, 'if they are in heaven then we shouldn't worry too much on that score.'

'That's as maybe,' replied Pat, 'but you must agree that a graveyard is about the only real monument to village folk who lived and died through the centuries.'

'We do have the parish records of course,' the vicar added, 'but they are kept in Carlisle and are far from complete.'

'By the way,' Pat said almost casually, 'do you know what a palimpsest is by any chance?'

'Sounds like Greek to me,' the vicar replied with a chuckle. 'I've a vague idea it has something to do with evidence of the past in the landscape, am I right or am I right?'

'You are dead right,' Pat answered, 'and so you should be standing in the midst of past parishioners! But since you are so erudite this morning, how would you explain the idea if you were going to use it in one of your sermons?'

The vicar thought for a moment, picking a few weeds from the gravel path as he considered a response.

'Well, in a sermon I would give a few illustrations. A graveyard is certainly a tangible reminder of those who lived in the past, and so are the marble tablets erected on the church walls to local families. But getting away from church, how about a campsite in the Lakes – an ephemeral canvas village, here one week in summer, a mere palimpsest of yellowy, grassy imprints the next.'

'Hey, that's a good one,' Pat exclaimed, delighted that someone else was able and willing to share her big idea. 'Any more?'

'Not really, apart from the decaying evidence of the Industrial Revolution on Tyneside and Teeside, with its shot towers, derelict shipyards, slag heaps and pit villages. Then there is always the prehistoric stone circles scattered around the north of England attesting to early beliefs and workshop before St Bede arrived to spread the Christian gospel. Which reminds me,' he added, 'it's a fact that many of our church festivals do originate from earlier pagan ceremonies.'

They chatted for a few minutes before going their separate ways. Pat felt a wee bit better for their conversation. She had dutifully taken part in the everyday social activities of village life – bring and buy sales, school fetes, harvest festivals, pageants, carol singing. It had been enjoyable at first, especially when the children were young. Now it bored her. She certainly couldn't see Port Carlisle as the end of the rainbow in her life. People were friendly enough but also decidedly gossipy; you couldn't lift a finger without everybody knowing about it. It was safe but suffocating.

She couldn't have survived without the sea. With a sense of relief she ran the last few yards down to the water. She stood on one of the massive sandstone blocks which marked the old canal wall. The tide was in, covering the miles of muddy inlets and salty marsh. The oyster catchers wheeled above her. It was a blue grey scene. In the distance was the Scottish settlement of Cummertrees dwarfed by the atomic power station at Chapelcross, near Annan. The Scottish river Esk and English Eden joined forces in the middle of the estuary.

Pat thought of an incident she had heard about a few years ago when a local doctor had gone out in a canoe and not returned. His family had feared for his safety. He had been carried miles down the coast by the swift and dangerous currents and only rescued a day later by an RAF helicopter. Drownings were not uncommon on the Solway as the tides swept in fast, and unwary visitors had little idea of local conditions. Pat stood on the edge of the water for several minutes. Anyone watching her might have thought that she was considering throwing herself into the waves. But Pat had always felt that suicide was such a futile act. Anyway she remembered the botched job that John Stonehouse had done when things had got too much for him. And whatever did happen to Lord Lucan? She recalled the absurdity of Leonard Rossiter, alias Reggie Perrin, trying to escape his misfortunes by dashing into the Channel from the pebbles of a Sussex beach.

It was threatening rain and she promptly turned back towards the village and home. She had had enough fresh air for the day, but there was still a nagging urge to get away from it all. Maybe if she had lived in the canal era then she could have caught the boat to Liverpool, but those days had long since gone. Instead she got changed quickly and prepared to drive into town. She checked the telephone for recorded messages and slightly to her surprise heard her husband's voice. He must have rung home on his mobile. He was calling to announce that he would be late back. He was going to have something to eat at the golf club and watch the cup final there. Pat was furious. She had been hoping that they would go out for a meal together that evening.

She decided she would go into town, and then drive on and see her daughter near Penrith. Her mood of despondency and dissatisfaction returned; her husband's 'take it or leave it' attitude was just far too casual for her liking.

She drove fast towards Carlisle, only slowing down to cross

the bridge over the old railway line at Drumbeugh. There had been some sidings there and the whole area was littered by old lorries and cars in Milburn's breaker's yard. The shells of vehicles were piled high in an untidy palimpsest of the car industry. Robert was always saying that even the slightest change in land use throughout Britain had been passed by some planning committee, but in this case the damage had been done before the prissy planners had gained control. Pat was still thinking about her crossword clue again. She couldn't get the palimpsest idea out of her head. She noticed an election poster for Donald McLean, the Conservative candidate in the forthcoming general election. It had been stuck to a tree at a prominent junction. She began to muse over the laws of the country as a palimpsest of legislation passed by successive governments over the centuries.

She drove past the road sign marking the limits of the city. 'Carlisle the Border City – Worth a Closer Look'. A closer look at what? The uniformly drab estates which ringed the town? The thirties semis built ribbon-like along the trunk roads radiating out from the core of the city? Or the red brick Victorian streets which she passed through as she approached the town centre with the Valium Hotel on the right (palimpsest of names?). Driving through these zones of urban development was like cutting through an onion. The countryside had been engulfed in successive periods of house building. But in the mediaeval centre the layers were vertical, with the modern city being built on Roman foundations. The street plan of this walled city had not changed much in two thousand years.

In Caldewgate, where the canal basin had been located, textile mills had sprung up. One or two still remained and the famous Dixon's chimney towered over the neat terraced houses. Pat had passed the 'Jolly Sailor' thousands of times but until today she had not associated it with the canal. Her 'palimpsest' spectacles were leading her to see things in a different light. Likewise the castle standing beside the inner

city ring route. Built on the banks of the Eden by William
Rufus it had dominated the town in the early part of its history.
Mary Queen of Scots had been held captive there in 1542. It
had been besieged by the Roundheads during the Civil War.
The populace had been forced to eat rats to stay alive. Only
remnants of the city walls remained intact. Even in the last
century Dorothy Wordsworth had noted with disapproval that
the walls were 'broken down and crumbling in places'.

The city had changed even in Pat's lifetime. The derelict
mediaeval lanes had been torn down and replaced by a post-
modern version with boutiques and card shops. The city centre
had been pedestrianised, with the old town hall being turned
into a tourist information centre. The old Sands fairground
had been replaced by a smart new leisure centre and concert
hall. As for the Palace Cinema where Pat had spent some of
her early dates in its double seats, its life as a bingo hall had
ceased and it was now derelict. Le Galls, the well known ladies
hairdressers was now a wine bar, and Gordon Easton's toyshop,
a building society office. In all the town she knew so well was
brighter but blander. Some famous local landmarks had
disappeared altogether. Her Majesty's Theatre was now a car
park. The Coop emporium in Botchergate was forlornly empty
and blighted. Other buildings had survived the postwar waves
of 'progress' – the covered market remained, though sadly
gentrified, the Turkish baths stood firm over the railway
viaduct and, much to Pat's abiding pleasure, Brucciani's ice
cream parlour was as popular as ever.

Pat parked and walked through the streets of her home
town. She was greatly attached to it. She had grown up in the
city and knew it as a child, adolescent, student, young
housewife, shopper and member of the teaching profession.
She knew she was bound to meet someone she knew. She was
dying to talk to someone. She wanted to share her recently
acquired palimpsest insights with someone who would be
interested. She often met one of her old school friends in town

for a drink or meal. Maybe she would bump into Lizzie Stoddart, Dorothy Dixon, Leila Brown or Jennifer Glaister. They had been her pals at the High School and had stayed in touch. But none of them were to be seen in Le Galls winebar or any of the Italian restaurants.

Naturally her circle of friends today was not the same as it had been earlier. She had kept in touch with some and lost others. Not surprisingly old boyfriends had moved to the edge of her life since she got married just over twenty years ago. Her early dates had been with boys from the Grammar School. They had found plenty to do in town, occasionally going to the dance hall down Botchergate but usually hanging around the coffee bars. John Heslop, who had lived near her in Stanwix, was one who she still saw occasionally. They had gone out socially as a foursome with their respective spouses on a couple of occasions. Her first real boyfriend had been Peter Thompson but he had gone off to college in London. His parents had divorced and left the district. She had long since given up any hope of seeing him again. Goodness knows what he would be like anyway after all this time.

Pat reflected on her friends as she passed amongst the shoppers in English Street. Perhaps she had too many acquaintances and not enough real close friends in whom she could confide. Why wasn't Robert more of a friend? Maybe she had relied on her family too much, not cultivated some of her teaching colleagues. They had made friends on holiday but contacts rarely lasted more than an exchange of Christmas cards. Most of Robert's friends were from work or golf and she did not really have much in common with them. No, her circle of friends was definitely too small and predominantly female. Once again she found herself thinking of the past and regretting not having kept in touch with people she had liked.

If Carlisle was a palimpsest of the history of the north of England, then her present network of friends and acquaintances was a palimpsest of her social development or lack of it since the early years. Certainly some intense friendships had been blotted out by the routines of married life.

Her morning walk had given Pat an appetite, but it was too early to call on her daughter. She decided to go for a sandwich in the antique market café, housed in the former Baptist church in Portland Square. There were three floors stuffed with antiques and collectables of all sorts from expensive jewellery, to piles of tin boxes and crockery valued at a pound or less. Household implements jostled with sports equipment, linen with silverware, and football programmes with military uniforms. Pat was very partial to Clarice Cliff pottery but it was getting rather pricey these days.

Here was yet another palimpsest, she thought, as she wandered round amongst the goods. Of all the belongings of the populace of Carlisle during the last hundred years or so, there remained this motley collection. Objects worn and used every day or kept for special occasions in the front room. Whilst most had been broken or thrown out as worthless, these objects had been hoarded in attics or stored away in outhouses. They had survived to be put up for sale in this one market. A veritable palimpsest of past possessions from different decades gathered together by wily antique dealers and hopefully bought by avid collectors at a huge mark up. Pat was in no mood to buy, but lingered over a stall specialising in musical instruments and records. A Victor Silvester number was playing on the wind-up Parlophone gramophone.

Pat was lost in her thoughts but was startled by a voice behind her.

'May I have the pleasure of this dance?' She wheeled round and found a tall, middle aged man standing beside her. She stared at him in disbelief.

'Good God, it's Peter Thompson!' she exclaimed in amazement. She was amazed that she recognised him so quickly.

'Right first time,' he said, 'and when did we last enjoy a

dance together? I think it was more than a few years ago.' They laughed and chatted for a moment trying to catch up with twenty years of news in a matter of minutes. Meanwhile the quickstep had been replaced by a sugary melody. It was Pat Boone singing *April Love*. Their song when going out in their sixth form days.

'What a pleasant surprise and coincidence,' he said. 'I'm only here in the city for a few hours and I meet you.' Pat was so overcome she could hardly say anything. Instead she politely asked him what he had been doing in the intervening years. It turned out that he had stayed in the south after his University days. His parents had left Carlisle and retired to the Channel Islands, so his connection with the city had all but ended. He had tried quite a few jobs since then but was now a successful antique dealer based in Richmond, London. Peter didn't offer any information as to his marital status and Pat didn't feel like asking.

'What a lucky break,' he repeated, 'a couple of hours in Carlisle to buy antiques and I bump into you. I have only visited the city two or three times in twenty years. What a happy coincidence.'

Pat felt a wee bit overwhelmed by seeing a person whom she had resigned to never seeing again. He had aged – his hair was grey at the temples and he had a fuller face than before but his mannerisms had not changed. It was his smile and voice which made her feel that she had met a real friend again. Peter suggested they should go for lunch.

'I noticed an Italian restaurant across the road where the coffee bar used to be – let's go!' It never occurred to Pat to decline, for one reason she didn't have anything else to do at that precise moment. But more importantly she was dying to find out more about him.

He ordered a bottle of chianti, and they ate lasagne and salads.

'Do you remember when we all used to spend hours

drinking coffee in this place after school? We were meant to be swatting for exams in the municipal library at Tullie House.' Pat told him all about their mutual friends. They chatted amicably over lunch and as she felt the effect of the red wine Pat felt increasingly comforted and excited. She could hardly wait to tell her old school friends about this chance meeting.

During a lull in the conversation Pat could not resist asking her old boyfriend and now middle-aged, knowledgeable antique expert sitting opposite her, if he was aware that his livelihood depended on palimpsests. To make a living from spotting bargains in provincial auctions and selling them at London prices.

'What's that got to do with palimwhatsit?' he queried, feigning ignorance. She explained the idea.

'You see what you buy and sell represents a fraction of the possessions of those living in the past,' she explained. 'Most have disappeared but some items have become antiques.'

'I agree,' he answered.

'When you think of it, every home has a real mixture of ancient and modern family heirlooms and bargains bought in the most recent sales.'

Pat was delighted that she could at last share her preoccupation with someone who showed a real interest. Over coffee she expanded on places they both knew.

'Take the Lake District for example. It is made up of a series of geological strata like the Lindstock sandstone and Skiddaw slate. Its scenery was formed by the ice ages and as ice sheets melted they left drumlins – glacial lakes. It had seen six thousand years of occupation by successive invaders. Its villages and fields show the impact that they made. Its landscape has been scarred by the mining and industry. Today its military defensive walls' role is not against the Scots or two world war ammunition depots, but nuclear plutonium production in the Cold War era!'

Pat's treatise clearly impressed. Peter seemed amused and

interested. He agreed that evidence of the past was everywhere. He gave some examples of his own which elaborated on the theme.

'Take Prague, or Istanbul or Florence, for example, they have all preserved their architectural heritage, and yet there are parts of all our European cities where the record of the past has been all but wiped out. If you visit Bucharest, as I did recently searching for icons, you will see that the Ceausescu regime wiped out the pre-Communist urban landscape apart from a few churches, now I suppose the landmarks glorying Communism are themselves being torn down as Western commercialism takes over!'

By this time it was after two o'clock and the waiter was getting restive. Peter asked for the bill. Then gave Pat a quizzical look asking – 'I'm not sure how we fit into this grand interpretation of things but I, for one, almost feel I am back in the 70s. She almost jumped up with excitement.

'That's exactly it. Our experiences of those days when we studied have shaped our personalities forever. We are whoever we were yesterday.'

Pat almost blushed when she admitted, 'You were the one that I really admired and I was devastated when you asked Fiona Turnbull out in our last term at school.'

He laughed and replied, 'Well if only I had known. I was too nervous to invite you out as I thought you were so much in demand at the time. You were certainly the most popular in your year. I honestly never thought I had a chance.'

'It sounds like a case of missed opportunity all round,' she admitted to her companion. Once the bill had been paid they looked at each other as they started towards the door.

'What now?' he said. 'I am driving to Keswick and Cockermouth to view some antiques this afternoon. I'm staying the night at the Pheasant Inn at Bassenthwaite. You are going to see your daughter by all accounts.'

This was in the form of a statement and half question, a bit like an Australian sentence rising in intonation.

'Yes,' she said without conviction, 'I suppose I should be getting on.'

He clearly detected her mood – that she was loathe to let the meeting end.

'Well, I'll tell you what, we are both driving down the M6, me to turn off to the Lakes and you to head towards Langwathby in the Eden Valley.'

Then much to Pat's surprise and delight he made a suggestion:

'We will set off together down the motorway. If you follow your plan and take the Penrith turning then I will wave goodbye. If you decide you would like to spend the rest of the day in Lakes in the company of an old school friend, then follow me.'

'And,' he added, laughing, 'if you go straight on heading south then I'll know you are as indecisive as ever!'

Pat didn't know if he was serious or not. She made no move to reject the plan outright. They soon reached their cars. Again by coincidence, her Metro was parked a short distance from his Audi estate.

She followed him down Warwick Road, past Brunton Park, the home of Carlisle United, then the new Tesco supermarket. It occurred to Pat that at this point, Robert would be sitting down to watch the cup final. However, her attention was on Peter's car in front. They passed alongside each other at the Rosehill roundabout. She could see Robert making signs to her. He was pointing to left and right, and then holding his hands open in an inviting or questioning gesture. The traffic on the motorway was fairly light and Pat drove steadily.

Her mind and mood however was in a state of some confusion, but her meeting with Peter Thompson had certainly banished the mood of depression that had overtaken her earlier in the day.

Normally she knew she would have relished the chance to

catch up with her daughter's news and discuss the forthcoming birth. But she also felt she would like to hear more about the two decades of Peter's life.

They passed the Southwaite service station and the turning to Unthank. On the side of the motorway the fields were full of stock – Ayrshire cattle and Cheviot ewes. The Pennines lay to the east and Lake District fells to the west. Blue, grey lines of hills appeared.

Her turn off to Langwathby would come soon. The motorway signs gave plenty of warning. Ten miles to Penrith and the Lakes.

Junction 41 came and went. Pat pondered over what to do. She was settled, respected, married and middle aged. She knew she was still attractive, but restive in her career and marriage. Her world was in Carlisle, and its once bustling port on the Solway. Through her family she belonged to its past. There was her house and garden she loved. She treasured the history of the place and her roots. She was part of it all, and could not imagine any other way.

On the other hand she had enjoyed the company of a man who she had yearned for as an 18-year-old. When they had first felt each other's physical presence and tender emotions. She had received an invitation, however lightheartedly it had been made. To accompany Peter, and to rekindle a close friendship. It was a case of custom and common sense versus curiosity and daring.

She must have unconsciously slowed down for Peter, who was still ahead, pulled over to the slow lane. The sign for junction 42 appeared – his exit. She could see him looking in his driving mirror.

He waved. But that didn't help her to come to a decision. Pat thought of her past and future. She could almost see her present life on the manuscript of that crossword magiboard; or were there glimpses of an alternative plot underneath?

She saw the Audi slow right down and flash its warning

lights. They stopped on the hard shoulder a few yards from each other. She could see Peter writing something.

He got out and came towards her. She rolled down the window in anticipation. He stopped beside her window and passed a card in. It was an old, very faded business card – Peter Thompson Antiques, 10 St Margarets Road, Richmond; plus telephone and fax number. Pat could see he had scrawled a few words on top of the hardly visible print of the card.

She eagerly focused on the message. It read – 'Dear Pat, see you at the Pheasant, if you fancy it!'

She sat for a few moments gazing at the latest and certainly the most intriguing example of a palimpsest that she had encountered that day. When she looked up he had got into his car and was joining the traffic. Pat waited a moment or two and then, with a sense of mixed emotions, she drove on.

Early years at Postcard Corner

A day in the life of
Nicolae Ceausescu

*A*t 5.32pm on the evening of 25th December, 1989, a burst of automatic fire rang out in a desolate courtyard on the southern edge of the Carpathian Mountains. Two elderly people in raincoats crumpled to the muddy ground. No proper trial, no term of imprisonment, no chance of exile.

It was the end of an era for twenty million Romanians, including those who lived in Constanța, the Black Sea port some two hundred miles to the east of this place of execution. This city had once been the called Tomis. It was here that Ovid had been banished, and it was here (in Dobrogea), the land between the mighty river Danube and the sea, that Phil also felt a bit of an outcast. He felt cut off from his family and friends back in Boston, and had not really settled in the town he was spending his Harkness Foundation scholarship year.

Constanța was drab and disappointing. Like hundreds of other cities in Communist Eastern Europe it seemed, to the outsider at least, grey and depressing. Endless tower blocks of peeling concrete, grossly overcrowded trolley buses; long queues outside half-empty shops; unhelpful and unfriendly officials.

The local populace seemed tired and dispirited. No laughter in their voices, no colour in their clothes. The stink of garlic on the breath and the fumes of cheap motor fuel as harassed shoppers struggled for the basic necessities of life. Youngsters pestering for dollars and jeans. Begging Gypsies on the street corners. Even the students seemed unwilling, or afraid to speak up or step out of line.

Life was hard in the Socialist Republic of Romania. But for the urban poor and village peasants in this Balkan country that had always been the case. For the elite in Bucharest, the capital city, who had '*pile*' or influence, it was a different matter. The leadership of Party and State lived well enough. All this was a source of concern to Phil. His roots and outlook were to the left of the American Democratic Party, and he didn't like what he saw being done, ostensibly in the name of socialism.

He had set out from the US ever so enthusiastically. His aim was to see the country from which his grandfather had emigrated. To study how the country had changed since the Second World War. And find out, at first hand, what life was like behind the 'Iron Curtain'.

His first few days spent in a plush hotel near the centre of the capital, and in the company of the American diplomats, had been fine. He had also been treated by the authorities, initially at least, as an honoured guest from the west.

But that was weeks ago. Now the early freshness of his adventure had worn off. His room in a student hostel was bare and noisy. The food in the canteen – comprising mainly cabbage soup, fatty pork, tasteless black bread, chewy cheese and sugary puddings – was awful. His Romanian language classes were long and boring. And no-one showed the slightest interest in his proposed research project. In fact it was worse than that, for the very mention of the early construction of the Danube - Black Sea canal made local officials wary and uncommunicative. All they would say was that it had transformed the regional economy.

All this was doubly frustrating for Phil because he was impressed by some of the developments that he saw all around him. There were new hotels, crèches, and public parks. Unlike the States the streets were clean and crime free. Although there were plenty of grumbles about everyday hardships, in the media at least, there seemed some sense of national pride, purpose and progress.

To make any official visits you had to be in possession of an '*adeverință*' – a special pass. Phil was getting impatient at the delay and so one morning had set off north along the coast on a borrowed bicycle to visit Năvodari. This was the place where the original canal had been started – with, it was rumoured, forced labour in the 1950s. He knew that there was a chemical plant and a children's holiday camp there and was interested to see how heavy industry and tourism could coexist together as neighbours in this planned economy.

The factory was not a pretty sight, and worse still a plume of yellow sulphuric smoke billowed from its brick chimney. That particular day the wind was taking the foul-smelling gases out to sea and away from the hundreds of kids who were playing on the beach. Phil had misgivings about the pollution and the quality of the water for bathing but he had no equipment on him to make any measurements.

It was on his return journey that Phil made a discovery that worried him even more. He was following a dusty road alongside the abandoned canal when in front of him he saw a huge waste dump. It was clear that the scooped out basin, created with the blood and sweat of political prisoners, was piled high with building materials and household waste. But what caught Phil's attention were the pools of brightly coloured chemical waste that lay unprotected in the stifling summer heat. He knew that the Năvodari plant made sulphuric acid. What he saw in front of him looked suspiciously like dangerous chemical waste, probably containing nitric acid, and possibly cadmium, arsenic and other highly toxic materials.

Phil remained on the scene for a few minutes taking notes. He even stumbled over a pile of asbestos, and at that point decided to get the hell out of it. He had read that this early canal project had been constructed in former years by 'enemies of the state'. He figured that if he made a fuss of what he had seen it would be him who would be classed as such! Especially as the new Back Sea - Danube canal, which had been at last completed following a different route, was soon to be officially opened by none other than the President himself – Nicolae Ceausescu.

After his secret excursion up the coast, Phil had thought it wise to remain in town. The next day, after a breakfast of hard bread, Bulgarian jam, and Chinese tea he set off on foot to inspect an urban renewal scheme which local officials were anxious for him to see. It was a sunny morning as he walked up Lenin Boulevard towards the town hall where he had an appointment with the black suits in the municipal building known to the locals as the White House. He also wanted to pop into the tourist office to check out trips to the monasteries of Moldavia and the Carpathian mountains.

He stopped on the way at a '*cofetărie*' and had a sticky pastry and small cup of Turkish coffee. Nearby stood a kiosk which had crates filled with empty milk and yoghurt bottles. A short, elderly man with spiky grey hair sat smoking beside his ramshackle premises. He must have been up for hours serving his patient customers. He greeted Phil with a smile.

'*Bună dimineața, Domnul.*' (Morning, Sir.)

He chuckled, clearly enjoying a rest from his earlier exertions. Phil noted the badge on his none-too-clean overalls. It announced 'Șerban Vasile' to the world.

'*Ce față.*' Phil greeted him, more out of courtesy than any desire to get into a conversation.

'*Bine, mulțsumesc, nu rău pentru un pénsionăr batrin.*' (Fine thanks and not bad for an old pensioner.)

Phil offered him a Marlboro which he lit up with evident satisfaction. Phil made good his escape and left Vasile joking with the lady who ran the coffee shop.

He passed the 1st Mai stadium where *Sporting Club Farul* (the Lighthouse sports club) played, and a semi-ruined synagogue. Most of the Jewish population of the city had either been deported to death camps by the Iron Guard during the war or fled to Palestine after it.

Entering *Ştefan Cel Mare* street, Phil spotted a queue outside a shop. He remembered the advice given by Miss Beale at the embassy in Bucharest.

'Always,' she had urged him, 'join a queue whenever you see one.'

He promptly did so and found himself being pushed into the shop and up to the counter. To his amazement it was fur hats that were the source of shoving and elbowing. Clearly such prized possessions were much sought after, regardless of the season. Phil tried on a grey fox hat. It fitted, but in a second had been yanked from his head by a rather distinguished older gentleman who had followed in his slipstream into the packed shop. After a brief impasse the two of them bought identical Russian hats and they escaped the crush out into the blinding sunshine.

Mr Marinescu introduced himself to Phil with an old-fashioned bow.

'*Sînteţi străini?*' (Are you foreign?), he asked, proffering a yellowing card.

Phil read – Ing Marinescu Auriel, Apt 119, Scara 5 Bloc F13, Tomis Nord, Constanţa. Having taken the card he was promptly invited to visit. Phil declined politely saying that he had an appointment, and also wanted to see the arrival of the Romanian President who was due in the city later in the day.

At the mention of the name of Nicolae Ceausescu, the old man scoffed and looking around to see that no-one was listening he exclaimed in perfect BBC English – 'My dear Sir, please do not waste your time on that odious fool ... You would be better employed spending your afternoon in the puppet theatre!'

Phil was left in no doubt that he had met a senior citizen who harboured no great love for the Communist regime – and more surprisingly – was prepared to say so out loud. He took his leave and promised to visit him later.

He passed the '*Tutungerie*' (Tobacconists) at nr. 47 and spied some cigars in the window. They must have been imported from Castro's Cuba in a barter deal for trucks. He bought one and lit up. The rich tobacco made him feel a lot better. He glanced at the billboards outside the municipal library. On one side were photographs showing Ceausescu visiting state farms and receiving foreign dignitaries – evidence of socialist progress on all fronts. In contrast on the adjacent panel press photographs from the capitalist world had been pinned up. Strikes and violence on the streets of Belfast were prominent. Phil recoiled at this blatant propaganda and turned his gaze to what the local House of Culture had to offer. Steve McQueen was appearing in *Bullit*; language classes were being offered in Russian, French and English; and a folklore concert was to be held that very evening in the main concert hall to celebrate the visit of the country's leaders to Constanța.

However it was a small, home-made fly poster that caught Phil's attention. A blues concert was being given by Harry Travitian in the library at 7.30 that evening. Entry ten lei, tickets for sale on the door. Very curious indeed, he wondered – who on earth was playing the blues in this backwater of the one-time Roman Empire?

Phil was in no doubt where he would be that evening. But who could he invite to come with him?

He tucked his precious fur hat into a carrier bag and entered the state tourist office – '*ONT Littoral*'. Two women were seated in the sparsely furnished office. They had a telephone between them and a few pamphlets were scattered around on their desk. There was a large map of the Socialist Republic of Romania on the wall. Phil recognised the tell-tale fish shape of the country. One of the two women was in her fifties and had henna dyed hair, wore a traditional Romanian blouse and looked distinctly unfriendly. The younger travel agent he couldn't see very well as she was on the phone and had her face turned away from him.

After a few minutes' wait the older woman turned her unenthusiastic attention to him

'*Ce doriți, Domnul?*' (What do you want) she asked coldly.

'*Vreau niște informați despre excursele in Romănia.*' (Romanian tourist information, please) Phil replied in his best textbook Romanian.

'*Rodica, stai puțsin y vine imediat,*' (Rodica, come here) she barked out to her younger colleague, who promptly put down the phone and smiled at him.

'What can we do for you?' she enquired in good English with just a trace of an American accent.

'I was hoping to obtain some literature on other regions of Romania,' he repeated.

'Certainly,' she said but added playfully – 'I hope you are not going to leave us so soon.'

Under the watchful eye of her boss Rodica plied Phil with brochures and quoted some prices. She warned him that he would have to pay in hard currency. By this time her colleague had disappeared and only then did she pull out some half-prepared Black Sea resort leaflets from under the desk.

'Would you be so kind as to give these a glance? I am afraid that the translation into English is not good enough.'

'*Desigur, Doamnașoara Rodica,*' (Sure thing, Rodica) Phil responded gladly and took the clutch of papers over to a table. This wasn't the first bit of proof reading that he had done since his arrival. He had been horrified to see the following sentence in an official publication on the construction of the Iron Gates, Danube hydro-electric scheme – *This major dam has been completed with millions of tons of cement and GRAVY!*' In that case it had been too late to remedy the script.

The first pamphlet he examined was one about Mamaia. It had a colourful cover, but there were plenty of phrases that Phil quickly identified as literal translations from Romanian – *'Mamaia is full of antique vestiges … An animated place with lacto bars, ale houses and jake boxes … some tourists lie on their sheets, spreading odorous oils on themselves … others start from the beginning to look for friends and have joint programmes with them … they will wander along the sea shore admiring and comparing the Romanian beauties with the lovelies sent by various European nations to these shores as messengers of perfection ….'*

In a few minutes the Mamaia leaflet had been re-written – *'Mamaia is full of archaeology … it has plenty of lively pubs, bars and restaurants ….'*

Rodica came and joined him at the table and placed another leaflet in front of him.

'Mangalia,' he read, *'with its health giving climate and mud, where you can stay in the mud for ten minutes until you feel your skin getting crisp! Cold water bathing is recommended to treat a number of affections!'*

Phil laughed and once again made some swift corrections. He enquired of Rodica: 'Affection or afflictions – what is most common in Constanţa?'

She seemed to blush and promptly handed him yet another draft leaflet.

'At the Intim bar the dancers are so suave, the jazz band so animated, that the announcing of the closing hour will seem a brutality!'

'A relief more like,' he suggested to Rodica. She laughed, and gave him a gentle cuff with the papers.

At that point her supervisor returned and their close scrutiny of next year's tourist publications ceased.

Reluctant to leave, Phil asked Rodica about Harry Travitan and his concert that evening: 'Is he from Bucharest or abroad?'

'Certainly not,' Rodica retorted. 'He is Mr Jazz of Constanţa. He is a local librarian who has never even set foot, let alone played the piano, outside the country.

'Well, I'm going to the gig,' he said. 'Maybe I will see

you there?'

Before she could reply she was engulfed by a gang of Polish tourists demanding to know where the nearest camp site was to be found. He made to leave and as he left the now crowded office he heard Rodica laugh and shout – 'Always use our head when buying a hat.'

Phil made his way to the White House, to meet Mr Marinescu and watch the parade. Suddenly he felt that Constanța was not such a bad place after all.

Meanwhile Vasile Șerban was on his way home. Although well past retirement age, he still enjoyed his work. It got him out of his tiny flat and away from the complaints of his neighbours. Because he was secretary of the block residents' association they all came to him to sort out their communal problems. They gave him a bad time when the lift broke down; when the central heating didn't work; when the corridors weren't cleaned; when rose gardens were littered. As a loyal Communist he did his best on the front line of socialist reconstruction, although the officials in the White House were a fat lot of use.

Vasile had no fond memories of the pre-Communist years. His pay had been pitiful if he had work, and his home had been a wooden house without running water, electricity or an inside toilet. He often thought that Romanians today didn't know how lucky they were. That's why he had joined the Party and worked for it all these years. And it had paid off. His son had gone to university and become a violinist in the National Orchestra in Bucharest. His daughter was a teacher in Tulçea. He had free medical care and a holiday with his trade union in the mountains every year. All right Romania wasn't as well off as the West but at least people didn't suffer poverty and violence. And under Nicolae Ceausescu's leadership the country had paid off its foreign debt, and made progress. And look at the investment that was going into tourism on the Black

Sea coast – foreign visitors were flocking to the resorts. He recalled his meeting earlier in the day with the young American.

Today he would go and cheer the Party leadership he decided. Not because he had to, although that was the case with his '*muncă patriótica*' (community work) that he organised every weekend for his reluctant neighbours in the old Railway Estate.

He helped himself to a cold beer and sat on his balcony watching the Saturday crowds below.

In the public library however, Harry Travitian was in a bit of a tizzy. His concert was due to kick-off at 7pm and it was already well into the afternoon. The library hall was locked and there was no sign of Mrs Popescu who was in charge. No doubt they had all been told to go to welcome the President on his visit to the town. Harry could not care less about the big-wigs from Bucharest. All he was worried about was his precious concert. For weeks he had been preparing for it. And tonight was the night to convince his sceptics that the blues were worth listening to. He knew only too well that the Communist Party did not approve of jazz. Indeed it had been banned in the Soviet Union under Stalin as decadent. This, despite the fact that the music originated amongst oppressed black Americans in the Deep South. In his defence, Harry had reminded Mrs Popescu that Paul Robeson, who had been a victim of capitalist racism, had fled to the German Democratic Republic. After a fair bit of arm twisting, Harry had been given permission to play on his concert.

He had planned the programme carefully, starting with some well-known numbers by Bessie Smith and Leadbelly and Fats Waller. Then he would introduce Willie 'the Lion' Smith and Jelly Roll Morton.

Harry finally got into the room where the concert was to be held. It was dry and dusty and no way like the whorehouses and speakeasies in which the blues had originally been performed. One minor feature of the room did worry him. On the wall, above the upright piano, a large photograph of President Nicolae Ceausescu was prominently displayed. As indeed it was in every office, factory and school in every village, town and city, and region in Romania. Harry felt the portrait jarred with jazz. Could he really play his raunchy Western music right under the nose of the 'esteemed' leader? He knew the President was in town that very day, and Mrs Popescu would see its removal as an act of treason. Could he get away with slipping it behind the piano for a couple of hours? The trouble was he had no idea who might turn up in the audience – if indeed there was one at all.

But the rehearsal of this ambassador of Romanian jazz was rudely interrupted by a loud knock on the door. Surely it wasn't the *Securitate* (Secret Police), calling already to put a spoke in the wheel of his beloved concert? It couldn't be Mrs Popescu as she never knocked. Instead a fresh-faced young man stuck his head round the door.

'Hi, I'm Phil Luca. You must be the one and only Harry Travitian!'

Harry stood up from the piano, momentarily confused by the sudden arrival of his young brash visitor. Harry gave a welcoming wave of his arm towards the piano.

'But you are far too early for the show.'

'That's OK,' Phil replied. 'I only dropped in to check out the venue. After all,' he added with a smile, 'it's not every day you get to have a ball in a public library.'

Phil paused as he gazed around the hall, his eyes resting on the presidential picture above the piano.

'Hey, so Ceausescu himself is coming to the jam session?' he asked jokingly. Harry felt unsure how to respond to this political irreverence.

'Yes,' he said quietly. 'I was wondering what to do about that.'

The jazz man was uncertain to confide in this young American. He had been in trouble before for spending time with foreigners – even tourists in the resort hotels where he regularly played. But somehow he knew that Mr Luca was on his side.

Phil thought for a moment and then offered a solution.

'Why not brighten up the place with a couple of flags – Romanian and American?' he suggested. 'You could just happen to have them hanging over the offending picture!'

After a moment's hesitation, Harry agreed and Phil said he would go back to his room, collect the Stars and Stripes, and bring it back in good time for the concert. They shook hands and Harry resumed his practice.

As Harry practised his way through his programme, the tumult from outside was deafening. The noise of the large crowd greeting the leaders of Party and State, as they were driven to the White House in their large black ZIF limousines, was drowning out his blues rehearsal.

Harry swore and jumped up to slam the window closed. He continued with a rendering of W C Handy's '*Hard Times*', oblivious of the noisy throng outside the library.

And there was one other citizen of Constanța who was doing his best to ignore the Ceausescu visit and that was Auriel Marinescu. He reached the '*Trei Brăzi*' bar and ordered a glass of white wine. He winced at its sour taste, and complained to the waiter about all the best Romanian wine being exported.

'What can I do about it you old fool?' was the unkind retort.

But Auriel stayed in a good mood; despite this rudeness, he knew it was all too true. Lowly state employees were indeed not encouraged to make life more pleasant for their customers. He saw his young American friend arrive – he seemed to have some flags tucked under his shirt.

'Hello Mr Phillip, come and have a beer,' he beckoned, taking a seat as some distance from the few other drinkers.

The older man embarked on a litany of the faults he saw in the Ceausescu regime.

'You must know that most Romanians live on the breadline,

178

while the dictator and his clan live sumptuously in their villas.

It is the Ceausescu family that has ruined our lives and country these past thirty years. He is bossed about by his wife Elena, his two brothers Ion and Ilie are in charge of the army and agriculture. And don't forget his son, Nicu, who lives a playboy life here and in Paris. We don't have democracy, and we don't have a decent life. Our once rich country has been reduced to penury and so have I!' Mr Marinescu exclaimed.

'One day I was a successful businessman in the oil industry, and the next a 'capitalist lackey' and exploiter of the proletariat! My house and car were confiscated. I was accused of sabotage and sent to work on the construction of the canal. I returned in poor health and since then have eked out a living giving private English lessons.' Phil listened sympathetically to Auriel's life story. He could see why the old man was bitter.

He raised his glass and offered a toast. 'To better times.'
He went on … 'You never know what tomorrow will bring. Who knows, the people may rise up and kick the Ceausescus out. Maybe one day Romania will have free elections and join the European Community!' Auriel shook his head. He recited a saying from the time that the Turks ruled the Balkans. 'Those who bow their heads avoid having them cut off.'

He mumbled. 'We are powerless prisoners in our own country.'

He pointed to the crowd making its way to the centre of town to listen to the Ceausescu speech.

'You see that lot, they would lose their jobs if they didn't dutifully clap and cheer. If they protested they would end up in jail.'

Mr Marinescu's tirade, fuelled by cheap wine and aided by having Phil as a compliant listener, was beginning to attract the attention of the other patrons of the bar.

He contained himself with difficulty, but couldn't resist one final jibe at the regime that had deprived him of so much.

'Take the Black Sea - Danube canal,' he said, pointing in the direction of the port.

'What a waste of money. It will never pay its way. It was built to satisfy the megalomania of the Bucharest bosses, and will remain forever as a their foolish and cruel legacy.'

With that, Mr Marinescu gathered up his meagre shopping, shook hands with Phil, and strode off, fighting his way against the flow of people heading for the main square.

Watching his tall hunched figure disappear from sight, Phil felt chastened by the one-sided conversation. He couldn't help comparing his own good fortune with that of this intelligent and spirited gentleman who had suffered so much from being in the wrong place at the wrong time.

Meanwhile back in the tourist office, Rodica was day dreaming. She was looking forward to the evening and meeting the young American.

Some of her female acquaintances had gone out with boys from abroad – mainly Italians, who had access to 'Western' currency, jeans and perfume. Rodica had resisted this line of romance, partly she had to admit, because as a worker in the tourist industry she was able to get hold of these valued commodities. Everyone in the office had been given time off to watch the country's leaders come to town so Rodica slipped out to have her hair done.

The women in the salon were a mouthy bunch.

'Who are you going out with tonight?' They pressed her to tell all.

'No-one you know,' she replied. Which was certainly true.

'You're not getting tarted up for Nicolae then?'

'Certainly not,' she replied. 'I've met someone new to the town and out to impress.'

Since she wasn't more chatty, the staff turned their attention to the official visit.

'Why doesn't Mrs Ceausescu make life better for us women then?' they chorused. 'No contraception allowed, only abortions and not enough money to go around when we do have the kids. They urge us to get the population of the country up to twenty million.'

'I bet Nicu has enough French letters to go round all his girfriends,' chipped in the girl who was sweeping up the dark hair strewn on the floor.

'But you must agree there are more opportunities for women these days, and crèches around. Both my doctor and dentist are female,' Rodica added. And there was a murmur of agreement from one or two of the staff in the room.

But the hairdresser next to Rodica didn't buy that argument.

'It's all right for them – they have money, all we have is long hours, poor pay, and husbands who won't lift a finger in the house.' This last interjection was greeted with general approval from customers and beauticians alike in the dingy salon.

Rodica kept her silence. She knew life was hard for them, and even more so for village women. But she wasn't going to let that spoil her night out. She read a magazine and emerged half an hour later into the bright afternoon and, with the help of a touch of henna, looking and feeling good.

It was getting towards four o'clock when the official cavalcade finally swept into town. Throughout the day along the route of the canal from Cernavoda at the western end of the canal the Ceausescus and their party had been met by orchestrated cheering crowds. They alighted from their limousines and were greeted by local dignitaries with the traditional and customary offering of bread and salt.

The crowds chanted their well-rehearsed welcome – '*Bine ați venit, Tov. Ceausescu, bine ati venit.*' (Welcome Comrade Ceausescu).

An old man was pushed forward, and placed within hearing and sight of the visiting press corps.

'*Am optzeci și opt ani, dar in viața mea n'am cunoș un conducător mai popular și mai impunator decît dumnavostră.*' (I'm 80, but in all my life I haven't known a more popular leader than you!) He croaked.

Flowers were presented by the young red-scarfed and white-shirted socialist pioneers

Ceausescu mounted the podium. He stood in front of a familiar banner. It read – '*Triasca Partidul Comunist Român ... Triasca Comunismul.* (Long live Romanian Communist party ... Long live Communism!)

For the fifth time that day N C embarked on a long and rambling speech. He lauded the construction of the canal as a magnificent socialist achievement and praised the workers who had built it. His twenty minute speech ended in prolonged applause. His name was chanted over and over again. As usual Elena stood by his side. She was no Eva Peron, but a plain and some would say, a serious minded chemist.

The press next day, notably the Party paper – '*Sciûntea*' – *reported 'O atmosferă de cald entuziasm ... o efervescenta atmosferă sărbotoreasca.*' (A warm, enthusiastic celebratory atmosphere). The speech was greeted with – '*aplauze puternice și prelungite.*' (Prolonged and powerful applause).

In the crowd of several thousand residents of Constanța, were Vasile Șerban and his neighbours from the old Railway estate, Phil Luca and Rodica Stoica, who had spotted each other and had got together for a night out. Intentionally absent was Mr Marinescu who was drinking tea and listening to the BBC in his dingy flat.

Not far away from the throng, but on his own for the moment at least, was Harry Travitian – the master of blues. He was putting the final touches to his evening jazz session. He sang softly to himself the lines of Roosevelt *The Honey Dipper*, Sykes' famous twelve bar blues number –

'*There's nineteen men living in my neighbourhood.*
Eighteen are fools and the other one ain't no doggone good.'

Postscript

Not many weeks later in November 1989, the Congress of the Romanian Communist Party met in Bucharest. President Ceausescu pledged to continue the policies that he had followed in the 24 years that he had been in power. His two-hour speech was interrupted by no less than 67 standing ovations

Yet less than a month later, after he had returned from a brief visit to Iran, he faced a less rapturous crowd from the balcony of the Presidential Palace. There was unrest in the western Romanian city of Timişoara, and swift currents of change were breaking the political geographical log-jam of Eastern Europe. There was heckling and sounds of gun fire to be heard on the fringes of the crowd. Amidst scuffles and booing the meeting was abandoned. A couple of hours later Ceausescu and his wife fled by helicopter from the capital amidst scenes of violence and lawlessness.

On Christmas Day the couple were summarily sentenced to death by a military tribunal. They were found guilty of genocide, and promptly executed by a firing squad. The senior judge at the hastily convened military court – General Giça Popa – was later to commit suicide.

Today the rest of the Ceausescu family and their close associates have been released after brief terms of imprisonment. They have (all too) quickly resumed their careers in business and public life. The imprint – some would say the scars – of the Communist years are there for all to see.

Phil Luca – if he exists – would have married Rodica and be Professor of Environmental Studies at Duke University, North Carolina.

Vasile Şerban still lives in his flat in the Old Railway estate in Constanţa. As a pensioner he has little money. He dislikes the changes that have come with capitalism, harks back to community mindedness of the old days and complains about the behaviour of youngsters in the locality.

Auriel Marinescu died exactly a year after the execution. His only satisfaction was to outlive the dictator who, as he saw it, robbed him of the good life.

Harry Travitian is now a successful musician, and is based in the German city of Dusseldorf. He plays regularly in jazz clubs and festivals throughout Europe. Last year he made a 'pilgrimage' to New Orleans and the Mississippi Delta to savour the birthplace of the blues.

All that these people had in common was that they were there, that hot summer day in Constanța, when Nicolae Ceausescu presided over the opening of the '*Canalul Dunare – Marea Neagra*.'

Early years at Postcard Corner

Grand Café de la Promenade

Vendredi, 23 Août

*A*nna turned off the busy Carcassonne-Beziers highway. She was fed up with the dust and fumes of the D 11, with its shuddering lorries and speeding holiday traffic.

Soon she was pedalling contentedly through the vineyards. Row upon row of *Sauvignon* and *Cabernet* grapes glistening in the warm evening sunshine. She relished the calmness and enjoyed the scent of thyme and wild lavender growing on the verges.

In the distance, set above the fertile plain, she could see the red brown outline of Montouliers – the village in which she had arranged to stay the night. It was to be her last stop before she reached the Mediterranean on her solo cycle trip from the Atlantic coast. She had planned her adventure for months, calling it her *Entre deux Mers* cycle tour. From the outset she had all sorts of doubts and fears about the whole expedition, but so far it had all gone brilliantly.

She had started at the elegant Basque town of Bayonne and sped through the pines of the dead-flat Landes. After struggling over the rolling hills of Gascony, she had reached the city of Toulouse on the fourth day. After that, it was a matter of following the Canal du Midi as it swung through the golden yellow fields of sunflowers and patches of blue alfalfa. As the valley opened out, vineyards took over as she turned east into the heart of Languedoc.

Tomorrow, the last leg of her journey was to finish at the port of Sète. Anna was then to return by train to England by the end of the month.

Despite generous applications of sun cream, her arms, legs and face were burnt. She was thirsty and tired. However, she was in good spirits and sat back on her saddle to ease her aching limbs. The prospect of a shower, tasty meal and glass or three of wine encouraged her to press on to the village.

She paused for a moment on the bridge over the canal. It was a placid scene, with a couple of fishermen idly flicking their lines over the murky water. Further along the bank a brightly painted holiday barge was tied up. On board, an elderly couple looked as though they were enjoying their early evening gin-and-tonic, or maybe it was *pastis*.

Anna accelerated down the slope from the bridge, past some newish villas which marked the outskirts of the settlement. Looking out for the *'chambres d'hote'* sign she barely noticed a large and rather pretentious house on her left. It was bounded by a thick juniper hedge. But, out of the corner of her eye, she did spot a tractor-trailer emerging from the lane beyond the hedge.

It never occurred to her that it would not stop. But it came on ... and on ...

The next thing she knew she was flung into the air. She crashed down onto the tarmac with her right shoulder taking the brunt of the impact. A few seconds later she felt a searing pain down her right side. As she lay on the road, blood trickled down her face and neck. For a few agonising moments nothing happened. Then she became aware of excited French voices, and blurred faces above her. She lost consciousness.

At the time, Mayor Henri Girault was dozing at his desk. He had had a good lunch. A letter lay on top of the pile of papers in front of him. It was from Madame Figol and demanded, in blunt terms, that the trees in the village square should be trimmed forthwith.

The Montouliers' *mairie* was an uninspiring building, distinguished from adjoining properties only by the tricolour which hung limply from a stumpy flagpole. There above the door was also the ubiquitous inscription *'Liberté – Egalité – Fraternité.'* Under the eaves clung the rounded mud nests of swallows which darted around the square. They represented the full extent of activity in this centre of communal life. Opposite the *mairie* a few familiar regulars were hunched at the counter of the *Bar du Paris*. Their desultory conversation did little to disrupt the quiet torpor of the Langedoc afternoon.

The quiet was shattered by shouting – a young lad rushed through the half-open door of the *mairie*.

'*Papa, un accident est arrivé ... une touriste est blessé ... viens vite!*'

The Mayor listened impatiently to his son's account and then reluctantly telephoned the local doctor.

Jacques Millaud was busy tending his beloved garden, but promised to go to the scene of the accident at once. Eventually, the English patient was helped onto a stretcher borrowed from the village sports centre. A little later her wounds were cleaned and bandaged, and she was given an X-ray in Dr Millaud's clinic.

Meanwhile, an animated crowd was gathering in and around the *mairie*. The *gendarme* were taking witness statements from any locals who volunteered them. They were making the most of the incident. Since it was clear that the victim of the crash was English, no time was lost in sending for assistance from the two English speakers in the village. One was Mary Dunbar who, with her husband Dennis, had bought and renovated one of the medieval houses overlooking the square. The second, and only fluent, English-speaking French person in the village was Gabrielle Bernard, the daughter of the former mayor. She was studying for an English degree at Montpeliers University. It was these two, more than willingly, who volunteered their services to cope with the incapacitated foreign cyclist who had arrived so abruptly in their midst.

Samedi, 31 Août

Anna lay in a painful state of semi-consciousness. An image of a spinning cycle wheel kept flitting through her mind. From time-to-time she felt cool water being pressed to her lips and face. She heard both English and French voices in the room.

Other sounds pierced the hazy grip she had on reality. Children shouting, a dog barking, the occasional whine of a motor scooter, and the regular, rather tinny sound of the village clock striking on the hour – not once, but twice, (to bring the peasants in from the fields she had learnt later).

During the last day or so, she had become aware of her surroundings. The white walls of her room took on a bluish tinge at night when the moon shone through the half shutters. There were several posters on the wall, including a map of France made up of pictures of regional French cheeses. Turning her head to the left, she could see the tiled roof of the building at the other side of the square. Below the peeling shutters of that same building, she could make out a faded sign which read 'Grand Café de la Promenade'. She stared at it blankly before sinking back into a fitful, sedated sleep.

Gradually, she got used to several visitors in her room. There was a tall, slim man, who wore spectacles and had dark, receding hair. She felt his strong but sensitive hands dressing her wounds, and noticed his brown arms as she was turned once or twice a day. He gave softly spoken instructions in French with a southern accent. She was later to discover that this was the doctor who had proffered professional advice so promptly on the day of her accident, and since.

There were also two women who spent a fair bit of time with her. One was a bustling English lady who changed Anna's bedding and gave her soup and cups of tea, and later on salads, homemade scones and other delicacies. This kindly person turned out to be Mary Dunbar in whose guest house Anna was recuperating.

During the quieter moments she also sensed someone else in the background. She was a pretty, dark-haired girl who sat reading. She curled her long legs round the elegant chair legs on which she customarily sat. Every now and then Gabrielle would ask her 'Mrs Spencer, do you want anything? A cup of tea perhaps?'

Anna's appetite, together with her recollection of where she was and what had happened to her, slowly returned. But, for the moment at least, she turned away all thoughts of the future.

Mercredi, 4 Septembre

It was about teatime that her family had arrived from England. Their journey to see her had been delayed because both her children had been away on a sailing holiday and out of contact. It had been several days before her husband and two children had got together and caught a ferry to France. They had driven down overnight and were now here to find out exactly what had happened to her, and make plans for her return home. By this time, Anna was feeling a wee bit better. Thankfully, limbs were not broken but only bruised. Her upper body was still extremely painful, but more worrying was the fact that she often suffered severe headaches.

Although relieved and pleased to see her family, Anna was somewhat anxious as to their reaction to her predicament. Her husband Geoff had initially been sceptical about her trip. She dreaded him telling her that she had been selfish and foolhardy.

Much to her surprise, the family did not say anything to that effect, even if they might have thought it. Her health and medical insurance cover dominated the conversation once the initial greetings were over. Dr Millaud was consulted as to when Anna would be in a position to travel. He was of the firm opinion that she shouldn't go anywhere for the time being. He had arranged for her to undergo tests for her head injury in a hospital in Beziers the following week, and ruled out the prospect of an immediate return home. It was agreed that she should remain as a guest in Mary Dunbar's house for the time being. Anna agreed to request her employers Zurich Insurance back in Portsmouth, to allow her unpaid leave of absence.

After her family had left, she felt in limbo. Few, if any, demands were made on her. She listened to the radio – thank goodness for the BBC overseas service – and flicked through French magazines given to her by Gabrielle. They seemed to be mostly about the social life of the British Royal Family and French film stars. In the afternoons she sat by the window and watched the comings and goings in the square below. She looked forward to Dr Millaud's visits, not least because he was in the habit of bringing her juicy grapes and delicious peaches from his garden.

She grew familiar with the everyday routine of Montouliers, the pattern of life which was no doubt commonplace in thousands of French villages, though probably modified marginally by the dictates of climate. The early rush of cars and greetings; the exchanges of women and old men on the way to the *boulangerie*; the shout of kids on their way to school; the bustle of the once-a-week, every week, village market; the early afternoon calm (especially here in the South of France); the return of life in the evening with the desultory conversations of elderly folk sitting on their doorstep; and the noisy banter of teenagers hanging around the fountain.

Directly in line with her bedroom window was the faded sign of the Grand Café de la Promenade. The letters had been painted in black on what had once been a magnolia background. Beneath it, the windows were shuttered and appeared to have been so for many a year. Beside the padlocked door were some broken signs – one for Kanterbrau beer. The whole place had a dilapidated air. But it was a handpainted sign which had been nailed to the door which drew Anna's attention. It said '*A LOUER TEL. 68912548*'.

Her curiosity as to the deserted Grand Café led her to ask companions about it. Mary didn't know much about the history of the place – only that it belonged to Madame Figol, and that it had gone out of business several years previously.

Gabrielle was more forthcoming. The Figol family had owned the premises for years, and Madame had run it as a bar more or less single-handed for the last two decades at least. Indeed, ever since her husband – who apparently had been its main customer – had died in the early 1970s. She had finally given up the struggle a couple of years ago. Since then it had remained as a dead and dusty backcloth to the village square. Gabrielle did not seem duly concerned about its demise. She explained that, since the opening of the Super U supermarket in the next village, several local shops had closed. She consulted her French-English dictionary before solemnly pronouncing 'Madame Spencer, my village is a backwater.'

She went on to explain that, whilst in the village the old folk watched television or the world go by, the youngsters spent most of their time in neighbouring Beziers or Narbonne. Montouliers still had active rugby and *pétanque* clubs, but its *Salle des Fêtes* was pretty moribund and the atmosphere of the *Maison des Rétraites*, was symbolic of the entire village.

Gabrielle pointed out the lonely figure of Madame Figol sitting on her chair in front of the door leading to the apartment above the Grand Café. She wore black and it seemed to Anna that, if she was mourning, then it was probably more for her dying village and closed bar, than her long since departed husband.

Lundi, 14 Octobre

The *vendage* – the grape harvest – was over. The leaves of the plane trees and vines had turned golden brown. The tourists had departed their holiday homes and campsites. There was much bustle in and around the village Cave Co-opérative winery, but precious little elsewhere.

Anna felt left behind. However she felt, and certainly looked, much better. Her aches and pains had all but disappeared, although she still suffered from headaches towards the end of the day. Thankfully, her hair had grown over the unsightly head wounds which had previously made her reluctant to stray far from her place of abode.

Her daily excursions took her through the narrow, medieval streets of the village, with their secretions and smells. She extended her outings onto the paths which led out into the surrounding vineyards. Her, she took a delight in the warm Autumn breezes which rustled the tinder-dry shrubs and seed pods of wild flowers. She spent time in the 15th Century church and in the adjoining cemetery. Here she discovered the families who were bound up in the history of the village. The same names appeared on the war memorial. No less than 27 '*enfants de la commune*' had died 'gloriously' for France in the First World War. She imagined them setting off for the front, amidst scenes of patriotic fervour, and having their short lives ended so abruptly in the Flanders' mud. There was also a small plaque with the names of those who had been deported or killed fighting for the Resistance during the German occupation in the early forties. The list included a Dr Claud Millaud and David Fowler, a British army officer. It was Gabrielle who had informed Anna that the former was the father of the present village doctor. He had been a leading figure in the local brigade of the *Maquis*, and had been captured and deported. He never returned from Belsen. As for Major Fowler, he had apparently been parachuted in, one night in August 1944. He had been spotted and gunned down in the vineyards, about half a mile from the village, before local help could reach him.

It was also Gabrielle Bernard who, after some prompting, told Anna about her own father. In the cemetery, Anna had seen a simple granite stone with the inscription '*Michel Bernard – Humaniste et Socialiste, Maire de Montouliers*, 1967-95'.

It was he who had masterminded the recovery of the local wine business in the years after the war. He had persuaded the owners to replace their gnarled old vines with new *Chardonnay* and *Merlot* varieties from the new world. He had also insisted on investment in new plant in the co-operative village winery so that, today, the local red and rose wines had achieved recognition both home and abroad.

Anna gradually built up a mental picture of the family clans in the village. These included the Mousty family, who owned many hectares in the locality, as well as the remaining local bar and garage. Then there was the equally powerful Giraults, with Henri the present Mayor and his tearaway son, Paul, who had crashed into Anna weeks ago. Paul had dropped out of agricultural college and now spent most of his time racing around in his flashy BMW. Anna's presence was a constant reminder of the Mayor's son's misdeeds. The court case was still pending, although it seemed to have got bogged down in the French legal system.

Clearly there wasn't a lot of *egalité* in the village, but what about *liberté* and *fraternité* ? Anna was at liberty to walk about the village, which she did regularly, being careful to say '*bonjour*' to all and sundry. She was also taken out on excursions to places of interest in the locality. She visited the Abbey of Montfroide, the colourful Saturday market at Pezenas, and the green, foothills of Les Montagnes Noires to the north.

During this time she felt that her two French companions remained polite but slightly distant. Gabrielle was shy and respectful, though attentive and clearly very anxious to improve her English. Meanwhile, her doctor, she sensed, kept a professional detachment. He was always immaculately turned out and, like many continental middle-aged men, carried his personal belongings in a leather satchel. He wore elegant light brown shoes and, as Autumn progressed, wore a cashmere sweater around his shoulders. Anna enjoyed his ready smile and slightly studious manner. Also, when the opportunity arose, being taken out in his powerful Renault Mégane.

She began to take an interest in him as a man rather than as the person at the other end of a stethoscope. As a patient and now, at the very least, as a close acquaintance, she liked him. In particular, she liked his hands and voice. She found his soft lilting accent soothing. He was invariably polite and concerned; Anna knew very well that, without him, her life in Montouliers would be far less appealing than it was.

As far as the local populace was concerned, communication was not so easy. She had difficulty in understanding the coarse, local Languedoc accent, especially amongst the older folk. After the usual greetings, her conversation rarely exceeded a few words of small talk. One evening, she did initiate a halting conversation with Madame Figol, who was sitting knitting with her cronies in their usual place in the square.

'*C'est un dommage que mon café est fermé,*' the grey-haired lady had replied to Anna's tenative enquiry about the Grand Café. Later that evening, as she rocked herself gently by the window, Anna mused over Madame's words. Why didn't someone reopen the Grand Café; turn it into a restaurant, bistro, or even a *salon du thé*? Back home in Southsea she had seen many empty shops being transformed into lively café-bars. If it could be done in English cities, why not here in France? She had spent many happy evenings with foreign visitors in English pubs, and they seemed to enjoy the atmosphere. She had a friend who had opened a tea shop down in Spice Island, Old Portsmouth, and made a real go of it.

Then it suddenly occurred to her ... why couldn't she do something like that in sleepy old Montouliers? Couldn't she give the charming but dilapidated building opposite a future; make it a centre of social life in the village once again?

A few days later she mentioned the possibility to Mary Dunbar, who was making one of her intermittent visits to her holiday home.

'A nice idea but definitely a non-starter', was her immediate response.

Anna's spirits sank as Mary reeled off a number of reasons why she thought that it would not be a realistic proposal. It would cost a packet to refurbish, there wasn't scope for a second bar in the village, the locals wouldn't use it and the tourists were only around for a few months of the year. Finally, the village, or to be precise, the mayor and his cronies would not take kindly to the English 'taking over' like that.

In spite of this cold dose of realism, which she had half expected, Anna couldn't put the notion out of her mind.

Her two French confidants, regrettably, were hardly more encouraging. The doctor reminded her that it was her first priority to get fit and well again. He jokingly offered to bet her a case of *Fitou* that, in six months' time, she would be back home across the Channel. Neither was Gabrielle's response any more reassuring. Although she admitted that she and her university friends did spend a lot of time, and occasionally some money, in the brasseries and piano bars in Montpelliers, she also urged caution. Her friends, she pointed out, would not be seen dead in a place like the Bar du Paris. They liked Carlsbergs, cokes and *crêpes*, but then only in places that were considered to be 'cool'.

'*Montouliers ... c'est tres different que Montpelliers,*' she remarked in her serious manner.

Anna knew perfectly well that there would be major barriers to anyone reopening the Grand Café. For herself to do it, these obstacles would be magnified. Commercially, the proposition was definitely risky. Furthermore, her personal circumstances were far from ideal, not least because of her commitments at home, and the fact that she barely knew the village in which she had been a guest these past weeks. She couldn't imagine what her friends at Zurich, or her family, would say to the idea. The had all been surprised about her cycling trip, what on earth would their reaction be to the madcap scheme of her staying on in France to open up a café?

Notwithstanding the doubts which remained firmly lodged at the back of her mind, Anna couldn't resist asking Gabrielle to contact the local *notaire* to find out more about the property. Her curiosity had been aroused, and her imagination stimulated by the possibilities involving the Grand Café Gabrielle returned the next day with the answer which really made her excited and nervous. Yes, the premises were available '*en bail*', which meant on a lease at a price of 2,000 francs per calendar month, subject to negotiation. The entire contents of the establishment were available for sale at a nominal sum. There would be no problem with the licence, as it was still held by Madam Figol, who was only too willing to have it transferred to a new operator.

Jeudi, 5 Novembre

Not surprisingly, her enquiries about the Grand Café did not go unnoticed in the village. A couple of days later, a letter was pushed under her door. It was from the Mayor. In it, *Monsieur le Maire* wished Madame Spencer a speedy recovery and expressed the sincere hope that she would soon be well enough to return home to England. There was no mention of the Grand Café, or indeed of the pending court case in which his son was involved, and related to the accident which had caused her prolonged stay in the village in the first place.

This subtle warning shot did not stop Anna from continuing her preoccupation with the Grand Café. A few days later she witnessed an event which gave a further impetus to her thoughts on the matter.

Jacques had invited her to go along to watch the local rugby club play. He knew that her son, Peter, was a schoolboy international, and that she had a passing interest in the game. A few dozen spectators watched Montouliers lose narrowly to Argeliers. It was a free-scoring game, marked by numerous tries and periodic outbreaks of ill-tempered fisticuffs. Some of the foul play was spotted by the harassed referee.

But it was the *après-match* which astonished Anna. She had seen many Saturday nights in rugby clubs at home, when players and supporters mingled after the game, drinking and singing together. Not so here. She was surprised to see the players of both clubs jump into their cars and disappear. Even the local lads didn't hang around. Jacques explained that this was quite normal.

On their way home, they passed the Café du Paris. It was clear that the players weren't there. It was, however, obvious that some of its occupants had seen the game or at least had heard about the result, for several taunting jeers from its interior were directed at the club president. Anna knew that the local team had not won many games recently, and the abuse sounded neither friendly nor polite in tone. Her serious-minded companion declined to translate what exactly had been said and ushered her past, pretending to make light of the incident. As they entered the square, Anna tried to visualise the Grand Café as a place to celebrate or commiserate after a match. After what she had just witnessed, and with the building in its present state, it was difficult to imagine such a scenario. But she still could not shake off the sense that here was an opportunity beckoning.

Dimanche, 29 Decembre

Anna stood at the rail of the *Pride of Le Havre* as it cut through the swell in the Solent. It was wet and windy, and few people were to be seen either on deck of the battlements of Old Portsmouth. The Isle of Wight was barely visible in the mist. She felt the ship begin to roll as it entered the open sea, and soon the only sign of land was a grey outline in the distance. She was on her way back to France. She felt alternatively subdued and elated, anxious and excited. After days of deliberation, she had made her decision. She had agreed with her husband, consulted with her boss at Zurich, talked to her bank manager, and discussed the whole matter with friends who had lived in France. Then she had made up her mind.

She was on her way back to re-open the Grand Café.

Vendredi, 30 Janvier

A small knot of people stood in the square. Anna was reviewing progress with her builder and all purpose handyman, Phillipe Matrou. His firm, luckily short of work during the winter months, had been able to make a prompt start, and had been at work on the property for three weeks now. It didn't show much on the outside, although the shutters had been sanded down and made ready for repainting. Also, Anna had insisted on keeping the sign above the door, leaving it exactly the same as before. Any suggestion of changing the name of the establishment was out of the question. There would be no 'Café des Sports', no 'Café de la Paix', nor a 'Brasserie Londres'. All these possible names had been briefly considered but firmly rejected.

Inside however, a transformation was underway. Years of cobwebs and dust were swept away. The old teak bar had been cleaned and was to be revarnished; the marble-topped tables and wrought-iron chairs refurbished; plasterwork and plumbing were in the process of starting to be renewed; old bottles and jars found in the cellar were to be placed on newly erected shelves.

Anna had also bought reproduction photographs of Montouliers, taken at the turn of the century, ready to hang on the walls.

In the kitchen and bar, all had changed. New units and bar equipment had been supplied at great expense by a specialist firm from Bordeaux. Everything was beginning to take shape, and the Grand Café already looked bright and cheerful. In a few weeks it would all be ready. Anna's plans had already progressed further than she had dared hope. Madame Figol had watched the work intensively and, as far as could be guessed, approvingly. She wasn't the only one to take an interest in the proceedings. It was amazing how many errands had to be taken which necessitated crossing the square and how many conversations just happened to be held right in front of the open doors of the Grand Café. One old farmer even crashed his Peugeot into the fountain in his anxiety to take a good look at what was going on. One evening, Anna witnessed from the window of her room the Mayor and a coterie of councillors deep in animated conversation, clearly an unofficial inspection of the changes being made at the heart of his domain. Even the village dogs seemed to give the Grand Café some respect. They no longer peed against the corner of the building or littered the pavement outside it with their turds. Maybe it was the smell of paint and a few buckets of watery disinfectant which had done the trick.

Anna sensed that incredulity and scepticism was rife in the village. For years the locals had witnessed nothing but closures, and they were obviously having difficulty coming to terms with this new 'foreign' development on their doorstep. In contrast, Dr Jacques and Gabrielle were full of admiration. Both had been very helpful in settling the inevitable hassles which had arisen as the work progressed. In fact, Anna could not have managed without them. She felt they were like '*les trois Mousquetaires*' in this venture.

As far as the doctor was concerned, Anna now treated him as a friend. Although he was a quiet person, she soon found out that he wasn't someone who suffered fools or knaves gladly. He quickly saw off an electrician whose lunch break seemed to be longer in duration than his working hours. Anna enjoyed her time with him. Whenever he met her, he started with the catch phrase – '*Toujours ici quand il faut,*' (Always here when needed).

The mystery of the distinctly absent doctor's wife was cleared up by Gabrielle. Apparently, Madame Millaud spent most of her time in Paris. It was said, though not by the demure and discreet Gabrielle, that their marriage was over in all but name. The doctor spent occasional weekends in the capital, but for the most part seemed content to practise medicine in the commune and pursue his hobbies of rugby and gardening.

There was no doubt in Anna's mind that she had come to rely on him, first as a doctor, and now as a man who gave her the confidence to see her project through. There was certainly no turning back now, at least as far as the café was concerned ... as far as the courteous doctor, well, time would tell.

Over a cognac in the three-quarter finished Grand Café they mapped out their allies and opponents in the village. Maybe friends and foes was a more apt description. Aligned against them were the hostile forces of the Mayor, his family, and considerable following. They had been completely against the refurbishment project from the start, but had not yet found an opportunity to put a major spanner in the works. The Mousty clan were also antagonistic and it was rumoured that those who drank in the Café du Paris had already been warned off transferring their custom elsewhere.

On the other side of the fence there were, apart from Jacques and Gabrielle, and individuals who had been working on the café, a few villagers who could be counted on to actively support the project. She sensed that most people were merely courteous, and curiously awaited to see how it all turned out before they gave their verdict.

'Fair enough,' Anna had remarked to Jacques, 'it would be exactly the same if a French woman opened a restaurant in a Yorkshire or Hampshire village.'

Of Madame Figol, there was little sign. Anna was told that this was more to do with the old lady's arthritis during the damp winter, than the commotion going on all around her. Clearly, Madame Figol's continued support was crucial to the success of her plans. She was held in high esteem by all, and her blessing of the new Grand Café was absolutely vital.

The following day, she received a visit from a reporter and photographer from *Midi Libre*, the regional daily newspaper. She suspected that Jacques had used his sporting journalistic contacts to get a bit of free publicity. Speaking to the young reporter, Anna was careful to make the point that she was counting on her place being good for the village and tourism. When she went to get a copy of the paper in the *tabac* the next day, much to her surprise, she was told they were all sold out. This was surely an indication that there was indeed intense interest, perhaps even pride, in what was going on in the square. On the other hand, perhaps someone had been hoping to get some ammunition from the article to use against her. If they were, they were disappointed, for the column was entirely positive. It praised the brave Englishwoman who had overcome a serious injury and was trying to resurrect village life.

Samedi, 1 Mars

The official opening was fixed for 11.00am. As to who should be invited to perform the opening ceremony, Anna could not bring herself to invite the Mayor to do the honours. She had decided to ask Madame Figol.

'*Mon Dieu, je viendrai un film star,*' Madame Figol had replied. After some persuasion, she had agreed to cut the tape at the appointed hour.

The Grand Café looked a treat. The old furniture had been cleaned and polished. The decor had been kept simple on purpose – with white walls which offset the solid dark furniture. A piano had been installed in the corner, and the bar had taken on the appearance of an altar, with the rows of bottles and spirits creating a fine display.

Outside, she had fixed up hanging baskets, full of early Spring flowers. The whole place was draped with bunting – Euro, British and French flags. But who exactly would come to the opening?

A few of Anna's English friends had promised to drop in. Gabrielle had rounded up some of her old school friends, including some of the local rugby club. Even some of her sophisticated university friends had agreed to drive out to the village to see at first hand what was going on. Flyers had been posted in all the surrounding villages. Invitations had been sent to everyone in Moutouliers offering them a 50% discount on all liquid refreshments bought on the opening day.

Fears and hopes chased across Anna's mind as she lay in bed early on the morning of opening day. She had consumed several glasses of red wine the night before to try combat her nervousness.

She certainly felt a sense of pride in what she had achieved so far. It was a bit like seeing her family growing up; buying their first flat; the kids' first days at school; their son getting his 'A' level results, and so on – and yet it was different, altogether a more intense, personal sort of pride and pleasure.

She had spent freely and had found, to her dismay, that her French bank account had to be continuously replenished. Fortunately, the sale of her mother's house in Reigate had provided the necessary funds. More worrying though were two incidents which had occurred during the past week. They severely dented her confidence. On Tuesday, two officials arrived unannounced from the *préfecture*. They were accompanied by the Mayor, of course! They breezed into the Café unannounced and uninvited, and demanded an immediate inspection of the premises prior to opening. As usual, the Mayor's breath was bad, very bad – a cruel mix of garlic and pastis – which made Anna keep her distance. After an hour of inspections, the officials ordered that changes had to be made to the storage of wine and the toilets. First, the wine had to be kept at a certain temperature and not in the containers in which it had been bought from the local *cave*. Anna readily agreed to this dictat, even though she doubted its authenticity. As far as the toilets were concerned, they were deemed not to be up to scratch for the disabled. Here Anna put her foot down. She had been forced to use the most appalling toilets in France, and she knew for a fact that the facilities at the Café du Paris were, to put it mildly, very basic. Only after an hour of entreaties, together with the intervention of Dr Millaud, did the official relent and agree that the opening could take place on time.

Even more worrying was an incident which had taken place the previous night in the square. Anna had been awakened by shouting. Looking out of the window, she saw in the moonlight that paint had been daubed over the windows of the Grand Café. '*FERME*' had been painted in large red letters. She had a fair idea who was responsible for this act of vandalism but didn't have any proof. She got up early in the morning and cleaned the graffitti off before the village stirred. Although this antagonism upset her, it merely strengthened her resolve to make a success of the Grand Café.

Whilst most of Anna's energies and thoughts went into the preparations for opening, she could not help thinking of home as well. Her son, she knew, was looking after himself perfectly well at college, and her 17-year-old daughter was commendably independent for her age. But she knew, from her own experience, that anxieties and insecurities lay beneath the surface at their age, and their mother was no longer on the spot to offer support when needed. As to her employers and her husband, both had, so far, been very tolerant. Her decision to stay in France, at first greeted with disbelief, had now been largely accepted. They realised that they couldn't stand in her way. But Anna was well aware that she ran the risk of burning boats on the other side of the Channel. She sensed that there was likely to be a limit to the patience displayed by all who were not directly part of her adventure in the South of France.

Dimanche, 1 Juin

The opening had been a great success. Almost a hundred people had patronised the Grand Café during the day. Even at the 'Happy Hour' prices, she had taken several thousand francs over the counter. It was nice to put money back into her bank account for a change. Quite a few elderly visitors from the village had dropped in, more out of curiosity than anything else. They marvelled at the English tea service. At least a dozen ex-pats couples living in the vicinity turned up for lunch. Even the Mayor put in a brief appearance before leaving to attend to 'urgent' business at municipal HQ. Later in the evening, the younger set had arrived to try out her wide range of imported beers. Jacques had played the piano, and student songs had been sung with increasing abandon. There had even been some dancing which spilled out onto the square, much to the delight of Madame Figol. Having performed the opening ceremony, she had retreated to her usual seat to watch the comings and goings with undisguised approval.

During the day, Anna kept firmly in charge of the bar and preparations of the food. She kept a clear head to supervise her part-time staff. But, as the evening wore on, she relaxed. She allowed herself a couple of well-earned glasses of wine. Although she had been on her feet all day, she didn't feel tired as she chatted to her guests. One of Gabrielle's friends had taken over at the piano and was playing Stevie Wonder numbers. A few couples danced, and Anna felt in the mood to join them. She sought out Jacques who was sampling a malt whisky she had recommended.

'*Monsieur le Medicine,*' she asked '*voulez vous danser avec moi?*'

'*Toujours ici quand il faut,*' he joked.

He held her lightly. He was wearing a pale cream shirt and brown trousers. As always, he was immaculately dressed and studiously polite. It was a strange experience for her to be held as a dancing partner by the same man who had skilfully tender her medically for so many weeks. For a moment she forgot all that and enjoyed the feeling of his strong hands holding her around the waist, and his warm body touching her breasts through the thin silk of her blouse. She smelt the faint aroma of his *eau de cologne*.

All too soon, she had to resume her duties as the café-manager, as the wearisome task of clearing and washing up called. It was well after midnight before the Grand Café was shipshape again. Anna retired to the empty house opposite, happy in the knowledge that at least the whole thing had got off the ground.

As she lay trying to digest all that had happened that memorable day, it was the few brief moments dancing with Jacques which remained most vividly in her mind. She felt that her body had been reawakened. Her needs as a woman had been aroused by the man who had, up to now, responded to her needs as a patient.

The following days were fairly quiet. A few tourists dropped into the Grand Café – mostly to have lunch before continuing their wine tasting outings through the district. A Dutch couple showed a real appreciation of the place and, after staying most of the day, left promising to return with friends. They said they would spread the word in the village in which they lived. The smart young lady from the local branch of the *Crédit Agricole* also called in for lunch one day, whereas before she would have promptly returned to Beziers once her duties had been performed. There was also a steady trickle of locals but, overall, nowhere near enough customers to ensure that Montouliers' latest enterprise could be said to be viable. In particular, Anna noticed with concern that the youngsters in the village still congregated under the neon lights and around the formica topped tables of the Café du Paris.

Listening to the overseas service of the BBC, as she did regularly, Anna knew that the value of the pound was strengthening against the franc. Consequently, there would very likely be an influx of British tourists into France during the coming summer months.

She had several large signs erected on the main road, as well as beside the Canal du Midi. She also placed notices in all the camping grounds within a radius of twenty miles of the village. Her efforts seemed to pay dividends, at least on a modest scale, for several French and English cars nosed their way gingerly into the square, seeking the newly opened place to eat and refresh themselves. They had heard about the café which boasted an Anglo-French cuisine and the largest selection of English beers and Scottish whisky in the South of France. Anna's cooking had always been excellent, and increasingly she experiement with Languedoc recipes. She learnt how to make *Aigo Bonuido*, the garlic and herb soup on bread, as a tasty snack. Also, dishes such as *Farcileau*, vegetables and dumplings with garlic, olive oil and tomatoes; *cassoulet*, a stew with bits of spicy Toulouse sausage and local ham from the Montagues Noirs. Then there was *Omelettes aux pignons*, another dish she soon mastered. *Cabeçous grillé, à la fleur de citronelle et salades aux noisettes rôties* (goat's cheese, grilled with lemon liquor and roasted hazelnut salad) was the culinary experiment she liked most.

She also made some mistakes – confusing *rognons* (kidneys) with *rognons blancs* (testicles), much to the hilarity of her staff.

Her wine list was mainly either from the Montouliers' Cave Co-operative. But she also ordered supplies of *Corbieres, Minervois* and *St Chinian*. Even her French friends were surprised at her growing knowledge of local cuisine.

As spring arrived, the rugby season was drawing to a close. While Toulouse and Toulon had done well in the newly emerging Heineken European Cup, the fortunes of the Montouliers' club were still languishing. With two games left until the end of the season, they were in danger of being relegated from the first division of the regional Languedoc league. Whilst their backs occasionally sparkled, their forwards were so poor that the team rarely got possession of the ball, and thus the club didn't score many tries. They also lacked a reliable place kicker. President of the club Jacques Millaud grew increasingly despondent. The honour of the village was at stake. Montouliers had always had a good team, and the ignomy of being relegated would be keenly felt by the whole village, at least all those who mattered in it, and that included Anna.

She knew that her son Peter was a good player. By now he had finished his university exams and thus Anna rang him up and suggested that he might like to come over to play a few games in France. After all, several French players were playing in England and vice versa. He jumped at the chance. Once Peter arrived, it did not take long for Jacques to complete the registration forms.

On the first Tuesday's practice and training session, the team greeted him with only mild interest, indeed more like indifference. It wasn't their fault that they didn't recognise his Loughborough University shirt, nor had any idea that he had played as a substitute for England's A team against the mighty All Blacks reserves. However, it did not take long for their white limbed foreign player to make his mark. In the twenty minutes practise game which ended the session, Peter took over the pack in which he was playing Number 8, scored a try, and impressed them all with his kicking. Anna and Jacques watched afterwards as he practised his kicking skills to the grudging admiration of the locals.

His selection was decided in the Grand Café shortly afterwards. Some of the committee felt that he should wait before being selected, but Jacques was adamant that he would play the following Saturday against RFC Servian from down the valley. At an extra training session on the Thursday evening, Peter's kicking and fitness, not to mention his skill, again shone out. He also made a point of working with the Montouliers' pack to bring more cohesion to their efforts. And all this in good French. The locals began to realise they might just have an asset on their hands.

At 4.00pm on Saturday afternoon, the *stade* was fuller than usual. It was a local derby, and everyone knew that Montouliers had to win, or at least draw, to have any chance of staying up. The first half was scrappy and littered with penalties. The new

English kicker calmly slotted all the penalties that came his way. At half-time the score was 14-9 to the Servian club who had scored two tries following some indifferent tackling by the Montouliers' centres. In the second half, Peter took charge of his forwards and, holding the ball from the set pieces, they ground their way forward into enemy territory. He picked up the ball from the base of the scrum and launched a series of short, fierce attacks. This ploy was as unexpected as it was effective. The opposition became frustrated and ill disciplined and, after a pushover try and an exchange of penalties, the final whistle went with the score at 22-22. There was little attempt to conceal the satisfaction on the faces of the Montouliers' players and supporters. They lived to fight another day in their battle to stave off relegation. That night, some of the team, including Peter, were to be found in the Grand Café with their friends, discussing the game and the merits of English and French rugby.

The following week, the last of the season, training was even more intense. This time, there was no hesitation amongst the players to listen and learn from their guest star. He instilled the basics of ten-man rugby. This went down well amongst the forwards at least. They practised the rolling maul and a couple of back row moves which involved the wing three quarter cutting in on a diagonal run. Jacques told Peter that their opponents of the final and crucial match of the season were Beziers Renault, a works team with a reputation for fluid, open rugby. All agreed to go along with the new controlled game being advocated by the English newcomer, even if only on a temporary basis.

Meanwhile, Anna lost no time in posting a notice all over the Grand Café announcing the game. She detected a new atmosphere around the village. Whereas before she had always been greeted politely, now people seemed to go out of their way to wish her '*Bonjour*'. She also noted with approval more men coming into the café to read the French sporting daily *L'Equipe* which she had ordered. Also, Peter and his team-mates came in to eat pizzas after training.

The game on the Saturday followed a similar pattern as the previous week. The big city boys arrived in their flash cars. They clearly expected an easy ride against a village team at the bottom of the league. The large crowd could not help but enjoy their pacey running and intricate moves. They scored a glorious try from a passing movement which started from within their own 22 metre line.

'French rugby at its best,' whispered Jacques, somewhat grudgingly to Anna.

However, the Montouliers' lads were holding up their own up front. Gaining possession, they held the ball ten metres out before advancing on the Beziers' line in a solid phalanx. They plunged over for an equalising try. The opposition disputed this score and, thereafter, nearly every decision made by the referee. Penalties followed but, with a few minutes to go, the score remained at 18-16 to the visitors. It had to be said that, in the excitement, the primitive village scoreboard remained unchanged.

Pinned down in their own half, Montouliers won a scrum. Peter picked up the ball and, instead of bullocking across the gain line, he put in a piercing grub kick diagonally behind the Beziers back. It found touch twenty metres from the opposition's line. At the subsequent throw-in Peter called out 'Twickenham' which was the coded name for the move in which the wing cut in at the back of the lineout.

The team chorused the cry 'Twick-en-ham', much to the amusement of the home crowd and the consternation of the opposition.

It worked a treat. Peter leapt like a salmon to catch the long lineout throw. He slipped it to the scrum half who dummied a long pass to the stand off. As the opposition cover fanned out, anticipating a passing movement across the field, he passed inside to the wing, who cut in like a knife through butter and scored under the posts. The final whistle went amongst scenes of wild jubilation on the pitch and touchline.

Rushing back to the centre of the village, Anna set out the beer in jugs, ready for the thirsty teams. Her young assistants put the production of food into overdrive. Celebrations went on well into the evening. Even some of the Beziers' players and coaches stayed on to share the evening's socialising. Jacques joked with them that they were out to poach his new star player, and it was true that Peter was the centre of attraction. Peter was indeed the hero of the hour, but more significantly the Grand Café had at last established itself amongst the sporting fraternity and young people in the district.

Mardi, 3 Juillet

The heat beat down on the lumpy Languedoc landscape. Very little stirred in the village. People in Montouliers paced themselves in the intense heat. Some of the early risers called in at the Grand Café for coffee and brandy. Lunches were served from 12 noon to 2pm, but custom at this time was still poor. Most locals went straight home to eat, and most tourists took picnics to the beach. A few wine-tasting tours stopped, including a minibus full of intrepid folk from the University of the Third Age. But most young people were away on summer courses, or working in the tourist centres on the coast. Anna began to wonder if her premises were in the wrong place, stuck inland away from the magnet of the Mediterranean.

While the Grand Café was ticking over, it was certainly not making a profit. Anna felt that, despite all her efforts, she was missing out on the potentially lucrative tourist trade. The editor of a provincial English newspaper, who had stayed with his family in the village the previous month, had written a well crafted article in the *Sunday Times* about her wonderful cuisine, but still English visitors did not arrive in any large numbers. Anna felt strangely flat. Perhaps she was expecting too much too quickly from the Grand Café and the village – after all, the place had been virtually dead for years.

However, the main cause of her discontent was not only to do with her café. Jacques' absence also had something to do with the general feeling of emptiness that she felt. He had gone on a sailing holiday with friends, including apparently his wife, off the coast of Turkey. Anna had to admit that she had come to rely on him heavily these past few months. She had almost taken his easy companionship for granted. That they liked each other was not in doubt, but there had been no further intimate moments between them since the opening, and this Anna knew she regretted. Neither had there been any news from England. Peter, her son, had long since departed back to join his friends travelling through the Greek Islands.

One of her former colleagues at Zurich sent her copies of the local paper, and she noticed with interest that the city council had organised concerts every weekend at a new bandstand which had been erected on Southsea seafront. She knew that in France such cultural activity was well established. She and her family had gone to many local *fêtes* in different regions of the country. One year, they had even attended a jazz festival in a village in Gascony called Marciac. She was also aware that the local midsummer fête was due to be held shortly in Montouliers in late August, and she became determined that she and the Grand Café would become involved in some way.

Anna got herself invited to the *Mairie* as plans for the fête were being hatched. Since her part in the success of the rugby club, she knew that they dare not ignore her anymore.

She marched boldly into his office. The demeanour of the organising committee suddenly became very formal. Minutes were read out and an agenda of items was solemnly taken. Under an item headed 'entertainment' it was suggested that a rock band called *Lightening* should be engaged to play for *le bal*. The elderly members were murmuring their assent when Anna interrupted them.

'*Monsieur le Mairie, pourquoi vous ne tenez pas un festival du jazz en Montouliers cette anneé?*' Before they had time to object, she followed this up with her offer. She would book jazz bands to play through the weekend of the fête, half of the cost to be paid for by her and the rest met from the municipal budget. She described how, in some villages, festivals attracted tourists and indeed how Marciac – now holding a major international festival – had started from very humble beginnings. The committee were impressed, if only by her offer of money and the prospect of tourists. It was eventually agreed that, whilst all the traditional elements of the fête should proceed as usual – the cycle race for youth and the old folks' outing to Narbonne – jazz should also be included for the first time, courtesy of the Grand Café.

Anna knew that the Mayor would not oppose her plans, as a few days earlier she had slipped into the *Mairie* for a serious word with him. She had offered him a deal – in return for giving his blessing to her idea of a jazz festival and ending his covert hostility towards the Grand Café, she would ask the police to drop all charges against his son. She also insisted that he should buy her a new bicycle and make an anonymous donation of 5,000 francs to the charity *Médicine sans Frontiers*. Since her insurance policy had paid for most of her medical treatment and accommodation, Anna could afford to be generous. But, her motives were not entirely altruistic, as she knew that the Mayor's tacit support meant a lot, even though he wasn't very popular in the village.

Anna spent the evening on the telephone. Through Gabrielle's contacts, she persuaded a modern jazz group from the University of Montpelliers to play for a nominal amount. Then she rang England. She knew the leading lights of her local jazz scene and, after lengthy conversations, she had struck a deal with a blues band and trad jazz band. They agreed to come down to the South of France for the weekend for modest fees and travel and accommodation expenses. She reckoned the whole package would cost her less than 30,000 francs.

Taking into account the Mayor's contribution and sponsorship, she predicted that she should not be out of pocket. With her contacts, and rough-and-ready business plan, she proceeded to arrange publicity for the event. The news of the festival spread fast. Just as with the opening of the Grand Café in the first place, and her imported rugby star son to act as a salvation to the village's sporting reputation, so people were soon quizzing Anna about the festival. The old folk were not very impressed, even if a few had heard of Louis Armstrong and Stéphane Grappelli.

Gabrielle, back from her English literature course in Brighton, was, in contrast, very enthusiastic. 'Just what the village needed,' she exclaimed. She agreed to be the publicity agent for the evet and, with her college contacts, promised that she would pull in a young crowd.

Apart from the details of the stages, tannoy systems, and the programmes, the only problem not taken care of was the Café du Paris. Anna had passed a scowling René Mousty several times in the street lately, and she knew only too well that he was likely to make things difficult for her in her latest venture. She played a trump card. One of her bands would play outside his café – her rival establishment. The Mayor confirmed that this arrangement was acceptable to all parties, and thus another plank was added to her village bridge building.

Thus the 'Languedoc-Montouliers Jazz Festival' was born.

Samedi, 23 Août

The previous evening, a couple of English minibuses had pulled into the village square. Sweaty bodies fell out, followed by instrument cases splattered with decals of past 'gigs' and festivals. The bands from abroad had arrived, and without further ado they piled into the Grand Café to quench their thirsts. Anna had ordered special supplies for the weekend but, watching the band members downing her complementary beers, she began to wonder if the order should be doubled. It was not long before the recently tuned piano was in action and a jam session underway. Ron, the leader of one of the bands, offered to take his trad band around the village on a march and they set off, followed by a crowd of noisy youngsters miming to the music. Anna remained in the café, preparing supper for her guests and making last-minute arrangements for beds. She was informed when they got back that the Mayor had been serenaded with when *The Saints Go Marching In*. Before they all sat down to a well-earned meal, she sent them off to play *St James' Infirmary* in front of Jacques' house. She had heard he had returned from his exotic holiday, and had her own reasons for wanting to lure him into the festivities.

On the Saturday, the first proper day of the festival, the village awoke to the blaring sound of its tannoy system. Little Richard was singing '*Wake up little Suzie, wake up*'. Anna had given some tapes to the *Mairie* to play whilst the bands were being refreshed between sets. She hoped that the early sound would not get anyone up too early and in a bad mood for the day's festivities.

Tables and chairs were arranged in the square and in the roadway between the *Mairie* and the Café du Paris. Bunting had been erected all over the village. The final touches were in place on and around the two stages. The young group from Montpelliers arrived minus only the tenor sax player who had been playing in Toulouse the previous evening, but who had promised to be there by midday.

As the morning sun grew hotter, a keen sense of anticipation gripped the populace, even those who hadn't the faintest idea what to expect from a jazz festival. At least something was happening and it was bigger, and most likely better, than previous years. Gradually, the temporary car park at the *stade* began to fill up. The two English bands struck up more or less simultaneously on the two stages. The crowd – it grew by the minute – sank their *aperitifs* and consumed *plats du jour* from the cafés and stalls.

By early evening, the village was full to the brim, drinking, listening, talking and, of course, eating. After all, it was a French festival, even if the music was mostly from across *La Manche.* The bands entered into the spirit of the occasion, competing in a friendly way for the attention of their cosmopolitan audience. Noisy, coke-drinking youngsters jumped around to the blues band. The *Spice Island Stompers* attracted the middle-aged locals and tourists, whilst most of the students, attracted by Gabrielle's flyers and flyposting, homed in on the discordant sounds of sax and trumpet coming from the modern French jazz group.

As the evening wore on, and the light faded, the streets and square took on the appearance of an impromptu dance hall. Some danced with partners and others without. Anna emerged from the Grand Café, which had been full all day, for a breather.

It was exactly a year ago to the day since Anna had been carried into the village, bruised and bleeding. Now she felt a great tide of elation and fulfilment sweep over her. She felt like leaping up and down and shouting to the assembled company – 'Look at the wonderful Grand Café ... look at what I've done!' Instead, she simply leant back against the wall and feasted her eyes on the lively scene. The square was full of music, colour and laughter. Some figures were familiar and others total strangers. People were relaxed and clearly enjoying themselves. Solos played by the band members were generously applauded.

People glanced at her and smiled. She could tell that the event was turning out to be a great success. Just as the opening of the Grand Café had amazed her at the time, so did today's event. Rugby had broken the ice with many in the community, now it was the turn of the jazz festival to seal her place in Montoulier's social history. It wasn't that she had ever lacked confidence, rather that she had never achieved anything so real and significant in her life before. Bringing up a family was rewarding, and she had enjoyed her job, but this was altogether something special.

There was one person who she had not yet seen amongst the crowd. She suddenly sensed him beside her. Jacques slipped his hand onto her shoulder and gave her a gentle squeeze. '*Bon soir Madame la directeur. Toujours ici, quand il faut!*'

He gave a mock bow before guiding her purposefully into the dancing throng. The band was playing a slow version of *Around Midnight*. The mellow saxophone sounded over the Grand Café. All around people were dancing, but none so closely and fondly as Anna and her doctor.

Birds

Great Dismal Swamp
National
Wildlife
Refuge

Th...
Dismal S...
Can...

Virginia

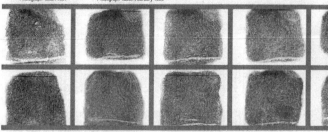

mp

WANTED
BY THE FBI

UNLAWFUL FLIGHT TO AVOID PROSECUTION - CRIMINAL HO
ROBERT RADHAMES-HERRE

Photograph taken in 1994

Aliases: Robert Herrera, Robert Porquin, Robert Radhames-Porquin, Robert Sosa, and "Lucky"

DESCRIPTION

Date of Birth:	August 28, 1977	**Hair:**	Brown
Place of Birth:	Dominican Republic	**Eyes:**	Brown
Height:	5' 10"	**Complexion:**	Medium
Weight:	140 pounds	**Sex:**	Male
Build:	Thin	**Social Security**	
Occupation:	Unknown	**Number:**	584-99-4
Scar and Marks:	None	**Race:**	Hispanic
Remarks	Member of "NETAS" street gang	**Nationality:**	Dominic
		Fingerprint Classification:	

CRIMINAL RECORD

No prior criminal history.

CAUTION

SHOULD BE CONSIDERED ARMED AND DANGEROUS AND AN ESCAPE RISK.

A federal warrant was issued on October 1, 1997, in the Eastern District of Pennsylvania, charging ROBERT RADHAMES-HERRERA in v
States Code, Section 1073, Unlawful Flight to Avoid Prosecution - Criminal Homicide.

IF YOU HAVE INFORMATION CONCERNING THIS PERSON, PLEASE CONTACT YOUR LOCAL FBI OFFICE OR THE N
OR CONSULATE. THE TELEPHONE NUMBERS AND ADDRESSES OF ALL FBI OFFICES ARE LISTED ON THE BACK.

RK

Early years at Postcard Corner

The Great Dismal Swamp ...
Don't go there

*T*he passenger seat of the Jeep was empty. Where was Ginny? It was well after 4 o'clock and still no sign of her. Jim had met every ferry from Norfolk since mid afternoon, but to no avail.

They had arranged to meet after work. Jim had left his office at the Portsmouth Convention and Visitors Bureau in New Hampshire in good time. He had worked extra hours all week in order to get away promptly for their date. Ginny was a staff writer for *The Virginian-Pilot* based over in Norfolk, Virginia. She had warned him that she might have to finish stories for the Saturday edition before she could join him for their weekend on the Outer Banks.

He tried not to be impatient, and drummed his fingers on the steering wheel in time with Grover Washington playing on Smooth Jazz FM. He had cleaned up the vehicle specially for the trip. His weekend bag was packed and stowed away in the back. Now he only needed her to appear on the ferry and they would be off. But where on earth was she?

Jim knew that she was writing a piece about the Bedsole homicide and that her editor had hinted that if she got it right, it might make the front page. She could still be at her desk for all he knew. But he couldn't help fearing that she might just have called it off at the last moment. After all, a weekend together down in North Carolina had only been a last minute arrangement.

They had been dating for a few weeks now. Jim was living temporarily with his parents in Portsmouth's Olde Towne, waiting until his apartment was ready. Ginny on the other hand shared a condo with some fellow journalists in downtown Norfolk. The problem was that they were separated by the Elizabeth River. Since the last ferry was at 10pm they were forever having either to go home early, or not drink, and drive the tunnel.

'Jim,' she had said irritably the previous weekend, 'I know that distance makes the heart grow fonder but why does one of us always seem to be rushing home early or staying sober when we meet?'

'Right,' Jim had responded without hesitation or indeed forethought. 'Why don't we get together over the weekend and get out of town?'

It had been agreed – just like that – as if they both had been thinking along the same lines. They went straight to the question of where. North over the Chesapeake Bay Bridge-Tunnel up the coast to Chincoteague or Assateague Island? Ginny had gone there with her family for many years and it held happy memories. Up the James River to visit the historic plantations and battlefields? Jim was used to directing visitors to those attractions. Or down over the state line to North Carolina's Outer Banks – to Kitty Hawk, Roanoke Island and Cape Hatteras?

In the end they had agreed to go south to stay at Nags Head, and explore the Outer Banks. Neither of them had said it, but they both well understood what it meant. A weekend away together could mean only one thing. They liked each other enough to go further.

But Jim still wondered whether she had cold feet at the last minute. He, himself, was in no doubt. He had to admit that he liked the idea of dating a reporter from the local newspaper, but far more important he liked her. She was 23, a graduate of Smith College. She had short brown hair, blue eyes, an athletic figure and a lovely smile. He teasingly called her 'Miss Tappahannock on the Rappahannock' ever since, in an unguarded moment, she had revealed to him that she had once won a high school beauty contest back home in Essex County. Jim had fallen for her in a big way. He readily admitted that to himself and his friends. He had high hopes for the weekend. To get to know her better. To show her the Outer Banks which he had visited many times before. To make love.

He had booked them into a small motel near the Comfort Inn. There on a Friday night they could dine and dance. But only if they got away soon. He checked that his cell phone was switched on, and waited.

Meanwhile staff reporter Ms Virginia Read was busy at her PC in a rapidly emptying press office. Most of her colleagues had already left for Happy Hour at the Irish pub around the corner. The weekend relief staff had not yet put in an appearance. She had promised to file her story by early deadline but it still wasn't quite right – not for the front page at least. The headline had already been written by one of the sub-editors – WILLIAMS FOR THE CHAIR? But her final paragraph still hit the right spot.

The story revolved around the murder of a Helen Bedsole, the 53-year-old, estranged wife of a well-connected local paediatrician. A young, petty criminal called Marlon Williams – who happened to be African American – had pleaded guilty to the charge of homicide. He had been handed down the death penalty by a Richmond judge back in 1994. Since then he had been on death row. He was due for execution this coming Monday, but his attorney had filed a final appeal to Governor George Allen of the Commonwealth of Virginia.

Ginny knew that her readers would remember the case. Not because a woman had been murdered, nor even that a black man was the alleged perpetrator. After all there were hundreds of homicides across America every month. The novelty of the case lay in its bizarre circumstances and impending outcome.

Williams had been supplying narcotics to Bedsole – or was

it the other way around? At any rate he had been offered three thousand dollars by the physician to kill her. The 20 year old had borrowed a bicycle and hand-gun, gone to the Bedsole family residence and carried out the killing. He had left his fingerprints at the house. He was picked up by Portsmouth's police chief in person a few hours later, and under questioning had soon implicated himself.

But the twist to this story – at least to Ginny – was that the eminent white doctor who had planned and financed the killing and who stood to benefit financially from his spouse's death, got off with a jail sentence. He had hired a smart attorney, obtained a jury trial, and was due for parole in 2016. Williams, in contrast, was to go to the electric chair the following Monday – unless the governor acceded to the final plea for clemency.

And all this on the weekend she had agreed to spend with Jim on the Outer Banks.

Thousands of column inches had already been written about the case. Now it was no longer a question of the relative guilt and blame as between the two men, but simply whether Williams should die. His lawyer claimed that he was of low intelligence and had been neglected as a child and abused by his father, a sergeant in the US Army. A final plea of mitigation was on the Governor's desk

What sort of weekend would he have with such a decision to make?

Ginny outlined the case for and against in stark terms. She asked her readers to give their verdict by telephone or e-mail over the next 24 hours.

Her earlier version had been sent back with one section edited out. In this paragraph she had referred to the racial overtones of the case. Would a jury – she had asked – have sentenced to death a white, petty criminal who had gunned down the wife of a prominent black doctor in the town? And would the governor be more likely to respond to an appeal which might have been lodged in such a case?

The editor had scrawled 'Don't go there' across the margin and added a cryptic note – 'Ginny have you forgotten who is the Mayor of Portsmouth?' She had realised her error at once. Mayor Hailey was quite black and very respected. Not the time to stir up the race issue.

Now she was rewriting her article for the final time. She was nearly there. She went to the refrigerator for a Diet Pepsi. Although she had gotten to know Jim well only in the last few weeks she knew his number by heart and called him.

'Jim, I'm terribly sorry, I've been held up. I'll be on the ferry and with you in less than an hour. Go have a drink.'

He sounded laid back. 'That's OK. So long as you're coming sometime tonight. I'll be waiting to catch a glimpse of you on the ferry and have the motor running.'

'Of course I'm coming,' she countered with a touch of impatience. 'I've got to put this article to bed and then we will ...' she paused feeling herself excited at the thought of going to bed with him ... 'get going' she added after a moment's delay.

Ginny sat still for a moment after she had put the phone down. She could hardly focus on the screen in front of her. She had been surprised and pleased when Jim had first asked her out for a date. He was a great-looking guy. Dark-haired and handsome. The looks of his Italian ancestors, and easy manner, instantly attracted her. And her girlfriends thought she was onto a real good number. They had gone on their first date to the Commodore Theater, the High Street art deco theatre in Portsmouth. They had ordered a salad and pizza and watched *Muriel's Wedding*. The movie had broken the ice, especially the hilarious attempted seduction scene between Muriel and her shy admirer.

When, a few weeks later, a weekend had been suggested by him she had been too bowled over to even think about refusing.

Perhaps it was the attraction of opposites. When he teased her about her past exploits as a cheerleader up at

Tappahannock High School, and she called him Silvester Stallone, because of his dark Italian good looks.

With difficulty she put the finishing touches to her article. The last of her colleagues were departing. She tried to ignore her friend Brad's plea to join him in the bar. 'Don't go there!' she thought to herself.

Across the Elizabeth River, Jim fed the parking meter with quarters, and paced up and down the ferry landing. He watched the ferries like a red-tailed hawk. He picked up a discarded copy of *The Virginian-Pilot* from a park bench and looked for Ginny's name.

There were articles about the rezoning of the 55 elementary schools in Virginia Beach; a new soccer complex to be built; and a planned extension to the Naval hospital bringing the payroll to over three thousand. He turned to a feature article on a Kosovan refugee family by staff writer Ginny Read. The refugees were shown at work. They had been found jobs in a hospital laundry at 6 dollars an hour. One was quoted as saying that they were very happy to be in America, although the sight of blood on some of the sheets they were cleaning made them feel bad.

Jim reminded himself to congratulate her when he saw her. It was a neat article – a good news story with a touch of pathos. She would get to the top he thought to himself, but then went back to thinking of Ginny. He couldn't wait to hold and kiss her. Never mind her journalistic skills, he wanted to get close to her. He could hardly get his head around the fact that they would be together for two whole days and nights.

Jim paced the waterfront restlessly. He noticed a sign in front of the Jewish Mother Restaurant and Bar. Wine and with Jazz ... Fridays 6 to 8.' As he stood by the entrance the musicians were unloading their instruments. He recognised Elly Shere. He couldn't miss her. She had the longest legs and shortest denim hot pants in town. Her crinkled fair hair flowed over her maroon tee shirt. She smiled at him.

'Hi Jim, coming in to hear my trio?'

He helped her with her music case, but was noncommittal.

'You know that I would love to but I'm going out of town for the weekend,' he said with genuine regret.

'Where are you playing next?' he said by way of conversation. Maybe he could take Ginny to one of her gigs. Or perhaps not, on second thought. He had known her quite well in the past, and it might show – definitely a case of 'don't go there!'

'See you then,' she shrugged and climbed onto the small stage. Jim headed for the exit, passing the glasses of California wine laid out for the early evening throng. He strolled over to the Post Office, still feeling a tinge of regret at missing a couple of hours of jazz and drinks to get the weekend off to a good start.

As he still didn't have a permanent address he checked his post office box. Only a communication from the *Readers Digest* and some junk mail. To kill time he glanced at the usual 'Wanted by the FBI' board. Although such notices were to be seen in every post office in the US he had never really looked at them closely before.

What an assorted bunch of hardened criminals they were. They looked out at the police photographer and post office users with disdain, contempt or just plain shiftiness. Underneath each one was their name, or to be precise their names, for many of them had several aliases. And their fingerprints. How, Jim wondered, could the public be expected to spot these desperadoes on the basis of recognising their fingerprints? Also listed were the felonies which they had allegedly committed and their criminal records. It all made frightening reading.

Amongst the least threatening was a Ramon Cardoza, alias Jose Quinonez, Ramon Garcia Jose Garcia, Jose Luis Tena and many more Spanish American names. He was a member of the NETAS gang, born in Rodeo Durango, Mexico, with a scar on his nose and a tattoo on his left shoulder – for Camela. Cardoza was wanted for illegal entry, unlawful flight to avoid prosecution and attempted first degree murder in Rapid City, South Dakota.

Next to him was James Kopp, a studious-faced white man with thinning hair. He was born on August 2, 1954 in Pasadena, California. He, the notice announced, 'walked with a limp, attended mass daily and did not bathe regularly'!

Kopp too was known by numerous aliases – James Copp, John Copp, Jack Cotty, and Jack Crotty, also as 'Atomic Dog' and 'Catfish'. He was charged with the second degree murder of a New York doctor and was cited as a class A felony drug dealer.

Alongside them was Terry Peterson; born Minnesota; carnival worker; arms and torso covered with tattoos – including roses, eagles, snakes and a panther. He had a 'Tweety Bird' on his right forearm and 'love' tattooed on the fingers of his left hand. Below was a chilling description of his crimes – he befriended single women living with their children in trailer parks and once he had gained their confidence had a record of molesting their young children. He was charged with criminal sexual conduct with minors, possession of narcotics and stolen credit cards.

Finally Jim's attention was caught by a James Bryant, together with Catherine Greig from Boston Mass. There was a quarter of a million dollar reward being offered for information leading to Bryant's arrest He was said to be a major organized crime figure in the Boston area and was sought for extortion, gambling, loan sharking and narcotics. He was known to have a violent temper and possess a knife at all times. He was likely to be armed and considered dangerous.

Jim reflected, in a somewhat detached way, on these and other fugitives looking out at him and the Portsmouth populace going about their everyday tasks of mailing letters, buying stamps and sending packages. Where were they all living or hiding? Scattered over the States on isolated farms or in seedy lodging houses? Going out only at night or in disguise? Watching endless TV chat shows, soaps, or sports recordings? Committing yet more crimes in other parts of the country? For the FBI it must be looking for a needle in the proverbial haystack or searching for a lost contact lens on a football field or in the bedroom.

Jim left the building. He could only wonder how they had gotten into their criminal ways, and the unlikely prospect of their being apprehended in this huge, sprawling and restless country. He pushed the whole business from his mind. He didn't fancy being a FBI agent or indeed a bounty hunter, and anyway, he had more pleasant things to attend to. Namely meeting Ginny off the ferry.

He thought about the weekend ahead with pleasurable anticipation. Showing her the long, deserted beaches; watching sea birds and dolphins; collecting shells; and swimming. She was bound to look gorgeous on the beach.

He planned to take her to Manteo on Roanoke Island, the site of the famous lost colony established in 1587 by Sir Walter Raleigh. It had disappeared without trace and the fate of the early settlers had never been discovered – including what happened to Virginia Dare, the first English child to be born in the New World. Some said they had been killed by Indians whom they had treated badly. Or maybe they had been swept away by a hurricane and tidal surge.

He looked forward to showing off his local knowledge, gained from personal experience and books he had read in the Visitors Bureau. He had even made a mental note that Ginny and Virginia Dare were connected by first name and that Read was an anagram of Dare. Might drop it into their conversation sometime! As far as the early settlers were concerned, someone should have warned them – Don't go there!' They had all died, probably of starvation their first winter.

As Jim sat waiting for the next ferry – she must surely be on the next one – he heard jazz blowing from the bar nearby. Again he was tempted. He might have a quick drink with Elly at the interval. No, he would not go in there, he again reluctantly decided.

Ginny paid her 75 cents and leapt onto the ferry. There were a few shoppers, tourists, and Portsmouth commuters aboard as the paddle wheels began to thresh the water. None of them, she thought, were looking forward to the weekend as much as she was. She had liked Jim from the start. He seemed almost too good to be true – neat, good looking, well dressed, polite, and attentive. And he kissed well. She had found that out on their date at the Commodore Theater. Some of her Norfolk girlfriends had certainly done the rounds but fortunately they had missed him. Perhaps because he had come back to work in his hometown only fairly recently and spent most of his time on the Portsmouth side.

Ginny had nothing against an experienced man, indeed quite the opposite, but she didn't fancy going out with ones who had known all the girls in town.

The Norfolk skyline gradually receded and so did thoughts of her work. The last press hurdle to jump had been to make sure that the photo editor came up with some good shots of the main protagonists in the Bedsole/Marlon Williams case. He had done exactly that and also obtained pictures of the electric chair and state penitentiary where the execution was due to take place. What's more he had traced Williams' mother and sister, and photographed them and a selection of local people who had strong views on the case. Excellent. The front page looked sharp and should boost the sales of Saturday's edition.

A huge gas tanker was lying off the Portsmouth Naval Yard. The dull metallic thuds of the construction work suddenly ceased as a shift ended. The vessel lay like a huge, beached whale, with lilliputian figures swarming over its deck and superstructure.

But Ginny's attention was not on the harbor, but on people she could just make out on the Portsmouth boardwalk. She saw the red jeep and Jim standing next to it. He was waving a folded newspaper! Behind lay Olde Towne. She rarely visited this side of the water although she had spent a few hours and dollars in the antique shops on the High Street. She'd gotten some costume jewellery for herself and some naval memorabilia for her uncle. Ginny slung her weekend bag over her shoulder and made her way towards the exit gate. She hadn't had time to change. She had packed shirts and jeans, but also a silky black dress in case they went out dancing at the Comfort Inn.

As she skipped off the ferry and walked up the wooden pathway, Jim pointed to his watch and pretended to scowl. But once within reach he kissed her lightly and took her bag.

'Jim, I've got to change sometime,' she reminded him.

'OK honey, but let's get going now and we will deal with that later. I've been hanging around for hours! I nearly decided to listen to jazz and drink some wine instead.'

'A good thing you didn't,' she retorted. 'And I'll have you know that I turned down several offers to go to O'Flaherty's bar.'

'Right, we're even then, so let's herd them in and ride them out.'

'What d'you mean them,' she replied, 'it's only us on the Outer Banks this weekend I trust.'

'Sure is us and the birds, and a few mosquitoes if we are unlucky.'

They got in and Jim drove below the speed limit through the town to Highway 17. They passed the rundown thrift shops and dingy gas stations of mid town and onto the leafy suburbs. On the right was the YMCA where he worked out, and on the left a Catholic church. A large banner had been placed on the lawn in front of the church. Its message read – 'Inactive Catholics come home'. Ginny pointed it out and asked:

'Jim when was the last time you went to church or Confession?' she put her hand on his shoulder and squeezed it.

'Come on tell the truth,' she teased.

'I went with my family at Christmas I'll have you know, and I might just go to Confession next week.' He looked across for her reaction. She laughed and said with a quizzical smile – 'You should be so lucky – what exactly are you going to confess about I wonder.'

He changed the subject. 'By the way did you get your article done?'

'Yep, sure did, it will smack 'em in the face in the morning. With any luck the telephones will be red hot as the good people of Hampton Roads decide if he should die or not. Not of course that it's their decision. You'd probably get a black-white split in opinion if they did.

'My guess is that Williams will go to their chair,' Jim said, 'it's too near the state elections for a pardon.'

Jim went on to tell her about the FBI fugitives he had spotted in the Post Office. 'Some of them certainly would not be shown much mercy,' Ginny remarked, 'but I guess not many of them will ever be tracked down. When you think that there are 275 million people in the US, and that's just the ones who fill out their census forms or have a social security number.'

Jim put his foot on the gas as they came to the edge of town. Tidy grass lots and split level suburban houses gave way to isolated cabins and farms, interspersed with farmers' markets, crossroads stores, and lots waiting development. The road followed the line of the Dismal Swamp Canal, but they did not notice it because their attention was caught by the blaze of colour in the open space between the divided highway. There were brightly coloured cosmos, poppies and corn flowers.

'The State Wild Flower Highway Programme at work,' Jim announced proudly. 'Just look at the colour.'

'It's great and must only cost a few dimes,' Ginny agreed. 'So Virginia is really for lovers then. So why are we going to North Carolina?'

She kissed him on the neck and placed her hand gently on his knee. Jim noticed that she was still in her work suit. 'Why don't you change as we drive?' he asked. 'I'll promise to keep my eyes on the road.'

'You better had, and don't crash the jeep by getting too excited.' Ginny laughed and took off her jacket and put a sweater on over her blouse. Jim could smell her perfume and that was enough to heighten his awareness of her. She wriggled out of her skirt and slip and into her jeans. Although their eyes didn't meet they both felt a touch of intimacy, and a keen sense of desire.

He looked around for his cell phone. Might just as well give the motel a ring to say that they were on their way. Where was it?

'Oh no, I've left my phone in that Jewish Mother place.'

'So you did go in there?' Ginny asked. 'You dope, what were you thinking of?'

'Of you, of course,' he said, although he knew that it had probably been Elly who had distracted him.

'Well, I didn't bring mine on purpose,' Ginny said, 'so we can't get in touch until we arrive.'

'So be it, I made a definite booking but said I wasn't sure what time we would arrive.'

The 17 highway was passing through the Dismal Swamp. Jim started to tell her about it. He quoted early explorers and settlers who had called it a vast body of dirt and nastiness. It was inhospitable, forbidding and treacherous to cross. But in the 18th century, at great cost, they built a canal through it to take lumber for the Portsmouth shipyard. The swamp became a refuge for Indians and later slaves fleeing from oppression and cruelty. It had attracted fugitives from all over the Eastern Seaboard. A hotel was built on Lake Drummond and became a wide-open joint for booze and a haven for runaway couples making the most of the more liberal marriage laws of North Carolina. Jim was getting into his 'get the visitor switch on' mode. But he noticed that Ginny didn't look too impressed.

'To coin a phrase, history is bunk,' she said and looked at the map. 'I'm more interested in finding something to eat. What about it?'

Jim went on, 'it's now a 100,000 acre wildlife refuge with plenty of facilities for birdwatchers, and hikers.'

'Look, it can't be far from that Lake Drummond hotel, why don't we go eat there. I'm famished.' Ginny sounded more enthusiastic suddenly.

Jim wasn't so sure. The last time he had been at Lake Drummond was over a decade ago when he had gone underage drinking with some of his college friends. He remembered that the hotel wasn't too palatial. Perhaps it had been refurbished. But he hadn't seen mention of it on any of the tourist brochures which had passed across his desk. They passed a sign for Elizabeth City – 20 miles, and another for Lake Drummond 4 miles.

'Come on, I can't wait,' Ginny shouted. Jim reluctantly turned off the highway, and onto a dirt road leading into the forest.

Here was a bit of unexpected adventure. The sun was getting lower and ducks flew overhead. The jeep was perfect for the dirt road. After a couple of miles or so Jim suddenly felt the vehicle start to shudder. He braked and came to a standstill. Maybe it was just the uneven surface. To his dismay he found that one of his rear tires was flat. Ginny took the news in good spirits.

'Get out and get under,' she sang, and pointed to the Goodyear tire held on the rear of the jeep with a stick she had picked up from the roadside. It took him less than ten minutes to replace the tire. Ginny was impressed. 'OK let's get to that restaurant before I eat you.'

While he had been changing the wheel she had applied mosquito repellent to his neck and arms. The smell was not nearly so nice as her perfume but the feel of her fingers on him made up for that. He got irritable when he was hungry, but not on this occasion. Around the next corner they came to a fork in the road. The sign had two pointers – Lake Drummond 2 miles, and the other Lake Drummond 1 mile. The road following the final sign looked marginally better, but they were in a hurry. He swung onto the shorter route.

Ginny was looking uncertain. 'I've got a feeling that we should have gone the other way,' she said quietly.

'How come?' he asked, 'I thought you said you could eat a horse!'

'Yes, but it's just an intuition, I think we made the wrong choice back there.'

'Too bad, it's done now.' Jim wanted to be seen to be decisive. In fact he was having misgiving about having left the main highway in the first place, but he kept it to himself. They drove on for a few minutes in silence through to inhospitable scrubby swamp.

Rounding a bend they came to a bridge over an inky-black creek. A crude barrier had been erected across the wooden bridge and a hand painted sign announced – 'Bridge unsafe for vehicles'.

Jim got out to take a closer look at the bridge. It was certainly in bad shape and some of the timbers rotten. On the other hand, tire marks went up to it and continued on the other side. He knew he shouldn't risk it.

'Let's walk to the lake and eat,' Ginny shouted, seeing him hesitate. 'It can't be more than a few minutes away.'

'OK. No way am I going to see the jeep end up in ten feet of water in the Dismal Swamp – what a way to spoil the weekend.' He felt himself shiver at the prospect.

Ginny got out. She carried her purse and was wearing her running shoes. He locked the Jeep and they set out at a brisk pace to find the hotel.

Around the next bend they saw lights in a clearing. Much to their disappointment, it wasn't the hotel or even a restaurant or diner, but a farm of some sort. There were outbuildings and a fence around the property. Lights shone out from the house which was situated behind a large barn. A number of rusting old autos and a school bus stood in the yard. It looked too old to be carrying children. Voices could be heard coming from the barn, and they approached to ask about the whereabouts of the hotel and the prospect of getting a meal. The door was closed so they peered through a slit in the shutters. An amazing sight greeted their eyes. Instead of a hay or farm vehicles, they saw a room full of men. They were all wearing tank tops or white tee shirts, some had shorts on. They were sitting played cards on an old door for a table or lying on bunks. The room was lit by a couple of naked electric bulbs. But the most extraordinary thing was that all the men were Chinese.

Jim felt Ginny grab his arm. 'My God, what are they doing here?' she whispered. He could only think one thing – they must be illegal immigrants. Why else would they be hiding out in semi-captivity in the Dismal Swamp? Both of them had read about gangs of Chinese being brought into the country in containers or secret compartments of freighters. Recently a batch had been discovered down in Savannah, Georgia. The problem was even worse in the Pacific ports.

They guessed that they had stumbled on a transit camp. No place to hang around any longer. But as they started to creep back to the safety of the road to get out of sight, they saw the door of the farmhouse open. Two men and a dog emerged. The men were smoking and cursing. They carried shotguns over their arms.

'OK, Leroy, got to get some of 'em out tonight. Our man is

waiting up in Baltimore. How we gonna choose which to take, they're all the same these goddam chinks.' As they unlocked the door there was a babble of voices from inside. There were shouts of 'We go New York ... We go New York.' Jim grabbed Ginny and they fled towards the road. They half expected the dog to raise the alarm, but it was barking at the noisy foreigners. They jumped across the ditch and hot footed it up the road. They never thought but to keep on going towards the lake, rather than back to the jeep.

For the first time they were frightened by the Dismal Swamp. Their feet were wet and they sweated in the clammy evening. Mosquitoes swarmed around them, but that was nothing compared to the dangers posed by the traders in human cargo nearby.

Somewhere nearby an owl shrieked. Ginny grabbed hold of Jim's hand even tighter.

'I'm sorry I ever suggested we come off the highway to this grim place,' he whispered.

'Don't worry, we'll surely meet some more friendly faces in a minute.' Jim tried to sound reassuring but he didn't feel it.

Around the next bend they saw another farm. This time it looked like the real thing. There was a vegetable garden beside the farmhouse, the yard was tidy, smoke was coming from the chimney. Somehow the place looked welcoming, but they were taking no chances. They walked hesitantly up the path. On one side was a field of corn and on the other a paddock in which a piebald horse was grazing. As they got within a few feet of the building they saw that a crop had been laid out to dry in front of the porch.

'Oh Lordy,' Ginny whispered, 'unless I'm mistaken that's a crop of marijuana.' Sure enough they both recognised the spikey thin leaves of the hemp plant. They had both tried pot at college and occasionally since. Ginny had even written an article about America's third largest cash crop. It had generated many letters as to whether or not it should be legalized. Most readers were against it. Presumably those who used it just kept quiet and smoked spliffs in the privacy of their homes.

Ginny laughed nervously. 'Let's get some,' she said half jokingly. But they hesitated and then turned back towards the road. To their horror a tall man appeared from behind a large pine tree. He too had a shotgun slung over his arm. He was dressed in faded denim and leather boots. He had a Cherokee Indian appearance.

'Hello strangers, what are you doing trespassing on my land?' he asked in a matter of fact, rather than menacing way.

'Sorry sir,' Jim blurted out. 'We're on our way to Lake Drummond, hoping to find something to eat, that's all.'

The farmer gave a short laugh. 'You're about a year too late,' he chuckled. 'The place got burnt down. You are wasting your time, it's a dump now. If I were you I would clear off before some of my neighbours get wind of your arrival.

'By the way, you sure you're not bureaucrats from the Department of Agriculture come to spy on me? You seen what crop I grow here, well it's my livelihood. I don't welcome anyone who might destroy all my hard work.'

He pointed the barrel of the gun at the house. 'You all can come in and have yourself some onion pie, but I'd get on out if I were you. As I said, the folks round here don't take kindly to strangers, least ways those they don't bring in themselves.'

'You mean the Chinese down the road?' asked Jim, sensing that they were relatively safe in the Indian's company.

'I don't know about no Chinese. I mind my own business, and they don't harm me and my family. To tell you the truth, I keep them supplied with pot and they leave me alone to get on with my life.'

Jim and Ginny were warming to their new impassive acquaintance. But they both felt they had better take his advice and go.

'And don't go back the way you came,' he advised. 'Carry

on round to the lake and then head back to the fork in the road. If I were you I'd avoid the bunch down the road, they are liable to get nasty if anyone treads on their patch.'

They made to leave.

'And don't go telling the whole world what you seen here. If I get busted, that's the end of my living. I'll have to quit the Dismal. My folks came here generations ago. I don't aim to have to leave now courtesy of the sheriff.'

They thanked him and made their way to the lake. The sun was setting and the red and yellow reflections on the water were picturesque. The beauty of the place was lost on them as they hurried past the derelict hotel. All that could be seen were a charred timber frame, rusting metal beds, and kitchen furniture. Sodden and half-burnt mattresses and armchairs lay about. The site was a real mess. Beer cans lay around, and several old trucks and autos were half visible in the undergrowth.

'So much for our candlelight dinner,' Jim joked to Ginny, but she didn't laugh. The place had a spooky feel about it and they ran past it.

'Good place to set a ghost story,' Ginny muttered.

They kept on going, but were surprised to see a trailer parked a few yards along the lakeside. They were skirting it as swiftly as possible when the door was flung open and a woman appeared.

'Help, help, he's dying, come quick.'

They stopped in their tracks as the woman ran towards them. She was both dishevelled and distraught. She wore a cheap, floral, cotton dress, and dirty sneakers. Her hair was long and loose. Ginny took a few steps towards her. Jim remained where he was.

The woman approached them. 'Come quickly, it's my man, he's out for the count.'

Jim still didn't move. Something told him to beware. 'Don't go there,' said a voice inside him. But the woman clutched Ginny's arm and pulled her towards the open door of the trailer.

Jim followed reluctantly. He knew first aid, and felt he had little choice but to follow them.

They were met by a disgusting scene. Clothes were strewn around, dirty dishes and pans filled the sink in the kitchenette. Empty coke and beer bottles lay on the unswept floor.

Two children huddled on one of the beds. On the other bed, a half-dressed man was lying. He was frothing at the mouth, sweating profusely and dead or unconscious. The woman stood by helpless. Ginny went to speak to the kids, who were aged around five and six. They shrunk back as she approached.

Jim held his breath. He took the man's wrist to feel his pulse. It was low but regular. He must have had a blackout or a stroke. The woman whined at his side but Jim paid no attention. He was looking at the tattoos on the man's torso and arms.

'He needs his pills,' the woman was saying, and shoved an empty bottle in his face. It was a common brand taken by diabetics to keep their blood sugar level steady.

'How long is it since he took his stuff?' Jim asked.

'I don't rightly know,' the woman replied. 'He took ill during the night and hasn't got up all day. We haven't gone into town as the auto won't start and I can't leave the kids.'

'No telephone?' Jim asked.

'Nope, it's never been repaired after the storm and no one round here gives a shit. They wouldn't help even if I asked them.' Jim and Ginny looked at each other. They each knew they would have to do something. But Jim was not fully concentrating on what course of action they should take. He was still looking at the man's tattoos. There were numerous animals and birds on his shoulders and upper arms. And a rose. On the fingers of his left hand L-O-V-E had been tattooed. One arm was hidden under the greasy blanket.

Jim couldn't help thinking back to the post office in Portsmouth. Surely this couldn't be one of the FBI's wanted men. But tattoos, a trailer woman with children, a diabetic. Some of it fitted at least. But then the there must be thousands of tattooed men who lived in trailer parks. Perhaps the unsettling events witnessed earlier were making him imagine things.

Ginny took a cup from the sink, and filled it with some coke. She forced it to the man's mouth and tried to pour it down his throat. He coughed and groaned.

'We need to get help and quick,' she said decisively. With a word or two of comfort and reassurance to the woman and a smile at the kids, she stepped out of the trailer into the fresh air. Jim followed. He had a quick look at the battered Buick that was parked between the road and the trailer. It had Kentucky plates – they could be false ones. He looked inside the vehicle. There were road maps, more beer cans, and the usual detritus of a travelling man. On the windshield was an out-of-date decal for an insurance company from Minneapolis. Jim was getting even more suspicious that the man lying in the trailer might just be none other than the fugitive whose picture he had seen a couple of hours earlier. Still he couldn't be sure, and anyway, they had promised to go for help.

The woman was standing forlornly on the step of the trailer. They set off up the road in the direction which the farmer had indicated they would be wise to take. This time they jogged at a serious pace. It was dusk and the forest was full of noises. It had long since lost any attraction. A minute or so later, they heard a vehicle approaching from the direction they had come. Jim grabbed Ginny and they plunged down into the ditch beside the road. They could feel the muddy ground oozing into their clothes and bodies as they lay together and watched the lights of a truck appear. As it roared past they caught a glimpse of two men in the front. In the back crouched half a dozen small dark-haired men. It could only be the Chinese and their guards they had encountered earlier. The truck's lights disappeared. They clambered out of the ditch, sodden and dirty, and ran on. They didn't say it aloud, but both had only one desire and that was to get out of the Dismal Swamp as quickly as they could.

Five minutes later they arrived at the road junction and turned back to look for the Jeep. Much to their relief it was there and apparently untouched. Jim approached warily nonetheless. They had had enough surprises already. He noticed some tire tracks and footprints around the vehicle. But as far as they could see, no-one was about. Ginny was getting impatient.

'For God's sake, Jim, let's get out of here and get help for that poor woman and her family.'

Jim got in and drove fast. Was he getting paranoid about the Dismal Swamp and its alarming inhabitants? Or had they really stumbled on a nest of vipers hiding out in this desolate corner of Virginia or was it North Carolina? He didn't like to confide in Ginny lest he should appear foolish or alarm her unduly. After all they were meant to be going on their first weekend together. If he panicked unnecessarily it might be their last.

Once again they headed south on Highway 17. Morgan's Corner was just a shack and they drove on towards Elizabeth City.

'Where shall we go for help Jim?' Ginny asked. 'The police or hospital? We need to get some paramedics up there pronto.'

'Sure,' he agreed. 'We best telephone once we get to town.'

Billboards on the roadside heralded the edge of Elizabeth City. They turned into a mall which had a filling station and pizza place which was open. Jim parked and sat for a second. He had to tell Ginny was he suspected. If he kept silent and it was Peterson at Lake Drummond, then things could go very wrong.

'Just a minute before we call, Ginny,' he blurted out. 'I have a feeling that the man lying in that trailer is a drug pusher wanted by the FBI for child abuse. And you saw for yourself that gang with the Chinese. And don't forget the warning by our Indian friend. Remember what he said – don't go there.'

Ginny was silent for a moment. 'If you are sure about Peterson or whatever his name was, then that's serious. But they still need help, and shouldn't we be alerting the police to what we have seen anyway?' She laughed nervously. 'Maybe it's the reporter in me but I smell a good story here.'

Jim was caught in two minds and he felt that despite her news-hounding instincts, Ginny might also feel the same way. If they got involved with the police then they could say goodbye to their planned weekend. They would have to go back to show them where to go. Besides they had half promised the farmer that they wouldn't stir it up, or he would get it in the neck.

Ahead of them lay the Outer Banks, behind the Great Dismal Swamp.

'Right it's time for action,' he said. 'You go and buy some pizza and I'll call the police.'

To his surprise she agreed, got out, and headed for the diner. He went to a phone booth at the edge of the parking lot. He knew what he was going to do. Phone the Chesapeake Police department, tell them about the sick man in the trailer at Lake Drummond and hang up. That way they would be doing their duty and yet not be ensnared in any of the dirty business that might follow. He got through and quickly but calmly told his story. He informed the incredulous cop on the other end of the line that he had grounds for thinking that the sick diabetic who needed urgent treatment might be a fugitive called Peterson.

Jim raced back to the Jeep and waited impatiently for Ginny. In less than a minute she joined him with a pizza box.

'Right we're off east on 158 to the coast. They will trace the call and be here in a minute,' he reminded Ginny. Sure enough, a few minutes later, a police car with its siren flashing passed them heading towards the mall. As Jim looked in the rear mirror he saw the police car speeding off into the distance, but he also saw a black Mercury in the lane behind them. He had a slight, yet distinct feeling that they were being followed. They drove and ate.

In less than half an hour they crossed the bridge onto the Outer Banks. It was just before 11pm when they reached Nags Head and the motel. He didn't think he had seen the Mercury, but he couldn't be sure.

The band was packing up in the forecourt of the Comfort Inn – so much for Friday night dancing. The woman at the motel reception came out from a back room when he rang.

'I thought you hadn't made it sir,' she said. 'I nearly gave your room to another couple.' She handed Jim the key and she offered them coffee and cookies. The fact that their clothes were still wet and they were covered with mud seemed neither to surprise nor worry her. She had seen too many guests come and go.

They threw their luggage onto the floor of the room and shut the door. Once again they looked at each other.

Jim went to Ginny and held her for a moment. They kissed. She broke free and kicked off her shoes.

'I'm going to shower first,' she said and disappeared into the bathroom.

Jim too, took off his dirty clothes. He unpacked and switched on the TV. He heard Ginny splashing and singing from the shower. As he listened to her he felt that at last they were due to enjoy each other. If anything, his feelings for her seemed to have been intensified by the events of the last few hours. It seemed a long time since he had waited for her at the ferry landing.

'Your turn Jim. Get on in here and get that mud off you,' she shouted above the sound of the splashing water. He needed no second invitation, stripped and followed her into the shower.

She had a sponge in one hand and soap in the other.

'Come on you dirty, hairy, swamp man, let's make a respectable citizen of you.'

She began to soap him down. They kissed and embraced as the warm water gushed over them. They explored each other slowly at first and then with growing passion. He led her out of the shower and onto the bed. They made love fiercely and swiftly. Afterwards they lay together. The sheets were damp but they held each other in a warm and intimate embrace. Later they made love again, before falling into a sleep in each other's arms.

Jim slept fitfully, he dreamed that he was being chased by a gang of Chicago mobsters. He couldn't get away from them. His car kept slipping and sliding on a muddy road by a lake.

Ginny was dreaming she was the wife of the Governor of Virginia. Her husband – he looked very much like Jim – had to decide whether or not to send Marlon Williams to the electric chair. But the condemned man had an uncanny resemblance to the Indian they had met in the Dismal Swamp.

Jim woke early. The sun was just up. He heard seabirds and, a few yards away, the sound of ocean waves crashing on the beach. The bedclothes were all over the place and their clothes scattered around the room.

Ginny lay sleeping peacefully. She lay on her front with her hands tucked under the pillow. Her hair was tangled. She looked beautiful. Jim felt a strong surge of affection for her. He felt like caressing and kissing her as he had done the night before. Instead he carefully got out of bed and found his swimming trunks. He let himself out of the motel room quietly and walked barefoot down to the beach. It was a perfect morning. A bright, blue sky and a light wind coming off the Atlantic. On the shore, sanderlings tiptoed up and down the sand, feeling as the tide ebbed and flowed.

Jim was a good swimmer. He struck out towards a wreck a few hundred yards offshore. It must have been one of the scores of boats sunk during the Second World War. After ten minutes he headed back for shore. Looking at the deserted beach, sand dunes and listening to the gulls and pelicans flying overhead the events of the previous evening seemed but a distant memory. Much fresher in his mind was the presence of the woman he had left back in the motel room. It was time to get back to her.

As he approached the room he noticed the door was open. Funny, he had left her fast asleep. The room was empty. She wasn't in bed, nor in the bathroom. Nowhere to be seen in fact. Clothes were still scattered around. Where was she?

He felt uneasy. He remembered the black Mercury which he thought must be following them. Had the gang from the Dismal Swamp found their jeep, waited for their return and followed them down to the Outer Banks? Jim's imagination began working overtime. Could they have been watching the motel and kidnapped her to make sure that they didn't tell the world what was going on at Lake Drummond?

He tried to put all this fanciful rubbish out of his mind. But where was she? He put on some clothes and went to the reception. The owner, the husband of the woman who had greeted them last night, stood behind his desk.

'How do,' he said. 'Sleep well?' he added with a wink.

Jim didn't take to his sleazy humour.

'Have you seen my partner?' he asked, with a touch of embarrassment.

'Nope, did she disappear then?'

'I think she must have gone out while I was swimming,' he replied, and then as casually as he could. 'You didn't see a black Mercury around here at all did you?'

The owner volunteered a grumpy 'Not as I can recall, you know we get a heck of a lot of visitors here, and I can't remember every auto that goes past.'

Jim went out and looked up and down the highway. No sign of her there. One or two of the roadside diners were open but no Ginny in sight.

He went back to their room. He would have surely seen her if she had gone for a swim. He began to regret leaving her in bed, and alone in the room.

As a distraction he turned on the TV. It was CNN News. There was a report on nationwide college rankings, the President of CalTech was being interviewed. He was quietly modest at coming above the better known Ivy League universities in the league table.

Jim was just about to switch off when the newscaster switched to the breaking story of a shoot-out in rural Virginia.

'We are hearing of a serious incident on the Virginia-North Carolina state border,' she announced. 'There is a siege at a farmhouse in the Dismal Swamp area. Federal agents have surrounded the property where, it is suspected, illegal immigrants are being held.'

There were shots of police cars, and heavily armed, crouching police officers. Jim stood stock still in amazement. What had happened? What had his phone call done? Was it Peterson, after all? How come the police had encountered the Chinese smugglers? And what would happen to the precious marijuana crop if police were swarming all over the area? Jim couldn't believe what he was seeing.

But his thoughts went back to Ginny. The TV switched to a breakfast food commercial. Jim sat on the bed with his head in his hands. What the hell was going on? All he had wanted was a short break here on the Banks. But instead they had run into a hornets' nest. If only Ginny hadn't been late. If only they hadn't turned off Highway 17. If only they hadn't contacted the Police. If only Ginny would appear. He remained motionless whilst the ads droned on for what seemed like ages.

Suddenly Jim smelled coffee. He heard a familiar voice. He leapt up and saw Ginny at the door. She had on a wrap, and was carrying a Dunkin Donuts bag and two coffee cups.

'If you go down to the woods today ... you're sure to get a surprise,' she sang.

She stopped when she saw Jim's face.

'You look as though you've seen a Dismal Swamp ghost and she laughed.

He switched off the TV, took a long sip of the steaming coffee, and held her tightly.

[PLATE VII.]

NICOLAI STENONIS
DE SOLIDO
INTRA SOLIDVM NATVRALITER CONTENTO
DISSERTATIONIS PRODROMVS.

A D

S E R E N I S S I M V M

FERDINANDVM II.
MAGNVM ETRVRIÆ DVCEM.

OBVIA | VLTIO | QVÆSITA

FLORENTIÆ

Ex Typographia sub signo STELLÆ MDCLXIX.

SVPERIORVM PERMISSV.

Early years at Postcard Corner

Steno

Foreword

*T*his is the story of Steno's doubts and dilemmas. You will never have heard of him, but, like us all, he faced some momentous decisions in his life.

In our case what we should do in school, which career to pursue, who we should marry, where to live, how many children to have, to go for promotion or change jobs, how to campaign on issues that you feel strongly about, how to cope with kids and ageing parents, when to retire and what to do in later life, where to have your ashes strewn .... (they say that those born years ago had limited choices – like using a corner shop, whereas in today's world the boundless opportunities presented to many is like a trip to a supermarket!)

But Steno lived in the 17th century.

He was a serious minded scientist and also a Christian believer. He had to decide if he should convert to Catholicism or remain as a Lutheran. If he should stay in Italy or return to his native Denmark. If he should publish his ground-breaking geological research and, in all likelihood, be accused of heresy and/or devote his life to Christ.

Niels Steenen was born in Denmark in 1667. He was educated in Copenhagen, and by all accounts was a serious -minded student who studied medicine. Such was the excellence of his scholarship that he was granted a doctorate 'in absentia' from the University of Leiden. Amongst his anatomical discoveries was the duct of the paratid gland (ductus stenonianus) which supplies most of the saliva to our mouths. (any ENT specialists will know what this is all about).

This brilliant scholar spoke four European languages and some Arabic and Greek. He travelled widely through the centres of learning. Steno – as he was called in Italy – found himself in Montpellier in the late summer of 1665. He conducted one of his public dissections in the Earl of Aylesbury's study. The Earl was to praise Steno as 'a man of genius and great personal modesty'.

Scientists down the ages and certainly in the 17th century, (including John Evelyn, Robert Hooke and Thomas Burnett) had to reconcile their work with their personal beliefs/disbeliefs and those of their peers. Their writings and public speeches had to be tailored to the dictates of the Church and civil authorities – not to mention the wishes of their benefactors. 'Publish or perish' had an altogether more sinister meaning at the time.

Let's not forget that amongst the conventional wisdoms of Steno's day was that God created the world in seven days and Noah's flood explained the existence of the fossils of sea creatures in the Appenine mountains amongst which Steno conducted so much of his pioneering work. Today many Christians see the Old Testament version of the creation as a parable, which need not be interpreted too literally.

Like churchmen over the centuries Steno was vexed by schisms within the Christian faith. Like many Protestants he was appalled by the laxity and worldly pleasures enjoyed by some Catholic bishops, and some of superstitious practices of the Church of Rome. But, as we shall see, the architecture, art and music of the Italian church also had their attractions.

It can be said with confidence that Steno was a virtuoso – 'virtuosi' were renaissance scholars who excelled in art, religion and science. But he was also a practical and generous-natured person who felt it was his duty to administer to the poor and destitute.

As we shall see, three hundred years ago, Steno faced difficult life, and possibly death choices, of multiple complexity

– including which church to belong to, and which side of the Alps to undertake his pastoral work. But above all to be a scientist or a 'man of the cloth'.

'Signor Steno, you know that I would give my life for your salvation, and your visits and our conversations have been to win you to the true faith'. Signora Arnolfini's words were short and direct.

'But I will not waste more of my time. Do not come to me again unless and until you have decided to convert to Catholicism'.

The imposing and influential wife of the Minister of Lucca to the Medici court turned sharply and disappeared into her house.

Her parting shot surprised and disconcerted Steno. He stood on the step of the grand doorway for a few moments – alone and forlorn.

Her impatient outburst was out of keeping with her usual pious and gentle demeanour, and it came as a blow from a lady he admired not least for her charitable work for the poor and sick. And he knew only too well that this was no idle threat. The formidable Lady Lavenia Arnolfini was very well connected, and could bring to an end his current well-placed situation in this warm and cultured city.

Steno turned and walked slowly from the house. He felt as if he was being forced into making decisions he was reluctant to take.

Nothing had prepared Steno for the stinging finality of Signora Arnolfini's ultimatum. After all she was the devout wife of the ambassador to the Medici court, a highly respected noble lady in Florentine society. One who was both pious and gentle – both qualities he greatly admired. Steno called her his 'Mother in Christ' for her generosity to the poor and willingness to tend to those in need. He knew she relied on the learned Father Savignani for her religious adherence.

Steno turned and gazed at the Arno. The autumn rains had swollen the river and, although his mind was in turmoil, he watched the rippling flow of the current.

Had any of the boatman plying their trade on the river nearby looked up from their exertions, they would have seen a thin, lonely figure standing quite still on the bank. If they had got closer they would observed the thin face, dark hair, wispy moustache, and pointed chin of this learned Dane.

What they also were not aware of was the existence of a letter in his satchel from the King of Denmark. In it he was invited – summoned – back to Copenhagen to take up an appointment as Royal Anatomist at an annual salary of 400 rigsdaler. Nor was this the only document on his person. He had his Bible, but stuffed inside it was a draft copy of his paper – ' La Evoluzione Geologica de la Toscana Seconda'.

Steno's usual calm disposition had been disturbed. He was stung by the finality of the good lady's ultimatum. The autumn rains had swollen the waters of the river. He experienced no solace from the fast flowing muddy torrent. He felt an inward struggle for his life and soul.

In his pre-occupied state of mind, Steno didn't see Father Savignani approaching. He, however, did feel a tap on his arm.

'*Cosa ce,*' the priest greeted him. 'Signor Steno, what is a scientist like you doing dallying by the Arno today?'

'*Buon Giorno*, senior padrev.'

Steno recovered his usual poise and greeted the avuncular priest.

'*Va bene,*' was the kindly rejoinder. 'Why don't you come round later for one of our little talks? I have just received a new batch of books from Rome; perhaps we can have a look at them together over a glass of wine.'

Steno readily agreed and they parted amicably.

A few minutes after taking his leave of Father Savignani, Steno reached the spot where a new bridge across the river was under construction. He paused to see if he could cross to the Palazzo Pitti. On his right the wan sun lit up the grey sandstone of the massive Palazzo Feroni. It was said that St Francis of Assisi had miraculously restored to life a child who had fallen from the window of the building. The thought of this supposed deed brought his mind back to the Signora's demand that he must become a true believer.

Although on his way to the Palazzo Pitti to get on wth some writing, Steno decided to try to clear his head by taking a detour down the Via Maggio towards the Porta Romana. In fact he was following the stream of peasants heading back home to their villages outside the city gates. Most of their wine, olives, vegetables and poultry had been sold in the markets and their panniers were empty and pockets full of florins.

Steno heard snatches of conversations. The strong country accents made it difficult for him to follow all he heard. But they were clearly relishing getting back to their farms and the Tuscan countryside in which their lives were embedded.

And Steno could hardly wait for him to join them. He hated the evil smells and raucous sounds of the city. He was dying to escape to the fresh fields and quiet bye-ways. He would love to be climbing up the steep valley sides of the Arno, exploring the caves and ravines, filling his satchel with samples of rocks and fossils, and sketching the landforms he knew better than any man on earth. He loved the terraced groves of cypress trees and vines, and green islands of irrigated gardens. Steno loved this southern European landscape he had discovered a few years earlier. The cold, wintry scenes of his native Denmark did not seem at all attractive at this moment in time.

Steno paused at the gates and watched the human tide disappear along the muddy track, heading south. At the gates were a rag-taggle of beggars, and thieves – all feeding off the honest toils of their country cousins. Steno gave some coins to the deserving disabled who clustered round him, seeking his attention.

He took one last look at the rural idyll beyond the gates

and resolved to make an expedition down the Arno's valley in the spring.

The words of his old tutor – Pietre Severinus came to him suddenly.

'Go, my sons, buy yourself some stout shoes, get away to the mountains, search the valleys, deserts, sea shores, and deepest reaches of the earth.' Good advice indeed and not to be taken lightly.

But as he trudged back into the city, he could not forget the letter he had received urging him to return to home and Scandinavia. The prospect of becoming Professor of Anatomy was also inviting in its own way. It would bring a regular salary and status, as well as first-class facilities for his experiments. Likewise the chance to spend time with his mother and sister's young family filled him with longing. He wanted to visit his old haunts and see the familiar landmarks – the Rundetarn and St Nicholas church. He missed dignified, ordered society of a homeland that he had left nearly seven years before.

But Florence certainly had its attractions. He spoke Italian and fitted in well in both scientific and ecclesiastical circles. He had built up a fine reputation and an expectation that he would stay and publish his much respected research on the origins and structure of the landscape he had studied so carefully. The prospect of leaving all this life behind troubled and saddened him.

And there was another reason for putting off the journey north across the Alps and German plains – the journey itself. It wasn't so much the long, days of physical discomfort – after all he was still young and pretty tough. He could put up with the cold and wet, and the jolting mail coach.

Rather it was the places he would have to stay on route which he disliked. The filthy 'albergos' with their flea-infested beds which strangers were expected to share. The greasy food of dubious origins, which had to be forced down every evening. And the rough company to be endured day after day. Steno could not help himself – he sought the company of upright and learned companions and did not take kindly to mingle for weeks with people not of his own choosing.

As Steno walked slowly and reluctantly towards the Palazzo and his work, his mind was weighing up the alternatives – convert to a new faith? Return to his homeland, family and scientific career? Stay and complete his researches? What did he want it to be religion or science, and where … in the south or north? These were no easy decisions to make, and all around him, at least here in Florence, were those who sought to prevail on his plans.

He saw the familiar figure of Vincenso Viviani ahead of him. There was no mistaking this tall gangly figure with his unkempt appearance. He had a sheaf of drawings under his arm. It was indeed the foremost engineer and mathematician in Florence, and a man whom Steno admired, and whose judgement he respected. Equally important he had the ear of prominent churchmen and politicians in the city.

They entered the grounds of the imposing building together.

'Nicholas, where have you been all day? I have been trying to catch up with you to enquire as to your intentions?'

'Do you want me to look at your treatise before it goes before the authorities?' enquired Viviani, placing a friendly arm round Steno's shoulders.

'Most definitely yes,' Steno replied without hesitation. 'I am not letting it anywhere the Holy Office without your approval. To do otherwise would risk it being banned, and goodness knows what would happen to me.

'It's nearly finished. I have only to re-write some conclusions on the Tuscan stratigraphy and explain how the remains of marine creatures are to be found high up in the hills and far from the sea.'

'Well,' Viviani paused and gave a quiet response. 'Remember to make sure that none of your pronouncements are contrary to the scriptures and the wisdom of the Church and the will of the Archbishop. Let me have the manuscript as soon as you can.' With that Viviani, his fellow scientist patted him on the back and said farewell.

Steno stood for a moment. He was fully aware of the thin line he had to tread in interpreting the geomorphology of mountains, indeed the timing of the origins of the great flood and the known world itself. Every scientist in Europe knew perfectly well that only a short time ago, in 1599 to be exact, Comenica Scandella and Giordano Bruno had been burnt at the stake for their heresy. And it was only 35 years ago that the great Galileo had died under house arrest after many years of being publicly attacked by the Church of Rome.

The last thing that Steno wanted to do was to upset those who he had met earlier in the day and to whom he owed his position. He sincerely wanted to show God's grace in his writing.

But in his introduction he had written – 'Untruths must be thrown out; new truths must be established; dark places must be illuminated; unknown facts must be revealed.'

Some, if not all, of the Church hierarchy were bound to be suspicious.

Steno sat at his desk as the light faded, surrounded by his specimens and discarded sheets of paper. He re-read the concluding paragraphs of what he hoped would be his magnum opus. He knew his thesis was sound – that the earth's strata and local geology had been subject to upward thrusts of gases, and scattering of rocky matter and also the slipping and downfall of upper strata which began to crack. And thus was formed the unevenness of the earth's surface, seen in mountains, valleys, water bodies and plains. His painstaking diagrams and sketches showed the processes and pattern of the resulting observed landforms. All was clear, but would it show God's handiwork and the beauty of creation to the satisfaction of those in authority?

He put his pen to paper to write the all-important preface.

He knew that at least would be read by all concerned.

He addressed it to the Grand Duke. He wrote -

'Speak to Earth and it shall teach you. (Job, 12, 8)

Please excuse this tardiness of mine, and in your kindness and goodwill, consider my treatise.

I offer the chief of what I have found, and trust that you will find my inquiry concerning sea objects found at a distance from the sea, whilst an old matter of contention, is delightful and useful.

I have set forth the processes whereby Nature and the Scriptures agree in relation to the chief causes of topography of your rich and wondrous kingdom.

I have set forth these things in Italian to please you.'

Finally he wrote –

'I am sending this text to you with my esteemed colleague Viviani, the reason being that I ask your leave to return to my native land as a true believer and loyal servant of the Church and your serene Highness.'

Steno folded the manuscript. He handed it to the clerk of the Academy. He blew out the candle and descended the stone stairs.

Postscript

*T*he events about which you have been reading – with such avid interest, at least those few of you who have more than a passing interest in the struggles of science vs religion, Protestantism vs Roman Catholism, working/living in the Mediterranean or northern Europe – occurred in 1667.

So what exactly did happen to Steno you may wonder?

In that year he did indeed change from being 'a proddy dog to a mackerel snapper' (as my Mancunian mate used to put it to me). During the spring and summer of 1668 he undertook fieldwork in Tuscany. In April of the following year his famous

'Prodomus' was published, with the English edition coming out a couple of years later.

1672 saw this eminent European scientist return to Copenhagen – to take up the promised post of Royal Anatomist. However, much to his great regret he was passed over for the coveted University of Copenhagen chair of anatomy. Two years later saw him back in Florence tutoring, and entering sacred orders. He was soon made a Bishop and from 1677 onwards tended the Catholic populace of Northern Germany and Scandinavia.

Eschewing the trappings of the Church hierarchy he lived frugally as he journeyed tirelessly across his huge domain. Indeed he sold his bishop's ring and gave the money to the poor and needy. But his letters of time hinted at a unspoken yearning for Italy.

In the last year of his life he suffered from cancer and died aged 48 at 7am on Thursday, 25th November, 1686.

The archduke Cosimo arranged for his body to be conveyed by sea from Hamburg to Livorno. The coffin was enclosed in a chest so that the seamen thought that they were carrying a consignment of books. He was buried in the crypt of the Medici church of San Lorenzo.

In1953 his remains were transferred to a 4th century sarcophagus which had been excavated from the river Arno. His final resting place is the Capella Stenoniana.

Steno was canonised by Pope Paul II in 1988.

His science – medical and geological – lives on.

About the author

*A*lan Burnett was born in Cumbria, but since the mid sixties has lived with his family in Southsea. He studied at the universities of Durham, Indiana and Southampton, and taught human geography at Portsmouth College of Technology/Polytechnic/University.

In the '80s and '90s he was immersed in public life in the city of Portsmouth. For over a decade he held an advice centre at 99 Fawcett Road, Southsea and was Labour leader of Portsmouth City Council for three years and Lord Mayor in 1994/5. More recently he worked in London at Help the Aged's HQ as a research officer/campaigner for older people. He is currently Chair of Portsmouth Pensioners' Association.

For (too) many years he played rugby for Havant and also helped to organise the Nuffield Jazz club. He has travelled and worked in Europe, USA, Ethiopia and Borneo.

Alan is a season-ticket holder at Fratton Park, grows vegetables on his allotment, and reads to his four grandchildren. Although he has had academic and policy work published over the years, this is his first major work of fiction (faction?).

Author's Note

These short(ish) stories were mostly written in the early '90s. They are about travelling to new places and returning to familiar ones; growing up and ageing; men and women's lives; landscapes on either side of the Atlantic and the old 'Iron Curtain'; jazz and love; past and present personalities and ordinary folk; Portsmouth (UK) an island city of rich history and great character.

I hope you find them of interest.

Any profits generated from the sale of this book will be donated to the 'Pompey Clinic' for older people in Awassa, Ethiopia.

Disclaimer

Some of the main characters portrayed in these stories depict real people. Lord Nelson and Lady Hamilton, Robert Goffin, Peter Sellers, Nicolae Ceausescu for example. However, most characters (as well as incidents recounted) are imaginary. They do not resemble any actual person – living or dead – or their activities in Portsmouth or other real places in which the stories are set.